Falling for

Cass began her writing life in Regency England, enlisted Jane Austen's help to time-travel between then and the present day and is now happily ensconced in 21st-century Cornwall. Well, in her imagination and soul; her heart and physical presence reside in northern England with her ever-patient husband and Tig and Tag, their cute but exceptionally demanding moggies.

A bit of a nomad, Cass has called three countries home, as well as six different English counties, but her aspiration is to one day reunite with her beloved West Country. In the meantime, she writes feel-good contemporary romances set in Cornwall and, in doing so, manages to live there vicariously through her characters and settings.

An Ambassador for the Jane Austen Literacy Foundation, Cass is also a member of the Jane Austen Society UK and the Society of Authors.

Also by Cass Grafton

The Austen Adventures (with Ada Bright)

The Particular Charm of Miss Jane Austen
The Unexpected Past of Miss Jane Austen

The Little Cornish Cove series

New Dreams at Polkerran Point
Escape to Polkerran Point
Christmas at Polkerran Point
A Fresh Start at Polkerran Point
Falling for Polkerran Point

Falling for Polkerran Point

Cass Grafton

CANELO

Penguin
Random
House

First published in the United Kingdom in 2025 by

Canelo, an imprint of
Canelo Digital Publishing Limited,
20 Vauxhall Bridge Road,
London SW1V 2SA
United Kingdom

A Penguin Random House Company
The authorised representative in the EEA is Dorling Kindersley Verlag GmbH.
Arnulfstr. 124, 80636 Munich, Germany

A CIP catalogue record for this book is available from the British Library.

Print ISBN 978 1 80436 608 0
Ebook ISBN 978 1 80436 609 7

This book is a work of fiction. Names, characters, businesses, organizations, places and
events are either the product of the author's imagination or are used fictitiously. Any
resemblance to actual persons, living or dead, events or locales is entirely coincidental.

Cover design by Head Design

Cover images © Shutterstock

Printed and bound in Great Britain by Clays Ltd, Elcograf S.p.A.

Look for more great books at
www.canelo.co | www.dk.com

To Jane Austen

My entire writing career has been influenced, one way or another, by my favourite author, and as I'm unable to thank her personally, this book—inspired by Persuasion—*is my expression of gratitude to her for giving us Captain Wentworth!*

Prologue

"Once Upon a Time in the West"

The little convoy of cars descended a steep, winding hill, lower and lower until glimpses of sparkling blue could be seen between the tall trees clinging to the steep cliffs, and then...

'Ohhh,' Elinor Arbon gasped, desperately trying to take in the stunning view of a quaint harbour filled with fishing boats and pleasure craft – the sun glistening on tall masts – and backed by pastel-coloured cottages jostling for space at the bottom of the hillside.

Once parked up, the group of friends spread out on a quest to find groceries, but Ellie – having never been to Cornwall before – lingered, instantly enchanted by the charm of Polkerran Point. She leant against the harbour wall, warmth encasing her bare arms, enjoying the vibe as a busker played a medley of old, familiar songs to a small but enthusiastic audience.

Conscious of the heat burning through her top, Ellie dropped a pound coin into the young man's cap and headed back along the cobbled street, keen to find the others, but suddenly she came face to face with a giant shellfish.

'Greetings!' the creature said, jovially. 'Can I tempt you?'

Ellie blinked, amusement vying with a hint of trepidation.

To what, for heaven's sake? You're a giant prawn… or something!

The vision in fleshy pink stopped waving its tentacles. 'God, I'm sorry!' The voice was surprisingly attractive… for a crustacean. 'I meant into there.'

A rubbery appendage indicated a sign: *Polkerran Point Aquarium*.

Suppressing the urge to giggle, Ellie eyed the bobbing antennae.

'Not today, thanks. It's too nice to be inside.' Then she frowned. 'Aren't you boiling in there?'

'You really don't want to know.'

This time, Ellie did laugh at the resignation in the deep voice, totally at odds with the comical costume.

'Well, I'll let you get on. Bye.'

'Oh. Okay. Bye.'

Ellie set off, unable to resist glancing back as the sea creature accosted a young family trying to edge by.

'Greetings!' it began again in the booming voice.

Then, suddenly a bike shot past and swerved onto the harbourfront, the rider scooping up the busker's cap and pedalling wildly in his attempt to escape.

Until, that is, he was floored by something large and flesh-coloured.

'Oh no!' Ellie raced across the cobbles, just as the dazed youth tried to wriggle free of the bike, but then—

'Aaaargh! Get away from me!' Eyes wide, a look of horror on his face, the thief tried to shrink into the ground beneath him.

'Oh for God's sake.' Releasing a tentacle from the boy's arm, the man in the rubber suit flipped back the head of the costume. 'Stop overreacting and give that back!'

Ellie retrieved the cap and scattered money, meeting the gaze of the crustacean – or rather, the extremely good-looking young man in the suit, despite his dark hair being plastered to his head and beads of sweat on his forehead.

'Hey,' he said, beaming. 'It's you.'

The distraction didn't serve him well, however, as the would-be thief twisted free and snatched up his bike – which resulted in shellfish-man being knocked onto his back – and fled.

The busker joined them, profusely grateful as Ellie handed over the cap and its contents.

'Cheers!' he said with a toothy grin, before heading back to his guitar.

'Help?' called the man-come-creature. 'Can you get me up? I can't bend in this.' He remained on his back, the bulbous costume hindering his ability to do anything but flail around with his tentacles.

'Oh! Sorry!' Giggling, Ellie bent down and, using all her strength, rolled him over towards the kerb.

'Now stay still,' she cautioned, ignoring the spluttering from the head of the costume as she tugged at the wide zipper on the back.

Lordy, I hope he's got something on…

Once free, the young man huffed out a breath, then started to laugh.

'Well, that definitely counts as the weirdest day yet in my new role.'

Gosh, he was attractive. His thick wavy hair was a rich, dark brown, as were his eyes, and his damp clothes clung to a toned body, already tanned a gorgeous golden colour.

'I'm Will, by the way. And thank you.'

'Ellie.'

'I'd best get this back.' He scooped up the suit. 'Oh, hold on. Here. Look after Stewie for a minute.'

Ellie clasped one of Stewie's floppy rubber appendages as Will shot over to the busker, digging in his pocket to hand over some coins.

'We street people need to stick together,' Will claimed on his return, relieving her of her burden.

'Stewie?' Ellie questioned, trying not to chuckle as the antennae slapped him in the face.

'Yeah. Stewie the Shrimp.' He winked at Ellie. 'But you can call me Bouillabaisse.'

This time, Ellie did laugh.

'Well, it was good to meet you, Ellie. I— er, I don't suppose you're here long? You local, or a tourist?'

'Holidaying. On a post-graduation break with my mates, staying in a couple of vans up at Polwelyn?'

'Nice,' he said, those rich brown eyes holding Ellie's green gaze. 'Very nice.'

And with that, he was gone, disappearing inside the aquarium with Stewie. Her heart almost singing, Ellie turned her steps back towards her friend, Bella's, car to await the others. Perhaps tomorrow she'd visit the aquarium properly? After all, it did seem to have the most intriguing of species.

–

A week went by, the weather fluctuating between scorching sunshine and tempestuous summer storms. Ellie's hopes of bumping into Will again brought a frisson of excitement every time someone suggested popping down into the cove, as the locals called Polkerran Point, but luck wasn't playing ball.

Just as she was beginning to give up hope, a voice hailed her as she emerged from the ice cream shop, followed by Bella, and Ellie's cousin, Nicki.

'Ellie! Wait!' Will dashed across the street to join them. 'I'm so glad to bump into you. I've been wanting to buy you a drink as thanks for rescuing me the other day.'

Bella's eyes took a long, slow journey up and down his frame as introductions were made, then her friend smirked, relieving Ellie of her ice cream cone.

'And we're leaving. Bye, Will, nice to meet you. Enjoy your drink!' And hooking an arm through Nicki's, Bella dragged Ellie's spluttering cousin away.

Ellie couldn't stop smiling at this chance encounter. 'I guess we're getting a drink then?'

They settled on a bench outside The Three Fishes, each clutching a bottle of chilled cider.

'Cheers.'

They clinked bottles and once Ellie had elaborated on how long she was staying, it was Will's turn.

'I'm at an old family friend's place.' Will gestured back towards the centre of the village, where the castellated rooftops of a large, stone property could be seen towering behind the church. 'Alex – his family own it – isn't normally down here, but he's on garden leave between jobs.'

'How come you have so much time free?'

'Ah, I'm an actor. At least, I am when I've got work. When I don't, I take anything going. As you saw the other day. Thankfully, me and Stewie only join forces twice a week.'

Ellie found Will's life fascinating and the opposite of her own mundane one, and she hung on his every word as he outlined the roles he'd secured since leaving drama school.

His confidence, and his total belief that success was just around the corner, was intoxicating, and Ellie – swept away by the charming, boyish smile, the dark eyes alight with enthusiasm – was quickly in danger of being smitten.

'You have to grab life's opportunities, not let things stand in your way. The only person who can make things happen in your life, Ellie, is you. Success isn't going to find me, I have to chase it, and I'm twenty-six already. But what about you? What's next?'

Ellie leaned back against the bench, its scratchy warmth grazing the back of her legs. 'I did a BA in History with my friend, Bella, at Manchester. She's going on to do her teaching qualifications, but I discovered a love of art history so I'm doing a masters. I think I'd like to get involved in restoration or conservation.'

'Sounds far more soul-enriching than my ambitions,' Will said, his eyes scanning the jostle of boats bobbing in the harbour. 'Where are you going?'

Ellie blushed. 'Oxford.'

'Wow!' Will spun in his seat. 'That's fantastic. Well done!'

'I didn't expect it. I mean…'

'Own it, Ellie! Be proud.'

She drew in a short breath. 'Yes. At least, my parents are, and I feel I've repaid them a little for all their support so far. I'm just a bit nervous. I won't know anyone.'

'You'll love it, I'm sure.' Will drained his bottle, then almost choked as he caught sight of his watch. 'Damn.

Sorry. Got to dash. Due on shift at The Lugger ten minutes ago.'

And then he was gone, and Ellie walked over to the wall bordering the water, eyes fastened on his back as he strode towards the bridge.

Once he was out of sight, she called Bella, who came to collect her, but as soon as they reached the campsite, Nicki came flying out of the caravan.

'I've snagged us an invite to a party!'

Still thinking about Will, Ellie blinked. 'Party? Where?'

'At that manor house in Polkerran. I met this gorgeous man called Alex the other day, and he just phoned. Said we could all go along. Tonight. Come on girls, time to get your glad rags on.'

A taxi dropped Ellie and Nicki at the manor house, and they paused on the threshold to a huge room to appreciate the aura of glamour and money that exuded from the sophisticated gathering.

'I'm not sure we've dressed correctly,' she hissed in Nicki's ear, conscious of her Primark dress and wedges. 'And where's Bella?'

'She was having her hair plaited by one of the girls in the next van. She'll be here. Bella never misses a party. Oh, there he is!'

Nicki waved enthusiastically across the room as a sun-kissed, god-like man spotted them, and Ellie trawled behind her cousin, feeling horribly self-conscious.

Then, a hand landed on her bare arm. 'Thank God you're here.'

Pulse trilling at Will's voice, Ellie turned slowly, then tried not to be too obvious in her admiration as she took in this more smartly attired vision.

'Let's get a drink. I need someone sane to talk to. Alex's friends are all way too posh for my taste.'

They settled in a corner on a velvet-covered chaise longue and resumed their conversation from the other day.

'My parents aren't as laid-back as it sounds. If I've had one lecture on the precariousness of the acting profession, I've had a hundred. But,' Will shrugged, 'they've came to the university productions, and taped every TV show I've been in. They pay for my room in Alex's place in London. They know I need to be in town to be on hand for auditions and if I'm out of work, I turn my hand to anything on offer. As you'll have seen.'

'I'm sure you intend to repay them when you can.'

'Of course. Besides, we've got an agreement. If I haven't found success by a certain age, I'll give it up and find a proper job. The deadline is when I'm forty.'

Ellie burst into laughter as Will drained his glass. 'I'll get us a top-up.'

He sauntered away, easing through the throng, completely unfazed by the glamour and prestige, and Ellie's fascinated gaze took in the scene.

Nicki was across the room, flirting with Alex – Ellie recognised the signs, and wondered if he realised he was playing with an expert. She glanced at her watch. Would Bella turn up or decide to remain hanging out with their new friends up at the site?

Someone had turned the music up as Will emerged from the crowd, a brimming cut-glass flute in each hand. He handed one to Ellie, then held out his free hand.

'Come on.'

He drew her to her feet, leading her towards some double doors on the far wall.

'This is my favourite place when I stay.' Will shut out the noise. 'Take a seat.'

It was a beautiful room, elegant but also homely, with comfy-looking seating, an impressive marble fireplace, thickly patterned rugs on the stone flooring and a large circular table in the bay window.

The muted thump-thump of the music could be heard through the wooden doors as they sank onto a sofa.

'You don't mind? It feels like there's so much to talk about.'

Ellie had felt the same instant connection, and the conversation flowed as easily as the champagne, with Will finally fetching a bottle so he didn't have to keep leaving her – reporting that Alex was now wrapped around a woman he'd never seen before.

Perhaps inevitably, their talk frequently returned to art and films.

'I had the most amazing trip to Florence as part of my course,' Ellie enthused. 'The galleries were incredible. My mum was so jel. *A Room with a View* is her favourite film, and I love watching it with her. The cinematography is stunning.'

'And yet you've not been to Paris?'

Ellie shook her head, conscious the fizz was causing it to buzz. 'No. It was one of the scheduled trips, but I had a nasty bout of flu and they wouldn't let me travel. I was gutted.'

'I'll take you to Paris,' Will vowed. 'When I get my next role.'

Alex stuck his head into the room, demanding they rejoin the party, and Ellie was startled to discover his new addiction to be Bella, who'd obviously decided to join them. Nicki was nowhere in sight, but checking her phone, Ellie saw a text saying she'd left to meet a local for a drink, and not to wait up for her.

By midnight, Ellie was struggling to hide her yawns, mortified when Will caught her at it, but touched when he called a taxi and came outside to wait with her.

'Are you working tomorrow, Will?'

'Yes, but not with Stewie. I've got another stint behind the bar at The Lugger. It's the old inn by the bridge. Have you been?'

'Not yet.'

Ellie wasn't quite sure what else to say. Will seemed so exotic, for all his unemployed status – a shooting star, out of her reach. Had she been as boring as she felt?

Will ran a hand through his dark waves. 'I… actually, I was hoping to get a date. For lunch. Tomorrow.'

'Oh.' Ellie tried to look disinterested as a taxi pulled through the stone gates into the grounds, and she stepped forward, keen to end the awkward moment.

'You do know I mean with you?' Will addressed Ellie's back, and she swung around.

'Me?'

'Am I really so bad at this?' Will held her gaze in the dim glow of the car's headlights, and Ellie was stunned to see uncertainty on his features.

'Yes. I mean, no, you're not. I'm just… I'd love to have lunch!'

A relieved smile spread across his face, and he leapt forward to open the rear door of the taxi.

'Meet you on the harbour? Midday?'

Ellie nodded through the open window, raising a hand in a small wave as the car lurched across the gravel and turned for the gate once more.

Sinking back against the seat, she released a long breath. She was going on a date. With the most gorgeous man she'd ever laid eyes on.

–

The lunch was the first of many, with Ellie protesting at Will using his paltry wages – earned either behind the bar at the pub, sweating away in Stewie the Shrimp or selling tickets for the daily boat trips – on buying her treats, like ice creams or silly souvenirs from the tacky tourist shop on the front.

In return, Ellie did her best to eke her budget out, buying takeaways for them to enjoy, sitting on the harbour steps, feet dangling over the swell of water, or a couple of ciders at the pub.

Nicki was barely seen, spending all her time with Hamish, the local fisherman she'd caught, and even going out on his boat once, returning green in the gills and several pounds lighter from finding the undulating sea far less attractive when actually *on* it. Alex and Bella were likewise lesser spotted.

As for Ellie and Will, they became inseparable, spending every possible moment together, be it day or night. She also became aware of Will's proclivity for giving away money.

'But you don't have any!' Ellie exclaimed, as he dropped coins into whatever collection tin sat on the counter in the chippy, or the convenience store or local bar.

'So now I have less.' He shrugged. 'I have way more than a lot of people, Ells. And what's a few pounds here and there, if I've got it? Another shift with my mate, Stewie?'

Will, in the meantime, was amused by Ellie's attachment to her phone.

'You're always taking photos. It's a phone, you know, not a camera.'

'I'd love a good one, but I can't afford it right now. Besides, this is the iPhone4.' She waved it proudly.

Will's look was comical. 'So not the latest, then.'

'It was the best within my budget.' She gestured at the scenic harbour view. 'And it's so easy to take great shots with it. Besides, look at the light! There's something special about it here.'

'It's also why you constantly run out of battery, draining it by snapping away like there's no tomorrow.'

'Hush, now,' Ellie cautioned, laughing as Will pulled a sulky face, then grinned. She tugged his arm. 'Come over here, by the wall.'

'Why? What am I looking at? I want my beer!'

'It'll still be there when I'm done. Stand still. Look pensive. Now look over there. The camera loves you, Will.'

'And I love you,' he responded, kissing Ellie swiftly on her surprised mouth, then assuming a god-like pose on the harbour wall, reclining, head tossed back, eyes closed.

Heart thumping like the hammer currently pounding in the nearby boat yard, Ellie stared at him. Then, as delight coursed through her veins, she pocketed the phone and walked over to hug him.

'I love you too,' she whispered, as Will's arms held her close.

'Where are we going?'

'You'll see.'

'Will!' Ellie called as he strode on ahead, his long legs covering the uneven ground of the cliff path more easily than hers.

The sun was unrelenting, its strong rays beating through her cotton hat, her sunglasses slipping repeatedly down her peeling nose. The hawthorn hedgerows were high on either side, the verges dotted with cow parsley, and the scent of newly cut grass drifted over from a nearby cottage as waves pounded the rocks to her left.

Will had stopped now, searching along the hedge bordering the path on the coastal side.

'It has to be here somewhere.'

Fetching up beside him, sweating and out of breath, Ellie put her hands on her hips.

'What? You're being really frustrating!'

With a laugh, Will turned around. 'And you're impatient! I told you, it's a surprise.' He leaned down, pressing a firm kiss on Ellie's lips as they parted to protest, so she changed her mind, flinging her arms around his neck and pulling him into a longer one.

'You're a minx,' he whispered against her neck. 'Now behave.' He dropped a final kiss on top of the hat and resumed his study of the hedge. 'Aha! I knew it! Come on.' He pushed aside some branches to reveal a wooden stile. 'It looks like no one's used this for a while.'

As Ellie stepped up onto the stile and Will grasped her hand to steady her, she released an audible gasp.

'Oh, it's gorgeous!'

Below, at the bottom of some steps hewn into the steep hillside, was a deserted expanse of pale golden sand, peppered here and there with small rocky outcrops holding pools of water, sparkling in the sun. Beyond lay the sea, a vast, glistening blanket, dotted with tall white sails and accompanied by a soundtrack of waves hitting a distant cliff as seabirds called overhead.

They reached the beach eventually, and Will rested his arm on Ellie's shoulders as she took it in.

'I found it weeks ago. Alex has a small motorboat, and I came out on my own. There's a natural sort of jetty over there.' He pointed to where rocks had been piled by some long-ago hand to form a short walkway by more sheltered water, barely disturbed by the waves currently rolling in.

Turning in Will's arms, Ellie admired the crescent of sand, protected on either side by high cliffs.

'It's perfect,' she said softly.

'Come on, let's find a spot to pitch up.'

They spent the rest of the day on what they quickly decided would be 'their' beach, lying on a blanket from Will's backpack. He'd packed a picnic too, and a couple of bottles of the local cider.

It soon became a frequent place for their assignations, with Will borrowing the motorboat on occasion. Other times, they used the steep path instead, depending on their mood or the weather.

The sand there was finely grained and so soft. Ellie loved to dig her toes into it after they'd swum in the shallows, lying on their backs, hands clasped, skin drying under the sun's caress, Ellie's hair wet and thick with sand against her back.

Never had she been so happy and nor, it seemed, had Will.

Chapter One

"Back to the Future"

Autumn – Twelve Years Later…

Pulling into a space in the service station car park, Ellie retrieved her phone to scroll through any messages she may have missed while driving. Nothing too pressing, other than a flurry of voice notes from the bride whose wedding Ellie was due to photograph shortly, and she emerged from the car to look around.

It was early afternoon in mid-September, but strangely quiet, and Ellie hurried through the doors into the service area in search of a hot drink. Barely had she taken a sip of coffee, however, when her phone rang.

Nicki.

'Hey, what's up?' Ellie's heart lifted. It was ages since she'd spent a decent amount of time with her cousin, and she looked forward to seeing her. At least, she'd be looking forward to it if it didn't mean going back *there*, of all places.

'I didn't expect you to pick up. Wasn't sure of your ETA. Hamish has gone for his pre-op appointment, so I wanted to let you know where the key is if I'm out. How's the journey going?'

'So far, it's been great. I've stopped on the A30 for a caffeine infusion.'

A huff of laughter came from the phone. 'That's one long road, babes. Whereabouts?'

'I've just passed Okehampton.'

'Fab. You're about an hour away.'

Oh God…

Ellie's midriff clenched, a sensation she'd become accustomed to lately. Ever since, in fact, she'd found herself agreeing to return to Polkerran Point – a place she had vowed never to revisit.

'Ellie? Hello? You there?'

'Sorry.' She gave her head a small shake. 'Think I got on the road too early. What did you say?'

'You'll pass the "nearly home" trees soon. Well…' Nicki paused. 'I suppose to you they'll be the "nearly there" trees, like they are for the pesky emmets.'

'Don't start going all Cornish on me,' Ellie exclaimed before they ended the call.

She headed to the ladies' before resuming the journey, but as she washed her hands, Ellie caught sight of her wary expression in the mirror. The stark overhead lights were unforgiving, leaving nowhere to hide.

Stop it, she cautioned silently, sticking her hands in the wall-mounted dryer, letting the loud droning blast away her anxiety. *It's not like* he's *going to be there, is it? Besides, it ended years ago. Get over yourself.*

The admonition did the trick, and Ellie sailed past the aforementioned trees blissfully unaware of them, too busy belting out the latest Sabrina Carpenter in accompaniment to the radio, her mind busy with the photoshoots she'd had to reschedule and hoping the fortnight she'd promised to Nicki would fly by so she could escape and return to the routine of daily life in Oxford.

By the time she'd left the A30 at Bodmin, however, it was harder to stall the free-falling memories, and as Ellie passed sign after sign bearing names she'd long relegated to the past – Lostwithiel, Lerryn and then Polwelyn – her shoulders began to stiffen. When the car passed the entrance to the camping park where she'd stayed on her one and only foray to the area over twelve years ago, she stared rigidly ahead.

Once she'd driven down the winding hill into Polkerran Point, however, Ellie pulled up in a vacant space on the front, assailed by recollections she heartily wished she could toss into the depths of the harbour.

The quaint fishing village in September bore little resemblance to the place Ellie recalled. The previous visit had taken place in the height of a deliciously warm summer, and the village had been bustling with families and seaside activities. Today, there was a gentle, early autumn vibe, a suggestion that – now the schools were in session and visitors a mere trickle – life had resumed its lyrical out-of-season pattern. Opposite the harbour, people enjoyed coffee and cakes outside a stylish restaurant Ellie didn't recognise, the canopies pulled down low against the sun's wistful rays.

Sinking onto a vacant bench, Ellie drew in a steadying breath before exhaling slowly.

So *this* is how it felt to be back. She'd wondered endlessly this last month, after Nicki's cry for help, and speculation had done her no favours, merely stirred long-suppressed feelings, bringing a run of disturbed nights and a horribly reminiscent sense of loss on waking.

'Wasson, shag?'

Ellie blinked, her gaze flicking to the elderly man who'd taken a perch at the other end of the bench, but to her relief, he was chuckling into his phone.

Time to find Nicki's cottage.

Walking back to the car, Ellie paused for a moment, leaning on the harbour wall. Whispers of thin cloud – less dense than up on the moors – clung to a dusty blue sky. Water continuously slapped the stone steps by the moorings as boats bobbed against the jetty. The rattle of sail lines mingled with the calls of seabirds circling over the trees on the far side of the water, and as her gaze drifted across the undulating expanse of blue towards the horizon, she could see the top of a lighthouse on a stretch of rocks pointing out to sea.

'Beautiful,' Ellie whispered, whipping out her phone and taking a burst of images.

Five minutes later, and she'd arrived in the driveway of a large house at the end of the lane bordering the quieter side of the bay. It wasn't an area Ellie had explored much during that long-ago summer, and she looked around with interest. The gatepost bore a sign: *Westerleigh Cottage*.

Ellie stepped back into the lane as her cousin emerged from the much smaller property next door.

'Thank goodness you're here!' Nicki squeezed Ellie into a hug. 'It's been too long. Loving the hair, by the way.' She tugged one of the curls resting on her cousin's shoulder. 'And the colour.'

Ellie laughed as she followed Nicki inside. 'I'm told it's honey blonde, but it looks like weak coffee to me.'

Nicki and Hamish's home – Little Cott – was adequate for them and their two growing boys, Liam and Jason, but there was no guest room. Nicki's close friend, Anna Seymour, who lived in Westerleigh Cottage – a property so large she used to run it as a B&B before her own babies came along – had offered Ellie a room during her short stay.

'We are *so* grateful,' Nicki gushed as she made mugs of tea and carried them out to the small, walled garden at the back of the cottage, Ellie following in her wake.

'Hamish has been putting off this surgery for ages, but it's got to the point where the pain is too much.'

'How's he feeling?'

Nicki shrugged before taking the seat opposite Ellie. It was a relatively mild day, but she wrapped her thick cardigan more firmly across her middle. The enclosed space at the rear of the cottage didn't feel as though it ever got much sun.

'He's frustrated more than anything.' She sent Ellie a rueful smile. 'Not used to being inactive and fretting about the loss of income. We'll just be glad when the op's over.'

Ellie clasped her mug of tea. 'It's amazing back surgery these days means such a short stay in hospital. What was the plan you agreed on for when he's out?'

'He's going to his parents on the north coast. They've got a bungalow, and we don't even have a downstairs loo, never mind anywhere to shower or sleep. Hopefully, with the enforced rest and his planned physio, he'll be back by the time you leave.'

'He won't be able to go back to work, though, will he?'

Hamish had long had a fishing boat moored in Polkerran Point. Much as he loved his job, it was strenuous, physical labour, and although the hours were erratic and weather dependent, it was still the family's main source of income.

'No.' Nicki tucked a loose strand of hair behind her ear. 'It'll be months before he can go out to sea again, but Jem – he's the Harbourmaster – says there's desk work in the office a few hours a week, and it's not paid, but there's always a need for someone on rota at the National Coastwatch weather station down in Polruan.'

Knowing this period of time-out was coming, Nicki had managed to increase her hours at the Point Hotel, a smart residence at the top of the hill above Polkerran Point, where she worked in the hair and beauty salon. It meant she needed to do weekend shifts and couldn't always be around for the boys before or after school either.

'What time will Liam and Jason be home?'

'We've got a reprieve.' Nicki grinned at Ellie. 'I normally pick them up at three, but today's a free-for-all music club, and they'll be home about five. We take it in turns, so one of the other mums will drop them back here.'

They had a bit of a catch up, with Nicki dismissing any talk of what it was Ellie could help with to make life easier, assuring her it could wait.

'You know I can only spare about a fortnight?' Ellie cautioned. 'I moved what I could, but I have to be in Oxfordshire for a wedding two weeks on Saturday.'

'I know!' Nicki beamed at her. 'I'm just grateful to have you now. The op is scheduled for Monday, so by the time you go, Hamish should be able to manage stairs, even if he's not fully mobile. Come on.' She got to her feet. 'Let's go and get you settled next door. Then you can come back and help me wrestle the duvets back into their covers.'

'How old are they?' Ellie spoke quietly as she observed the two little ones snoozing in their respective portable cots beside one of the sofas in the gorgeous sitting room at Westerleigh Cottage.

'Nine months.' Anna, Nicki's neighbour and friend, whispered, coming to stand beside her, sporting an apron bearing the words 'Jam First', her attractive features flushed with the heat of the oven and her wavy brown hair tied up in a ponytail, from which tendrils were escaping.

'They are so sweet.' Ellie's heart swelled with delight.

They admired the sleeping babies for a few moments longer before quietly padding back to the kitchen island.

'They're less so at two in the morning. Bertie sleeps like a log now, but Emma is clearly going to be a party girl. She's always ready for a play, and her brother is already channelling his inner teen and does *not* like being woken up.'

Ellie laughed. 'Sounds like me and my sister back in the day. It's very kind of you to do dinner tonight.'

Anna placed a large casserole dish in the oven, then tossed her oven gloves onto the kitchen island. 'I love cooking, and it's ages since we've had people round. Nicki and Hamish need a bit of a break, too.'

'I'm so grateful to you, letting me stay in that beautiful room.' Ellie waved a hand towards the ceiling, but Anna shook her head.

'Nicki's always been such a supportive friend – it's the least we could do.' Her eyes twinkled. 'I'm glad you like the room. It used to be ours, but we moved down from the top floor once the twins arrived so we could be near at hand. The timing's perfect too, as a few weeks after you go home, we're off to the States. My best mate, Lauren, lives there, and she's getting married.'

They chatted a little about the challenge of a transatlantic flight with the babies, but once she was assured there was nothing she could do to help with the dinner prep, Ellie headed back to Little Cott to find Hamish returned, as well as the boys.

She played a frenetic game of *Angry Birds* with Liam and Jason and tried not to allow the slowly emerging memories any purchase. At least staying at Westerleigh – with its stunning views and its luxurious bedroom – was a far cry from the single bed in the shared caravan, and it was only for a fortnight, not a couple of months, like last time.

And he's *not here, either…*

Back round at Westerleigh, with everyone fed and the boys happily absorbed in the snug, Anna's husband, Oliver – a renowned social historian and author – opened another bottle of wine while his wife went upstairs to check on the twins.

The sitting area, despite its open-plan nature, was utterly cosy, with comfy-looking sofas and a low coffee table bearing a neat pile of bibs and a cute cuddly rabbit on top of a stack of books. There were a couple of sturdy wingback chairs either side of a striking hearth, clearly more suited to Oliver, who was not only extremely tall but broad of shoulder, too.

Ellie was delighted when a black cat jumped onto her lap, and she rubbed it under its chin, drawing a responsive purr.

Oliver grunted. 'Heathcliff's nose has been a bit out of joint since the twins arrived. She'll love you forever if you make a fuss of her.'

The conversation drifted between Hamish's convalescence plan and the progress of Oliver's latest book – a non-fiction historical series aimed at school-age children – and before long, Anna returned from upstairs.

'That was a gorgeous meal, Anna,' Ellie enthused. 'And I swear clotted cream always tastes better in Cornwall!'

'It's my downfall, too,' Nicki said. 'It goes surprisingly well with pumpkin pie, and Anna makes a corker.'

Surprised, Ellie looked to their host. 'I thought that was mainly an American thing.'

'Probably, but we always have so much to spare after the annual pumpkin trail, it seemed a shame to waste it, so I've been experimenting over the years.'

A small sound came from Oliver, and his arm stalled in mid-air as he raised his glass to his lips.

'What?'

Anna smirked. 'Oliver is my guinea pig. He never quite got over the pumpkin pancakes.'

'It wasn't as bad as the pumpkin-spiced granola you put on the table the next morning,' Oliver retorted, but his keen blue eyes held a warmth for his wife alone, and Ellie exchanged an amused look with Nicki.

'So what's the trail?' Ellie asked, cradling her glass in both hands.

'Carved pumpkins all around the cove. And local craft makers displaying their pumpkin-themed products, from food to art to clay or wood. Phee – she's a local artist, watercolours – does a map, which the book shop sells for a couple of pounds, all proceeds to the village school.'

'The local businesses all chip in prizes,' Hamish added. 'It's a lot of fun.'

'Wow. I'd assumed it would be pretty quiet at this time of year.'

Anna's eyes lit up. 'Never a dull moment in the cove! There's a scarecrow festival next, and then Hallowe'en, followed by Bonfire Night. It helps bring trade into the village either side of half-term.'

'And that's all before the circus comes to town next spring,' Oliver mused as he stretched his long legs out in front of the hearth.

'Really?' Ellie blinked. 'Where on earth will there be room for that?'

Anna chuckled. 'Can you imagine? Lions and tigers in the cove?'

Oliver made a small sound. 'More likely to be peacocks and clowns with this lot.'

Nicki grinned at Ellie. 'It's all local chit-chat so far. Alex Tremayne – do you remember him? He took over running the family estate last year. We all thought there'd be little change, to be honest.'

Ellie's skin went cold. How could she ever forget *that* name?

'Alex is known to not be fond of the cove,' Anna interjected. 'He's a city man, through and through.'

'And they're welcome to reclaim him whenever they wish.' There was steel in Oliver's voice, but Ellie's skin tingled as the past moved stealthily towards her.

'So what's the gossip?'

'A big rumour about a documentary filming early next year, down the coast beyond Fowey,' Hamish explained. 'Tremayne is allegedly keen for some sort of involvement for Polkerran. Lord knows why.'

Ellie's shoulders stiffened. Alex Tremayne… Will's housemate back then, the whole reason he'd been in Cornwall… and the man who'd ultimately ended all her hopes and dreams.

Chapter Two

"Ghosts"

Ellie sipped her wine as the others debated the pros and cons for the village if the rumours were true, her mind fighting the urge to return to those heady, summer days.

'Seems he's taking the investment in the cove seriously for now,' Anna mused.

Oliver grunted. 'It won't last. He'll soon be bored.'

'That might depend on Bella,' Anna said sagely, heading to the kitchen.

Bella?

'*Our* old mate Bella?' Ellie shot a glance at Nicki. 'I remember you saying last year she'd turned up in Polkerran.'

Close at university, Ellie hadn't seen much of Bella in recent years.

'Yes! She's not here all the time, because of her freelance teaching in Bristol, but she's been doing historical research for Oliver.'

A wail came from the baby monitor.

'And she's been a lifesaver with this latest book.' Oliver got to his feet. 'My turn.'

'He's such a lovely dad.' Anna spoke warmly, as she came over with a tray of mugs and a cafetiere. 'He had no idea he'd be cut out for it, but I couldn't have asked for more.'

'Are you okay?' Ellie's brow furrowed as Anna wiped away a tear.

'She's fine,' Nicki interjected, picking up the sugar. 'You'll get used to it.'

Anna gave a watery laugh as the wailing stopped. 'Nicki's right. Take no notice of me. The more content I get, the more prone to emotion I seem to be.'

Trying not to be envious, Ellie took a mug of coffee from Anna.

'Here's to happiness, then!'

They clinked mugs, and the subject turned to Anna and Oliver's upcoming trip to America, but as the evening drew to a close, and the family returned to the cottage next door, Ellie couldn't help but feel she may as well wish for the moon.

—

Over the next two days, Ellie's temporary new life settled into a pattern, and although the ghosts of the past lurked on every corner, she did her best to dismiss them.

Nicki's full-time hours meant frequent weekend shifts at the salon, which helped as it paid more, but meant she got less time with her boys. Hamish did his best to keep them entertained, and Ellie busied herself with the household chores, worrying about finding a moment to complete the editing process on a couple of recent shoots.

She tried not to think about the lost income from the rescheduled jobs. At least she had a little coming in from her greeting card commissions – a sideline that didn't make much profit, but fed her creative soul.

On Sunday evening, conscious of their impending separation, Ellie shooed the increasingly anxious couple off to The Lugger for a few hours, insisting she and Liam and Jason had unfinished business on the PlayStation. Despite being in pain, Hamish grabbed the chance, saying a pint of Doom Bar would set him up 'well and proper, mind' for the next day.

The following morning, once the boys were at school and Nicki and Hamish left for the hospital, Ellie set to work on editing a shoot on her laptop. There wasn't any space in Nicki's cottage, but Anna had kindly offered up the recent addition to Westerleigh of an elegant orangery at the back of the house. Whether accessed directly from the main sitting area or approached across the large terrace, it was a beautiful space, its stone base and tall windows complementing the house perfectly. An arched glass roof featuring white wrought-iron finials created a sense of fully being outside and stunning, natural light streamed in, even on a cloudy day.

A message came some hours later from Nicki to say Hamish was in recovery and she was heading home. As it was nearly time to pick up the boys, Ellie began to pack up her hard drive and leads, just as Anna appeared by the open doors onto the terrace, wheeling the twins in their stroller.

'Hi,' Ellie called. 'I'm just heading down to school.'

'I'll walk with you, if you like.' Anna bent down to tuck a blanket more firmly around Emma, who trilled some nonsensical sounds. 'These two aren't taking Mummy's advice about having a nap, but motion usually solves the dispute.'

They chatted comfortably as they walked along the narrow road running around the quieter side of the bay, and Ellie reflected on how easy-going Anna was. She felt as though she'd known her for ages.

'Nicki said you never came back to the cove after that one holiday. Did you not like it?'

A frisson shot through Ellie. 'Oh, you know.' She attempted nonchalance. 'You often think you'll go back to somewhere you had a great time, but life just runs away with you.'

They'd reached the bridge spanning the river which fed into the curved bay of water, and Anna stopped to check on the twins, who had done as she'd predicted and drifted off to sleep, and Ellie leaned on the parapet and stared across the shimmering wavelets towards the horizon. A stiff breeze blew in from the sea, where larger waves were decked in frothy flowing capes as they scurried towards the rocks, tossing ribbons of white into the air. Ellie wished she could do the same with the memories moving steadily inwards like the tide.

'I know what you mean.' Anna rolled the stroller to and fro. 'I stopped coming here for a long time after I left college and didn't have the summer holidays to spend in Cornwall. North Yorkshire was such a long way off.' She sent Ellie a regretful smile. 'I used to meet my aunt Meg in London all the time, as it was easier to get to. She left me – us – the house, bless her, and I'll always wish I had tried harder to spend more time with her.'

They continued into town, and Ellie headed to the village school to meet Liam and Jason, warmed by the friendliness of those collecting children of various ages. She allowed the boys to persuade her to walk to the small beach, accessed along the lane which ran parallel with the water on the busier side of Polkerran, towards the rocks bearing the small lighthouse. Wishing they'd chosen anywhere but there, Ellie fought the recollections circling like the gulls in the sky overhead.

'There's a cafe,' Jason said, as he all but skipped along beside Ellie. 'They do the most epic ice creams, Auntie Nellie.'

Ellie's lips curved at the name they both used for her, then frowned. 'Isn't it a bit chilly for ice cream?'

Liam rolled his eyes. 'Grown-ups say such silly things. If it's cold, then at least they won't melt like they do in the sun.'

'Fair point,' Ellie conceded.

Ten minutes later, they'd reached the tidal beach bordered by grey cliffs and topped with tall trees and, on one side, a stunning, Gothic-looking house which seemed to emerge from the stone as if they were one.

'That's Harbourwatch,' Liam added, as they headed straight to the quaint beach cafe built into the same rocks. 'Our friend, Mollie, lives there.'

As far as Ellie could recall, the property had been empty and covered in scaffolding when she last visited. But then, she'd not really paid it much notice, far more interested in the fingers intertwined with hers, as she and Will stretched out on the warm sand.

The cafe – which certainly hadn't been there before either – was takeaway only, but stocked a delightful range of locally made goods, and Ellie couldn't resist making a few purchases while the boys tucked into their treats, chattering about school and how they missed the water sports in the winter and what they intended to dress as for Hallowe'en.

'Can we skim some stones?' Jason begged, as Ellie offered him a wipe for his hands. 'This is a great place for it.'

Although she was a bit cold, Ellie nodded. 'Of course, just don't get your trainers wet or your mum will never forgive me.'

Both boys sped down to the shore to seek out the best pebbles, and Ellie picked up the discarded school bags and Jason's PE kit and walked over to where a couple of benches had been set on a raised plinth.

Gripped by mixed emotions, she refused to allow her gaze to move over to the secluded corner she and Will had favoured until they'd discovered *their* beach. A soft sigh fell from her lips, and she brushed the hair from her eyes. How bittersweet the memories were.

Ellie tucked her hands into her pockets and tried to focus on the waves rolling gently onto the flat sand, rippling where they encountered a few low-lying rocks. There were a couple of families over by the cliffs supporting Harbourwatch, busy rock-pooling, and a group of walkers chatting animatedly on a low wall, sipping their takeaway coffees.

Ellie's gaze drifted towards where the open sea met the smoother waves of Polkerran Point, just as a gleaming yacht, its sail billowing in the wind, rounded the rocks to her right, and she watched with mild interest as it rolled and swayed. Even at a distance, she could detect two figures on board. The vessel's speed slowed, assuming a more sedate pace and diminishing in size as it moved with ease towards the sheltered waters of the harbour.

Ellie shivered, then glanced at her watch.

'Come on, boys.' She waved at Liam and Jason, who dispatched their last two stones before tearing back up the beach towards her. 'Your mum will be back by now. Time we went home.'

Nicki worked the Tuesday, but once school was over, she headed over to Port Wenneth with Liam and Jason to visit Hamish. His surgery had gone as planned, aside from his complaining of an intense numbness in his legs, but they assured him it would ease off with time. Everything seemed on track for him to be released into his parents' care in a few days.

With free time on her hands, Ellie donned her walking boots and slung the strap of her trusty Canon camera across her body before heading out onto the coastal path. The strenuous walk did her good, helping to clear her mind of the past, and she clicked away, keen to capture the light on the sea, a stark contrast to the bracken-coated clifftops.

Hints of dusk creeping west were sufficient to direct Ellie back home, warmed from the exercise, pink-cheeked, her honey-gold hair teased by the clifftop breeze into escaping its silk bandana.

Ellie's phone rang as she walked down the lane past a driveway bearing a sign which read The Lookout.

Nicki.

'Hi. How's it going?'

'Okay.' Nicki sounded hesitant, and Ellie placed a hand over her other ear to listen more carefully. 'Hamish isn't too bright, but they're looking after him well. The boys have petitioned to see a film before we come home. Will you be okay? We'll be back around seven.'

'Of course! Shall we be naughty and get a takeaway tonight?'

'Sounds fab. The menu for Thai Dai's is in the drawer by the toaster. Or there's chippy tea from Colin the Cod.'

Pocketing her phone, Ellie hesitated when she reached the place where the lane from the cliff path joined the one leading up to Little Cott and Westerleigh.

It would be a good few hours before Nicki returned. Sitting alone in the cottage didn't hold much appeal, and Ellie had failed to get into her book every night since she'd arrived, so it would either be wasting time playing games on her phone or streaming mindless shows. Anna and Oliver had gone with the twins to stay overnight with her brother, who lived with his girlfriend on a tidal creek further up the river, so it would be equally lonely there, too.

Turning right, Ellie moved briskly down the lane, passing the quaint-looking Lugger Inn, adorned with hanging baskets filled with fading blooms, and started across the bridge.

'Beautiful,' she whispered, reaching for her camera again.

Ellie clicked away, but as she neared the harbour, she noticed a yacht – possibly the one she'd seen the previous afternoon – moored nearby. With its mast gleaming in a late burst of sun as it sank towards the horizon, it made for a stunning shot, and she reviewed her efforts on the camera display.

Reaching the harbourfront, the delicious aroma of garlic emanated from both the bistro and an unfamiliar waterside restaurant further along, to the accompaniment of voices and laughter and the tinkling of cutlery against china from those seated outside.

Ellie replaced her lens cap and leant against the harbour wall. A steady stream of customers emerged from the chip shop, paper packages clutched in their hands. Sea birds wheeled overhead, their piercing cries drifting upwards over the trees, whose gold and amber foliage created a patchwork across the hillside.

Suddenly, a chill swept over Ellie's skin as a voice floated across the water from the nearby jetty. Her hand shot to her throat, which felt strangely tight. Surely not... not now...

Pushing away from the low wall, Ellie darted across the cobbled street and into Karma, a smart coffee shop.

Forcing herself to breathe evenly, silently scolding her tummy for doing a back flip the envy of any budding gymnast, she hastily ordered a hot chocolate, then slowly edged towards one of the window seats.

'Oh God,' she intoned with dread.

If Ellie's eyesight didn't deceive her in the fading light, Alex Tremayne was now on board the stylish vessel she'd just photographed, a shaft of sunlight turning his hair gold, and on the jetty – one hand gripping the steel railing of the boat as it bobbed and weaved on the water, the other holding a coiled rope – stood the man who broke her heart all those years ago: Will Farmer.

Chapter Three

"Strangers in the Night"

'Are you okay?'

Ellie started, then dragged her hungry gaze away from this older, more rugged Will. A petite young woman with red-gold hair, accompanied by a pretty child, had paused beside the sofa. They looked vaguely familiar.

'You've gone horrid pale.'

'Yes. Sorry.' Ellie pulled herself together. 'I've seen you at the school, I think?'

The woman nodded, her chin-length curls bobbing. 'Phoenix, or Phee to most. Verity Blue,' she indicated the little girl. 'Started there this year after we moved back to the cove from Meva.' She had a warm, West Country burr to her voice and a friendly smile.

Ellie shook the proffered hand. 'Ellie. I'm here to help my cousin out for bit.'

'Nicki? I thought I'd seen you with her boys. Poor Hamish. He'll be missing being out at sea. Well, if you're sure you're okay, we'd best get on.'

Phoenix said goodbye, ushering her daughter out of the door, and Ellie's anxious gaze shot back towards the harbour.

There was no longer any sign of Will or Alex, thankfully, and her heart resumed its normal pace.

He'll doubtless be gone again soon. Just keep a low profile. Don't go out. Stay in your room. Don't even get out of bed.

'Idiot,' Ellie silently admonished, as she cautiously sipped the hot chocolate. Why did it taste like ashes?

She put it aside. Time to get back to Little Cott. Thank goodness her stay in the cove would be brief!

–

Nicki had been somewhat subdued when they arrived home, explaining that Hamish had little to no feeling in his legs at present.

Alarm gripped Ellie as she hugged her cousin. 'I'm so sorry.'

'It's okay.' Nicki attempted a more positive tone. 'We had been warned it was a possible side effect, but you just don't expect it to happen.'

'How long do they think it will last?'

Nicki shrugged as she dropped her bag onto the kitchen table. 'They said it's likely to fade over the next twenty-four hours or so.' She cast a wary glance towards the sitting room, where the boys could be heard arguing over the remote. 'I haven't mentioned it to Liam and Jason.'

Ellie made a cup of tea while Nicki attended to another message from Hamish. It put her ridiculous feelings over the sudden sighting of Will into perspective – after all, she wasn't twenty-one any more – and she determined to get over herself and concentrate on making some reels for her business.

'Bummer,' she muttered, as she took out her own phone. 'Dead again.' The charging lead was in her room at Anna's; she'd have to borrow Nicki's.

'Great.' Nicki tossed her phone onto the table and grabbed her mug.

'What's up?'

'I need to swap my shift in the morning. The surgeon wants to speak to us both. Hamish says he's been told there's nothing to worry about. How can that be right?'

'They must know what they're talking about. Come on. You need something to do. I know of an exciting pile of washing just waiting for us to get our hands on it.'

'You're right,' Nicki said, heading to the back porch, which doubled as a utility room. 'At least the op is over. He's going to be so frustrated waiting to be fit enough to take the boat out again, but at least we'll have a goal.' A flicker of disquiet touched Nicki's features as she sorted clothes from the washing basket.

Ellie sent her a sympathetic look. 'And you'll have his company again.'

'True. He'll be home again and here for the boys around school hours. And he'll need to get moving.'

Ellie tugged more towels from the tumble drier, enjoying the wafts of fabric softener as she flipped them over to fold.

'Sounds like you'll have the whip out.'

Nicki chuckled. 'Not sure he'll be up to *that* any time soon.'

Laughter burst from Ellie. 'And remind me, when do Anna and Oliver leave for the States?'

'Less than a month now, I think. Anna's godmother to Lauren's little girl, Mia. Aside from the wedding, she can't wait to get out there to see her.'

When they returned to the kitchen, Nicki plugged in the iron while Ellie opened the fridge.

'It's getting late. Do you want to forego a takeaway? There's some of that quiche left. We could make up a salad, and there's oven chips for the boys.'

Nicki draped an ironed school shirt over a chair and picked up another. Then, she slumped onto a stool. 'I'm so fed up. Since Hamish's back started playing up, I only ever go out now to work. No more sitting round Anna's table with the locals, no socialising. We used to have some fun girly lunches, me, Anna, Kate – she lives at Harbourwatch – and sometimes Anna's brother's girl-friend, Gemma, too…'

Ellie sent her a sympathetic look as she closed the fridge door, torn over what to suggest. Was she being mean, wanting to hide away? Surely Will, if he was even still in the cove, would be staying up at the posh hotel or with the Tremaynes, like he did all those years ago? She didn't even know if the yacht was his or Alex's. He was a hugely successful actor. Didn't they buy into those sorts of trappings?

Eyeing Nicki's forlorn expression as she stared at the crumpled shirt in her hands, Ellie's heart won out. Her cousin's wellbeing was far more important. She'd worry about her bank balance another time. Besides, she'd be home soon and able to resume business as usual.

'How about we head down to The Lugger? My treat.'

Brightening, Nicki dropped the shirt back into the ironing basket. 'Are you sure? We're so strapped for cash right now, and the cinema wasn't cheap. They do love eating at the pub.' She glanced at the clock. 'I'll call Seb and ask him to hold a table for us.'

A half-hour later, they settled into a high-backed booth opposite the bar of the inn, Jason and Liam both focused on the devices propped on the table in front of them, and Ellie and Nicki nursing a glass of wine each.

Once the food order was placed, Ellie settled back into the corner of the booth, her gaze uneasily scanning faces, relieved to recognise none of them.

'Cheers.' Nicki held up her glass and Ellie clinked hers against it, but as she raised it to her lips, the door opened and Alex Tremayne entered, accompanied by a tall, stunning woman with long black hair, and behind them, another man sporting a hat, low over his eyes. Yet Ellie would know the set of those shoulders, that jawline, anywhere…

She almost dropped her glass, grabbing the stem to steady it, then ducking her head as the group made their way to the bar.

Scooting to the far corner of the booth, she became aware of Nicki's concern.

'What's the matter? You look like you've just been slapped in the face.'

Ellie put a hand to her cheek.

'I'm serious,' Nicki said quietly, casting a quick look at Jason and Liam, who remained oblivious, sipping Dr Pepper through paper straws and continuing to stare at their respective screens. 'You're red as can be!'

'It's nothing,' Ellie lied. She all but trembled at the thought of facing Will.

Why, though? He let you down in the end, not the other way round…

Perhaps if she left now, while their attention was focused on ordering drinks…

'Ellie?' Nicki tugged at her sleeve. 'It's clearly *something*. Do you feel ill?'

She could hear the trepidation in her cousin's voice. The last thing she needed was for her support to keel over.

'I'm fine. Honestly.' Ellie's gaze was inadvertently drawn to where the group stood.

Nicki peered over, then looked back at Ellie, her brow furrowed.

'That's Alex Tremayne. Currently running the estate.'

Ellie cleared her throat. 'Yes. I remember him. Weren't he and Bella an item back then?'

Nicki looked a little uncomfortable. 'As I recall, he tried to be an item with everyone. Not that I was around much after I met Hamish.'

Warmth permeated Ellie's skin, intensifying as images flew through her traitorous mind of long evenings with Will, either in his room at Tremayne Manor, sitting on a secluded beach watching the sunset, or cuddled together in her tiny bed in the van. At the time, she'd been thankful for Nicki's absence.

Nicki was listening to something Liam had asked, and Ellie drew in a shallow breath, picking up her glass and welcoming the distraction as Gavin – who ran the pub with his husband, Seb – arrived with the boys' burgers, followed by a young girl with Nicki's lasagne and Ellie's fish pie.

'Alex could be here for any number of reasons,' Nicki continued, conversationally. 'The manor is his now, although his parents still live there. And Claudia,' she nodded towards the out-of-sight bar, 'is an old family friend. The other chap might be her latest. She gets through them like wet wipes. They're a monied set, but Alex is never here long.' She leaned forward to peer over. 'They've gone into the snug. Probably don't want to hang out with the plebs.'

Relieved, Ellie stared at her plate while Nicki passed ketchup to Liam and put far less salt than he demanded on Jason's chips. Her appetite had fizzled out, as had her hopes for not seeing Will again. Perhaps if they ate quickly, they could all leave before he emerged from their private sanctuary?

Nicki took a photo of her lasagne and glass of wine and started typing a WhatsApp to Hamish. Ellie picked up her fork and speared some cheesy-topped mash, but she stiffened as a figure passed by the booth.

Will still had the hat pulled down low as he selected a newspaper from the rack, then he turned to pass their table and all but froze, raising his head to reveal the glimmer of dark eyes as his stunned gaze met Ellie's.

For a second, the moment endured, before Will's features assumed a blank expression and he ducked his head, striding out of sight, followed by the sound of a door closing with a snap.

'Oh my God!' Nicki put a hand to her mouth as she swallowed a mouthful of lasagne. 'That was him, wasn't it? That chap you hung out with. Alex's mate. Went on to star in some big stuff – not my sort of watch. What was his name?' She narrowed her eyes. 'Bill something?'

'Will,' Ellie whispered.

'That's it!' Nicki shook her head. 'Well, Alex Tremayne never struck me as someone who people hung around for long. This Will must either be thick-skinned or thick-brained.'

Ellie was struggling to breathe evenly. The look on Will's face had said all it needed to. He knew her face, recalled exactly who she was.

And he clearly had no desire to be reacquainted.

Chapter Four

"Much Ado About Nothing"

Thankfully, Ellie saw no further sign of Will or Alex that evening, as no one emerged from the snug before she and Nicki left to take the boys home. The gleaming yacht – which Nicki confirmed was Alex's – had also gone from the harbour the following morning.

It had been a restless night, and giving in around four in the morning, Ellie sat up and nestled wearily against her pillow, laptop on her knees, desperately trying to calm the thoughts scampering through her tattered mind.

Why had Will been in Polkerran? Was this his first visit after all those years, or did he regularly come down with Alex? Surely Nicki would have found him more familiar, if he did… And would he be back, or would seeing Ellie – and she knew he'd recognised her – be enough to put him off?

Telling herself it was old history landed on deaf ears, and with no answers to hand, Ellie soon fell victim to searching social media, but Will was absent in his own right. The only things she could find were fan-led Instagram and TikTok accounts or Facebook groups full of older fans obsessed with every snippet of information or photo they could find. He'd been so successful, yet a search of IMDB showed nothing recent.

She'd known, of course, about his early roles – bit parts on stage and a small, recurring role in a soap for a few months – but her mind shied away from thinking about their conversations back then.

Any news reports focused around the premieres for the films and TV series that had catapulted him to fame. Beyond that, the few other links she found on Google were to older interviews. It was as if Will had vanished from the world.

Frustrated with having indulged her interest and keen to put the brief encounter behind her, Ellie buried herself in potential work, setting up a few video meetings to discuss possible shoots once back home and working on the reels she'd intended to post the previous day.

Once the boys were in school and Nicki had left for the appointment with the surgeon, Ellie returned from a brisk walk to find Anna's kitchen buzzing with people.

'Hey, come and meet some of the locals.' Anna beckoned her over to the long, scrubbed pine table by the window, and Ellie was pleased to see Phoenix sitting in between two elderly ladies, who eyed her with avid interest.

'This is Nicki's cousin, Ellie, who's been helping out at home, with Hamish in hospital. This is Mrs Lovelace and Mrs Clegg.' Anna indicated the two elderly ladies. 'They like to come for tea and a chat in the mornings.'

'Alright, my lovely? How be the young'un after his lunar composting?'

'Lumbar decompression, Mum,' suggested a lady seated in the window seat, bouncing Bertie on her lap. 'I've seen you in the village. Jean Lovelace.' She nodded towards the elderly lady with silver curls framing her wizened features. 'My mum.'

'Jean runs the ice cream shop in season,' Phoenix added, as she stirred sugar into her mug. 'And works at the Point Hotel in the quieter times.'

Ellie smiled at the only gentleman, seated opposite Phoenix. His weather-beaten features bore a mischievous air as keen eyes scanned Ellie's face.

'This is Patrick,' Phoenix continued. 'I'm not sure who keeps who in order, but these three muddle along together somehow.'

'Wasson, young'un?'

'All good, thank you. I'm lucky enough to be staying in one of Anna's beautiful rooms and spend my days in the orangery pretending to work while I get swept away by the view.'

'Would you like a tea or coffee?' Anna walked over to scoop up Emma, who'd pulled herself up and was making her way around the coffee table, little hands gripping the wood, tongue stuck between her lips in fierce concentration.

'No, I'm fine, thanks,' Ellie said. 'I've got a few calls to make, and Nicki should be back soon.'

She waved goodbye to the group in the kitchen and headed to the orangery, but as so often happened, she was drawn to the windows. It was a beautiful late September day, the sea gliding into the bay as though on a conveyor, barely a ripple breaking its surface. A small white boat could be seen not far below the cliffs supporting Harbour-watch – one which Anna had explained before now was Larry the Lobster's – and as she watched, he hauled up a large open-work pot and began to empty his catch.

Ellie turned her back. Thank goodness Hamish would be home the following week. She needed to leave Cornwall and its heart-wrenching memories and return to the even tenor of her days. No more fear of bumping into Will again, or seeing that dismissive look in his eyes; eyes that once held warmth, fire, love…

Trembling, Ellie's hands gripped the back of a chair.

'Enough,' she said, fiercely, closing her eyes, the murmur of conversation from the kitchen intruding. Then, she looked at her watch. Had she missed a message from Nicki? She should have been home by now.

'Don't you dare be flat again,' she scolded her phone as she tugged it from her pocket, but as she did so, it rang. 'Hi. Are you on your way back?'

There was a muffled sound, followed by a suppressed sob.

Ellie's heart lurched, and she pressed the phone to her ear. 'Nicki? What's wrong?'

'It's Hamish,' Nicki croaked. 'This numbness, it's more than that. He's got this…' She hiccupped, then sniffed. 'He's paralysed from the hips down.'

'What!' Ellie exclaimed, her skin awash with cold.

Snuffling came down the line. 'They're saying it's most likely temporary, but they have no idea when it will ease off. He's allowed to go to his parents as planned, but now we don't know for how long, and you're leaving next week.' Nicki wailed. 'I'll be all alone and unable to do enough hours.'

Expressing sympathy as best she could, Ellie sank onto the chair in front of the table doubling as her desk. Was she imagining it, or could she hear doors clanging shut? This wasn't going to be a quick fix. There was no immediate escape on the horizon.

Ellie could be stuck in Polkerran Point for a very long time.

Nicki had been frantic by the time she'd returned from the hospital, choked with worry over Hamish and fraught with anxiety over how to manage the situation.

'It'll be fine,' Ellie soothed, picking up her cousin's bag, which had fallen to the floor when she'd failed to hang it properly on the back of a chair.

'I called Mum, but she and Dad can't come down, not until half-term.'

Nicki's parents were both teachers in a secondary school.

'Look, sit down,' Ellie said firmly, steering Nicki onto a kitchen stool and taking the one opposite.

'Wait! Where are the boys?' Nicki's eyes darted to the sitting room.

'Over at Harbourwatch with Mollie. They were invited to tea. Listen. I'll stay.'

Nicki sat back in her chair. 'But your business, Ellie. You need an income as much as any of us.'

It was true, and the profit she made on the cards wouldn't cover the rent on her flat in Oxford, or the bills. Parking it for now, Ellie took her cousin's hands in her own.

'I'll find work. Something. But I can't walk away. I *won't* leave you.' Ellie swallowed quickly. What was she committing to here?

'Poor Hamish,' Nicki cried, fishing for a tissue. 'He desperately wants to come home, and now we don't know when he will.'

Ellie popped back to Westerleigh to do a few jobs on the laptop before returning to Little Cott, and Nicki spent the evening – when not exchanging messages with

Hamish — swinging between gratitude towards Ellie for extending her stay and guilt for disrupting her cousin's life.

'Anna would've helped if she wasn't going away. And the boys are always welcome at Harbourwatch, but Kate — she's a colleague and friend — works full time too. Matt — Anna's brother — and Gemma live on a tidal creek, pretty much only accessible at high tide, and are too remote to help with school runs, and although there are other parents willing to chip in here and there, it's so disruptive for the boys not to be at home to do homework or just… be themselves.'

'Please don't worry,' Ellie begged her as she washed up after dinner. 'I need to go and do this wedding shoot, but I'll be straight back. My other clients aren't tied by timing for the work we had planned, and they're being very flexible.'

She refrained from telling Nicki a couple of them — new, not regulars — had chosen to go elsewhere when Ellie tried to reschedule them a second time, and she didn't blame them. She'd probably do the same thing in the circumstances.

A further pressing dilemma had been where to stay. She couldn't impose on Anna and Oliver much longer. Besides, they were going away…

There was a small holiday let opposite Nicki's cottage, fronting onto the water, which would have been the perfect location, but when Ellie enquired about it, the cost was simply too much.

Perhaps she'd best pitch a tent on the beach?

—

Ellie came downstairs the following morning, weary from another disturbed night and thankful Nicki – who was on a later shift – had time to do the school run.

There was a pretty glass heart-shaped dish on the hall table, filled to the brim with a variety of shells.

'Aunt Meg's,' Anna said as she emerged from the snug carrying a cake stand. 'She was obsessed with collecting them.'

'They're lovely.'

'I picked my favourites for the dish.' She looked a little embarrassed. 'Don't tell Oliver – he thinks I had a clear out – but I couldn't bear to throw any of them away, so there's a much bigger store of them in a box in the cellar.'

Ellie laughed. 'Sounds like my mum. She's hoarded every card we've ever sent her. Little does Dad know what's actually in the large flat crate under their bed!'

It was heartwarming to discover a now-familiar domestic scene when they entered the kitchen – Oliver at the table, spoon-feeding Bertie, most of which appeared to be landing on the little one's bib rather than in his mouth – and Anna scooping up Emma to pat the wriggling baby's back.

'The kettle's just boiled.' Anna's brow furrowed as she surveyed Ellie under the brighter lights of the kitchen. 'Unless you'd prefer coffee. You look like you need it.'

'I forgot to put my toothbrush on charge. I don't suppose—'

'I have everything. Left over from the B&B days. I'll dig you one out in a minute.'

'Brilliant. Are you expecting the usual crowd?' Ellie asked over her shoulder as she made a welcome cup of tea.

'Sadly,' Oliver muttered, placing the bowl and spoon on the table and exchanging babies with Anna. 'Thankfully, there is growing evidence I am needed to do a nappy change.'

Anna sent him a loving look as he left the room, Emma nestled against his broad chest, then cleaned Bertie up before sitting him on the play mat and handing him his favourite teether.

'There are cakes in the usual place,' she added to Ellie, who opened the cupboard and soon had an array of Anna's home-made treats on the cake stand, which she placed on the table in the bay window.

An hour later – Oliver and the babies accompanying their dog, Dougal, on his morning walk – Ellie emerged from the orangery to find the locals around the table in the window indulging in their favourite things: a free coffee morning and plenty of village gossip.

Anna beckoned her over to the kitchen where she was making a fresh pot of tea, when the door to the boot room opened and another elderly gentleman entered, tall and with an erect frame which belied his age.

'Ryther!' Anna exclaimed, hurrying over to welcome him, and Ellie watched on in amusement as he kissed her hand with a flourish.

'Ellie, come and meet Ryther. He grew up at Harbour-watch across the water. His record company has been a lifeline for my brother.'

She shook hands politely, receiving a charming smile from a still-handsome face, aware of the elderlies at the table ribbing Ryther as they questioned where he'd been lately. Once Anna had installed him at the table, taking his coat to hang it up, she joined Ellie back at the island.

'He's not been well lately. It's lovely to see him back in the cove and looking so much better.' Anna poured boiling water into the pot. 'Come and join us.'

Sipping her tea, Ellie's attention drifted, not knowing any of the people being discussed, and she watched as two fishing boats headed out of the entrance to the harbour, furls of white icing trailing behind them.

Poor Hamish, she mused silently. *He must be so frustrated—*

'—they fillim folk, and I says to Cleggie, here, I says, didn't I, Cleggie? They'm no regard for us locals. Parking they gurt trucks any old where. Tommy the Boat was proper jumping.' Mrs Lovelace looked around the table, as though garnering support.

'Aye,' Mrs Clegg added, dipping a biscuit into her mug, which promptly broke and sank into the murky depths of her very strong tea. 'Bugger.'

'It was a small van, Mum,' Jean Lovelace interjected from where she sat between the two elderly ladies. She took a spoon and rescued the disintegrating biscuit, placing it on a side plate. 'And they won't be in Polkerran when they're filming, will they? Rumour has it, it'll all be down beyond Fowey.'

Two silver-haired heads peered at each other around Jean, then both ladies folded their arms in sequence and let out respective 'humphs'.

Ellie exchanged a grin with Phoenix.

'This is news to me,' Ryther said as he stirred his tea. 'But then I only returned yesterday.'

49

'Kate – she works at the hotel on events,' Jean explained to Ellie, 'says it's to do with Daphne du Maurier, so they'll be down that way.'

'I can't wait to see it,' Anna exclaimed, eyes shining. 'I love her books, and so much of Cornwall inspired them. I wish I still had the B&B.'

Mrs Lovelace sent her an affectionate look. 'You'd have been in your element, young'un, loving they classics as you do.'

Phoenix turned to Jean. 'What's the schedule, do you know? I'd heard it was the spring.'

'Those young'uns in the pub, they'm in the know.' Mrs Lovelace tapped her nose.

Mrs Clegg let out an inelegant snort. 'Spent half their time in The Lugger, and more than half their money, I reckons.'

Nicki, who had just arrived, joined them at the table. 'Gavin says the pre-production gang pretty much drank them out of stock last weekend.'

'Aye, truth 'tis.' Mrs Clegg took a slurp of tea, then fished up her sleeve for a tissue to pat her mouth. 'Saw the bins. Overflowing, they was, with empties.'

Mrs Lovelace nodded firmly. 'Right teasy, they was, when Seb ran out of obsolete.'

Ellie's brow furrowed, but Ryther mouthed, 'Absolut.'
Ah.

'The producer person's due in the area next week,' Anna added, beginning to stack the side plates. 'Dev – he's Kate's other half and Ryther's grandson – reckons he or she's an acquaintance of Alex Tremayne's.'

The mention of Alex brought her brief sighting of Will into full focus, and Ellie's gaze dropped to her clasped hands, conscious of movement around her as people began to stir and make moving noises. Why couldn't she control her reaction? This was ridiculous. It had all been so long ago...

But I've never forgotten him, have I?

Chapter Five

"Have I Got News for You"

It took a while for the teacups to be drained, but then there was a flurry of goodbyes and see you drecklys, Old Patrick ribbing Ryther about something from their school days.

Nicki touched Ellie's arm, and she roused. 'What's up? You've gone all funny again, like you did the other day.'

Anna began brushing crumbs into her hand. 'Would you like some water?'

'No, I'm fine, honestly.'

Nicki sent her an assessing look. 'You said as much last time as well. Come on. Fess up.'

Anna disposed of the crumbs and came to join them again.

'Would you rather I disappeared?'

Ellie hesitated, then shook her head. She liked Anna, and she needed people around her she could turn to should Will turn up again. Nicki had so much on her plate, it would help to have Anna in on the loop.

'I saw Alex the last time he was down,' she explained. 'There was someone with him, someone I used to... know.'

'More than.' Nicki turned to Anna. 'Ellie and Will – he's the 'someone' – had a summer fling many years ago here in the cove. He was friends with Alex at the time, and they were both in Polkerran Point the other day.'

'I'm so sorry,' Anna said softly, her kind hazel eyes on Ellie.

She didn't want to remember that devastating day when they'd split, or the fraught time that followed as she'd tried to mend things…

Anna's dark gaze hadn't moved from Ellie's face, and she stirred in her seat.

'Something about it still hurts, doesn't it?' She spoke gently, placing a comforting hand on Ellie's arm.

'I knew there'd be memories but didn't expect it to feel so raw. He…' Ellie rested a hand on her rib cage, where a dull ache had formed, as though she'd just gone several rounds with a kangaroo. 'Will cut me dead the other day. I don't know if he's still angry, or simply didn't want to remember me. It was more than a decade ago… people change…'

'But he hadn't?'

Ellie swallowed with difficulty. 'No. I mean, he's older, of course. I suppose he must be late thirties now. But there's no way I'd not know his face.' She smiled ruefully. 'Even with a hat low over his eyes and a shadow of a beard.'

When someone has haunted your dreams, is nestled in the deepest recesses of your heart, you don't forget…

Once Nicki left for the hotel, Ellie resumed her work on a Christmas card collection. Playing suitably festive tunes to get her in the mood, she hoped to shut out the burgeoning remembrance of the past, and when Anna popped her head around the door to ask if she wanted a cuppa, Ellie willingly put down her pens and joined her in the kitchen.

'The twins are taking a nap, so it seemed a good time for a spot of adulting.'

'Is Oliver not around?'

Anna poured hot water into two mugs. 'He's got a video thing with Bella and his agent. I'll be so glad when she comes back.'

'I hope I'm still here when…' Ellie's voice tailed away in awkwardness. 'Sorry. I didn't mean *here* here. In your home.'

'Nonsense!' Anna declared, passing a mug to Ellie. 'It's exactly what I've been wanting to have a chat about and now seems a good time. My brother, Matty, and Gemma can't both be here to pet-sit when we're away as there are animals to look after at Rivermills. Oliver and I hoped we might be able to persuade you to stay a bit longer and help us out? We're popping over tonight to stay with them, too. Normally, Nicki helps out with the pets when we do, only I don't like to ask at the moment. You can have a practice run, if you like?'

A rush of affection for Anna robbed Ellie of her voice for a moment, but then she smiled.

'I'd love to. It would be a lifesaver, to be honest. I couldn't afford one of the holiday lets, so I'd resigned myself to my having to sleep on Nicki's sofa.'

'Please stay in your room! It's no trouble at all, and as I say, we won't even be here for a couple of weeks. You don't mind looking after Dougal and Heathcliff? I hate putting them in the kennels.'

'More than happy.' Ellie hesitated. 'There's just one small problem, Anna. I have to head home to cover a wedding at the weekend, but I need to bring the rest of my photography equipment back with me. I'm hoping to find some local business to tide me over. The constant charging will up your electricity bill, so let me know the damage and I'll contribute.'

'Definitely not,' Anna dismissed the offer gently. 'You are saving us the hassle and cost of boarding Dougal and Heathcliff. And Oliver knows I'll just fret all the time we're away about how sad they will be in a pen rather than free to roam. Let's call it quits.'

–

When Nicki came home and began prepping dinner, Ellie headed back to Westerleigh Cottage to feed the animals and take Dougal for a quick walk.

On their return, she made a cup of tea, looking around at the homely, open-plan room. It would be lonely in the evenings, with no one to talk to or laugh with, but she had plenty to keep her occupied, between looking after the pets and continuing to help Nicki with the boys and housework.

Speculating over when Hamish would be able to come home was pointless. Even Nicki seemed to have calmed down now, accepting fate for what it was and simply hoping daily to hear of some improvement now he'd arrived at his parents' home in Wadebridge.

It was a mild evening with no breeze, so Ellie walked out onto the terrace, hands clasped around the mug.

The tide was incoming, and gentle waves slapped against the cliffs below Westerleigh Cottage. Settling onto the wall, Ellie sipped her tea, closing her eyes and letting the gentle rays of the setting sun caress her skin. Aside from the lapping water, the only sounds were the distant call of seabirds and the faint throbbing of the little red-and-white passenger ferry as it neared the jetty further down the lane.

The moment of peace was disturbed by a message notification.

Nicki.

When are you coming back over? There's something you need to see.

'You're not going to share a photo of Hamish's stitches, are you?' Ellie half joked as she walked into Nicki's kitchen five minutes later.

'Hah. Not likely. I've never forgotten how squeamish you are! Fancy a glass?' She raised the one she held.

'Always. Where are the boys?'

Nicki rolled her eyes. 'Gaming still. Come and look at this.'

She indicated an open newspaper on the kitchen table, and Ellie's gaze flew to the image. Will's handsome features stared back at her – did he but know it. He looked awkward, sullen almost, and Ellie's heart clenched as she read the headline above the feature: *Revealed. Surprise Producer Takes the Helm for Cornish Docu-drama.*

There was another man in the photo, perhaps a tad shorter than Will – who was well over six feet tall – and seemed mildly familiar, and Ellie read the line below the picture: *Will Farmer and Matt Locksley met up at Secret Gem Records HQ last month.*

Ellie's heart lurched like a buoy on choppy seas as realisation dawned. 'This is what the filming's all about? The Daphne du Maurier thing Anna's so excited about?'

Why did her voice sound faint? She all but flopped into a chair at the kitchen table.

'Looks like it.' Nicki seemed to notice Ellie's pallor, grabbing a glass and sloshing wine into it. 'Here, take a slurp.'

Doing as she was bid, Ellie reached for the paper with a hand that wasn't quite steady. Eyes fixed on the black-and-white image, she was thankful – despite the unpleasantness – that she'd seen Will already. She tried to skim the words, but a hint of tears clouded her vision.

'I don't understand… I mean, Will's an actor.'

Nicki shrugged. 'They often step behind the lens, don't they? Maybe he's giving it a go on something low key.'

Oh God. And she was trapped in the cove…

Nicki leaned towards her. 'Ellie, your skin's ashen. It's an ancient history holiday romance.'

Eyes wide to prevent the wetness clinging to her lashes from falling, Ellie tried to clear her throat.

'It…' She swallowed hard. 'It was an awful break-up. I struggled to get over it at the time.'

Sinking into the chair beside Ellie, Nicki held her gaze solemnly. 'I remember my mum saying your mum had been upset when you dropped out of your masters in the first term. This was why?' She tapped Will's image on the table.

Ellie's expression spoke for her.

'Oh, Ellie!' Nicki flung her arms around her cousin. 'How could I not know how much you were suffering?'

Summoning a watery smile as Nicki released her, Ellie shook her head. 'You were too busy being loved up down here and fighting your own battle with your parents over giving everything up to be with Hamish.'

Nicki gave Ellie's arm a squeeze.

'Well, the good news is they aren't filming until the spring, according to this.' She tugged the paper round so it faced them.

A slither of relief eased the tension gripping Ellie. The spring! That's what they'd been saying round Anna's table. Months away. Next year. Plenty of time for Ellie to be long gone.

'That's Anna's brother.' Nicki pointed to the figure beside Will.

Pulling herself together, Ellie studied the image of the two men, then frowned.

'But I haven't met him yet. Why does he seem familiar?'

Nicki spluttered as she lowered her glass. 'Come on, Ells. They were all the rage when we were leaving school. *You* had a massive crush on the drummer, remember?'

'Oh my God!' Ellie scanned the face of the man beside Will. 'You're right. BorderLine Beat. Wasn't he the guitarist everyone fell in love with? Silent, brooding, always in the shadows, letting that posturing lead vocalist grab the spotlight. What was the singer's name?'

'Harry. Bella was mad for *him.*'

Now she'd managed to control the quivering, Ellie read the article in the regional paper.

It seemed Matt had been hired to provide the soundtrack for the credits and the dramatised elements of the programme. There was very little about Will beyond mentioning the globally successful films and series that had brought him fame and fortune. The paper claimed it had reached out to Will's agent for a comment, but none had been forthcoming.

'Anna mentioned a brother,' Ellie mused as she closed the paper on the unsettling news.

'He and Gemma live upriver in a converted old mill – very secluded – with its own recording studio. Anna and Oliver go over and stay now and again, so Matt gets more time with the twins.' Nicki topped up their glasses. 'Suppose we ought to eat. The boys had theirs earlier.'

Ellie glanced over at the empty hob. 'What's on offer?'

Nicki shrugged, then sighed heavily. 'I'm fed up, Ells. I loved my life, working part time, being here for Liam and Jason, trips to the beach after school, cosy evenings with Hamish. It's not just the worry over our income; the boys would eat chips every day if I let them. Without Hamish to cook for, I can't work up any enthusiasm.'

'At least he's at his parents' house now and out of the hospital environment. Come on, let's get a takeaway and then we can watch some mindless TV together.'

Hours later, Ellie returned to Westerleigh, relieved to leave Nicki in better spirits after back-to-back episodes of *Married at First Sight*. She settled Dougal, then headed up to bed, Heathcliff on her heels.

'I'm not sure you're allowed—'

Heathcliff jumped onto the bed and began kneading the soft throw furiously.

'Okay. I won't tell if you won't.'

She busied herself preparing for bed, striving to close her mind to the recent revelations in the newspaper.

Yes, but what if Will turns up in Polkerran again? It isn't far from Fowey…

'Damn it,' Ellie muttered as she clambered onto the bed, careful to avoid where Heathcliff had now curled into a ball. 'Stop imagining it. Besides, what would you say to him after all this time?'

Nothing. And based on that first sighting, conversation is the last thing on his mind. At least with me, anyway…

'But—' she whispered, tugging the duvet up to her chin and switching off the bedside lamp.

No buts. I can't run away and desert Nicki. I promised. If I see him, he won't try to speak.

Accepting the facts didn't make it any easier. As if Polkerran wasn't already seducing her, lulling her back to those wonderful weeks when she'd fallen in love. The only time. Once and forever.

Ellie pummelled the innocent pillows into submission, curling up on her side, her cheek tucked into the soft mound.

'Just keep counting the days,' she murmured as her eyes closed, refusing to face up to the truth already staring her in the face. The recollections were stronger, more intense, than she'd anticipated. 'But I'm over it, aren't I? Over *him*?'

Unsurprisingly, the darkness held no answer, and Ellie fell asleep, memories curling around her like smoke rising from smouldering ashes.

Chapter Six

"The Great Escape"

With daylight came perspective, and Ellie found she was better able to relegate the resurfaced emotions around Will fairly well, determining to keep so busy she had no time to think.

'How is it Friday already?' She addressed her reflection in the hallway mirror as she tied up her hair before flying out the door to collect a protesting Liam, who insisted that, at nearly eleven, he was old enough to walk to school alone.

Watching him charge ahead, Jason skipping by her side, Ellie couldn't help but agree, but Nicki had concerns over leaving her eldest in charge of his brother.

On her return to Westerleigh, Ellie eyed the improvised workstation in the orangery, her heart swelling with gratitude towards Anna and Oliver, who had made it so much easier than it could have been.

Flicking through her photos, Ellie's lips curved upwards. She appeared to have a growing fascination with the local scenery. She put the camera aside, adding the finishing touches to a few cards she'd made the other day, dropping on the decorative pearly ink dots and stacking the cards in the slots of the stand to dry. She had a vague notion of putting together a portfolio to present to the local book shop.

Once she'd stopped for lunch, however, the more pressing dilemma of income resurfaced. As she munched on a hastily made sandwich, Ellie scoured Instagram for local businesses. It wasn't worth approaching the hotels or wedding venues, as they would have already secured services for any events likely to occur during Ellie's stay. The same applied to school shoots, which often took place in the autumn.

There was no point doing posts and reels until she had a grasp on what might work in this small community.

'Mini-sessions,' she mused as she swallowed the last morsel and headed to the dishwasher with the plate. 'But first I need a few evocative headshots.'

Feeling inspired, Ellie started to tap notes into her phone. Then, hearing a sound, she glanced over her shoulder.

'Hey, how was your visit?' Ellie looked to Anna's left and right as she hovered in the doorway. 'You seem to have forgotten something.'

Anna grinned. 'It was great. Gemma loves the twins, plus there's quite the menagerie out there for them to chatter at. We just got back, and Oliver didn't feel like writing, so he's taken them out with Dougal. It's such a beautiful day.'

They both looked out across the bay, which was bathed in soft light today, a weak sun trying its best to peer through hazy wisps of gossamer cloud and dusting the turning trees clinging to the steep hillsides with gold.

'How will it be as a place to work long-term?'

'Perfect. I'm so grateful to you both.' Ellie wrapped her arms around her middle and turned to stare out of the open patio doors. A yacht had just turned to approach the embrace of the cove, and her mind fled back to the recent sighting of Will.

'But?'

Ellie shook her head. 'I'm being stupid. I just wish... oh, I don't even *know* what I wish!'

Anna rested a gentle hand on her arm. 'This chap from the past?'

'I saw the article announcing him as the producer for this TV thing, so now I'm dreading coming face to face with him. But there's this stupid—' Ellie broke off, huffing out a breath. 'Idiotic, damn, bloody, ridiculous slither of *hope* that keeps tapping me on the shoulder, saying perhaps our paths have crossed for a reason.'

Anna eyed her with sympathy.

'I can't see that he'd be in the cove much. If they aren't filming until spring, I mean. I suppose there's a risk he'll stay at the manor, knowing the family, but the entire production is based in and around the Fowey area.'

All very true, but the trepidation remained, and as Anna left to unpack the overnight bags, Ellie set off to collect the boys from school, her mind as conflicted as ever over what the coming weeks might bring.

–

'No change,' Nicki admitted after ending her most recent call with Hamish.

'Give it time. It's only been a few days since he got to his parents. Let him rest, give his body time to recover. Come on. I need you.'

'Why? Where are we going?'

Ellie tugged Nicki out the front door.

'What about the boys?'

'We're literally going a hundred yards down the lane. They'll be fine for five minutes.'

They fetched up by a stretch of low wall, running along a gap between the closely huddled, pastel-painted cottages, revealing a perfectly framed view of the bay, with both Westerleigh Cottage and Harbourwatch acting as sentinels, perched on their respective cliffs at the entrance to Polkerran Point.

'Here, the sun's in just the right place.'

She urged Nicki to lean against the wall, taking quick shots face on, directing her to turn her head, then back, letting the breeze lift her blonde hair.

'Now swing back towards me. Perfect.'

Continuing to click away, Ellie started to tell Nicki about her latest encounter with Mrs Lovelace, whereby she'd asked her how life was in the 'organery', and captured Nicki's laughter.

'Okay, serious now. Just look over at the harbour. Turn your shoulder a bit further towards me. Think about something special.' Ellie moved around, capturing the emotions flickering across her cousin's face. 'There. Done.'

'Why were we doing that?' Nicki queried as they returned to the cottage.

'You're going to be my poster girl while I try to kick-start some local business.'

Nicki's phone rang, and she threw Ellie a sceptical look as she answered.

Ellie went to check on the boys who were, as she'd predicted, oblivious to their having left the building for five minutes.

Back in the kitchen, however, Nicki chewed on her lip, and Ellie's heart quickened.

'Is Hamish okay?'

Nicki blinked. 'What? Oh, yes. Sorry. Look, we've just had a last-minute invite to dine up at the Point Hotel tomorrow. With that Will, as producer of this upcoming production? He wants to talk to some key locals.'

A sense of foreboding crept through Ellie, and she sank onto the nearest kitchen chair.

'How are *we* invited?'

'Well, we aren't, exactly. There were a couple of places spare and my colleague, Kate, offered them to me. She's organised it, private dining room, low key, strictly no press. Look, I know you won't want to go, but I'd love the chance.' Nicki's tone was hopeful. 'The food is exceptional, and it'd be fun to be out, dress up for a change.'

Ellie sent her a comforting look.

'You go. I'll stay here with the boys.'

Nicki frowned. 'Are you sure?'

More than you'll ever know!

'Go for it, Nicki. You'll have so few chances to go out in the coming weeks. I'd just rather not.'

A reassured Nicki headed to the fridge to start preparing supper, and Ellie pretended to check the photos she'd taken, but her head was spinning. The hunger to lay eyes on Will had taken hold with a vengeance, but being ignored by him was more than she could handle.

–

The following evening, Ellie stood in the lane outside Westerleigh, waving off an excited Nicki.

Offering to babysit had been the perfect excuse, but despite the demands of two energetic boys, once they were in bed, her mind took the flying leap across the bay to the hotel. She tried losing herself in an old film showing on an obscure channel, but it wasn't much help.

'Hey, I'm back!' Nicki called as she came into the kitchen some hours later, and Ellie joined her with relief.

'How did it go?'

Did she even want to know?

'It was fun,' Nicki declared as she filled the kettle and reached for the tea caddy. 'And that Will created quite the impression.'

Ellie essayed a nonchalant, 'Oh?'

'Yeah, he was very unhappy about the leak to the local paper the other week, emphasising he wants to ensure the mayhem won't extend to the cove. He's sending the cast and crew to Fowey for accommodation next spring. However, he's aware of Polkerran's proximity and, by limiting possible trade in a quieter season, hopes to support the community as best he can in other ways.'

'How's he going to do that?'

'Making use of the hotel where appropriate, for meetings and dinners. More discreet, he anticipates. He seems paranoid about publicity.'

Ellie frowned. 'Won't he need it, though, when it comes to promoting the programme?'

'It felt personal rather than professional,' Nicki mused as she poured hot water into two mugs. 'He clearly doesn't want press snooping around the cove, either, and he's planning on using Polkerran's bakeries and cafes to supply lunches – despite them having access to a catering truck – and channelling some funds into local charities.'

Ellie was filled with a deep sense of contentment. Will had been thoughtful back then, the most gentlemanly man she'd ever come across. It warmed her heart to know that, despite the fame and fortune, he appeared to have retained his integrity.

Once back in her room at Westerleigh Cottage, Ellie stared out of the window at the lights shining through the fir trees in the grounds of the hotel at the very top of Polkerran Point. Her heart clenched in despair. She may have escaped being in the same room as Will tonight, but she couldn't avoid him forever.

Fate was not being particularly kind, Ellie mused, as she closed the curtains on the view. If only she could do the same on her troublesome thoughts.

—

On Monday, the usual crowd descended on Anna, and Ellie realised she'd begun to enjoy their company. It was an entertaining break from looking after the boys and working on her designs.

Ellie met Matt and Gemma when they called at Westerleigh, trying not to stare at the once-famous musician. They were an adorable couple, and clearly very attached to Anna, Oliver and the twins.

She also enjoyed chatting with Jean when she stopped to get ice creams for Liam and Jason, and often had a coffee with Phoenix after the school drop-off, discussing their mutual love of art. It was a gentle pace of life, undemanding, yet Ellie's emotions felt stretched, as though they were on too small a canvas in a frame unable to contain them.

One morning, after Ellie dropped the boys at school, she popped into the book shop, which sold stationery and other small gifts, with a sample of her cards, leaving them with the friendly girl behind the counter, who said she'd show them to the proprietor.

Stepping back into the street, Ellie looked around. It was quiet now they were into October. A man was busy digging out the fading plants in a repurposed rowing boat on the harbourfront, and a couple of fishermen in yellow overalls were unloading crates of fish from a nearby vessel.

Despite wrinkling her nose at the fishy odour drifting her way, Ellie walked over to watch the proceedings, which was her undoing.

'Hey, Ellie!'

She spun around. Matt had emerged from Karma and crossed the road towards her, and she took a moment to appreciate the absurdity of someone from a band she'd idolised as a teen being within her acquaintance.

'Hi,' she began, but the smile froze on her lips. Will had emerged from the cafe too, tugging his hat firmly in place and his attention on his phone, but as he neared Matt, he looked up.

'You've not met,' Matt continued, blissfully unaware of the undercurrents as anxious green eyes met unfathomable deepest, darkest brown.

We knew each other... once.

'Hi.' Will's tone was the politely dismissive one of following courtesy against his present inclination, and Ellie raised her chin, holding his gaze firmly under the rim of the hat.

Fine. She could play that game too.

She gave a cursory nod. 'Sorry, got to dash. I'll leave you two in peace.' Sending Matt a warm but apologetic smile, Ellie turned away, willing her limbs to move steadily, but not too fast, unaware she'd forgotten to breathe until she turned the corner towards the church, whereby she sank back against the wall of a small tea shop and drew in a sharp bolt of air.

'Well, that was fun,' Ellie muttered, pushing away from the support of the wall and walking briskly towards the church.

She hadn't explored it yet and now seemed the perfect time to make a plea for some divine intervention.

—

'Well, at least it's over.' Ellie picked up a plate, giving it a thorough dry before placing it in the rack on the pine dresser, but Nicki merely sent her a doubtful look.

'I assume you mean the first proper meeting rather than the entire memory that seems to have haunted you for years? I can't believe I didn't know about this.'

Huffing, Ellie selected another plate. 'I buried it deep.' *Or so I thought.* 'And this is just one of those awful coincidences. I doubt our paths will cross again if they aren't filming until next year.' Ellie's brow furrowed as she stacked the plates in the dresser, then placed the tea towel on the rail to dry. 'What I don't get is why Will is in Polkerran now.'

'Maybe staying with the Tremaynes is convenient? They were certainly close back then.'

Not wanting to think about it, Ellie inspected her nails. She had to stop biting them. She hadn't done that in years…

Nicki emptied the bowl of fading suds into the sink. 'He seems obsessively publicity averse, more so even than Matt. In fact, they were heads together a lot at the dinner. Probably comparing notes.'

Recalling online reports of fans hounding him, Ellie sympathised with Will. Avoiding notice would certainly account for the hat pulled down over his eyes…

Then, a sudden thought occurred to Ellie.

'Did Will recognise you? You pretty much disappeared after you met Hamish, but he saw you at the caravan a couple of times.'

Nicki leaned against the sink, drying her hands. Then she sighed. 'Look, I wasn't sure whether to tell you or not…'

Ellie's skin grew cold. 'What?'

'I thought I'd test the ground for you.'

'Oh God. What did you say?'

Nicki laid the damp towel on the radiator. 'Nothing, really. Just when Kate introduced us, I said I remembered him, that I was your cousin, and I believe he'd seen us in the pub the other day.'

'Nicki!'

'I told you I wasn't sure whether to mention it to you!'

Ellie held Nicki's gaze, her heart flapping like the pillowcases on the washing line outside. 'Go on. Hit me with it.'

Chapter Seven

"Working Girl"

Nicki bit her lip. 'He wasn't very gallant, said you were so altered, he barely recognised you.' Walking over, she gave Ellie a fierce hug. 'I'm sorry. Truly. If it's any consolation, you look way better, as though you've found yourself. That may be what he meant. Come on. We need to make up the beds.'

Ellie's palpitating heart calmed as she followed Nicki upstairs. It hardly mattered, and at least she now knew for a fact, Will had not forgotten her.

Nicki chattered on as they put clean sheets on the beds, trying to change the mood.

'I suppose it makes sense he wants somewhere away from prying eyes. Fowey is much bigger, hugely popular and draws loads of emmets come springtime. Kate says he stayed at the hotel here a few months back with a researcher. I suppose they were scouting out the locations and so on. Not that I ever saw him.' She grinned over her shoulder as they entered the boys' bunk room. 'Didn't get chance to do his hair or give him a manicure, sadly.'

Despite her misgivings, Ellie laughed, grabbing Jason's pillow to give it a pummel. 'Well, if you ever do, do *not* mention my name again.'

As they finished the housework, Ellie tried to relegate thoughts of Will to the back of her mind, something she'd become proficient at over the years. Didn't his dismissive attitude towards her deliver the closure she needed?

If only…

–

Ellie had become familiar with rough nights lately, but this time she knew it was self-inflicted. Unhelpfully, the film that launched Will's global success – released about eighteen months after they'd split – was available to stream online, as was one of his massively popular TV series. Although she'd watched the latter avidly the first time, she'd never revisited it until now and ended up bingeing several episodes of the series too before falling into bed with a pounding head and a heart once again in shreds.

Waking to find her cheeks damp and her mood low, it hadn't helped on opening the blinds to see a heavy grey sky and equally steely stretch of water outside the window.

Once she'd taken Liam and Jason to school and picked up a coffee, however, Ellie felt more herself, returning to Westerleigh determined to immerse herself in work. A heartwarming scene greeted her as she pushed open the door to the kitchen.

Oliver had a wriggling Emma tucked firmly under one arm, and a giggling Bertie under the other. Anna was busy at the island, cutting out dough shapes of some sort.

'Hey!' She beckoned Ellie over as Oliver headed out to the hall with his precious cargo. 'Come and join me. I'm making biscuits for the school sale on Saturday.'

Once the biscuits were in the oven, Anna led Ellie over to the sofas. There was an open laptop on the coffee table, next to a low vase of autumn foliage, a pot of baby wipes and a teething ring.

Scooping up the MacBook, Anna tucked her legs up on the sofa and balanced it on her lap. 'Is it insensitive of me to mention the documentary?'

Ellie clasped her hands in her lap, willing her midriff not to dive like a seagull after fish. 'Of course not. There's no escaping it, is there?'

'I suppose not. The cove is normally a restful place. It saddens me to see you stressed by being here.'

Ellie waved a dismissive hand. 'I'm good. Honestly. So, what's the news taking the village by storm today?'

'The production team are reaching out to locals through the community Facebook group. There's a mention of extras and who to contact. Seems they want all ages.'

'Are you thinking of putting Emma and Bertie forward?'

Anna laughed as she closed the laptop. 'I don't think Oliver would approve. You know they've roped Matty in to compose the music? He's in his element. They've also asked if there are any local photographers.' Anna sat up suddenly. 'Hey, why don't you—'

Ellie's expression was enough to halt the suggestion.

'Sorry,' Anna exclaimed, a hand to her mouth. 'I was thinking of you needing to compensate for lost business, but it was thoughtless of me.'

'You don't have to tread on eggshells around me,' she reassured Anna, who seemed truly mortified. 'It's messing with me a bit, but in reality, nothing's changed. We split up a long time ago.'

Ellie welcomed the return of Oliver with the newly changed twins, taking Emma onto her lap as Anna received Bertie from her husband.

'Are you off to work?'

Oliver had a Tardis-sized den at the top of the garden where he focused on his historical writing projects and managed his local property endeavour, the Seymour Trust.

'Bella's phoning shortly.'

Ellie's ears pricked up. 'Is she coming back? I haven't seen her in ages.'

'We hope so,' Anna said, bouncing Bertie up and down on her lap. 'Oliver's a lot less stressed when she's around. Bella's like his comforter.'

With a laugh, Ellie picked up a picture book from the coffee table and settled back, ready to point out the images to Emma. 'She was a bit of a firebrand. I'm intrigued to see this other side of her.'

'She has been prone to impulsivity in the past,' Oliver admitted as he dropped a kiss on his wife's cheek and headed for the boot room door, and Anna turned to Ellie to relate what had happened the previous year when Bella had re-encountered Alex Tremayne in the cove.

–

Ellie's most ongoing worry, once she'd managed to wrestle thoughts of Will into a suitably watertight place, continued to be that of income – or rather, her current lack of it.

Although she didn't doubt for a minute the production would pay well for any freelance work, especially as it was for a streaming company, the risk that it might mean working in tandem with Will was sufficient to make it a no-go. Ellie also wasn't blind to the fact he'd probably refuse to employ her anyway, and she didn't need any further rejection from him.

The proposed fortnight in Polkerran Point was no longer a simple break. Yes, Ellie was heading back to Oxfordshire at the weekend, but that was only to cover a wedding. There'd be no resumption of normal life.

She'd put a card in the window of the Spar, for both the photography business and her artwork, and hadn't held out much hope, but on the Thursday – the day before leaving for home – she took a call from a man called Marcus, who ran a glamping site up on Bodmin Moor.

The business had taken off beyond his dreams, and he'd now acquired a field above Polkerran which was being developed with a view to offering shepherd huts by next spring. He realised he needed to get some business cards and flyers made as he was heading up to a trade fair in London in November. Would Ellie be interested in coming up with a design for him?

It would only be a one-off job, but Ellie grasped the opportunity, scribbling down details. It was also out of the village centre, which meant less chance of running into Will.

They agreed to meet in Karma for an informal chat, and Ellie popped some examples of her work into the leather portfolio she never travelled without, wondering if she'd recognise Marcus from his voice.

'Idiot,' she admonished.

As it happened, there was only one person in the coffee house when she arrived, and as he greeted her the moment she opened the door, she assumed she must look like an Ellie.

'The portfolio.' Marcus gestured at the large, flat bag on her shoulder. 'Gave you away.'

Ellie grinned. 'Occupational hazard.'

She studied Marcus covertly as he ordered coffee at the counter. He was of average height, with dark-blond hair and dressed for life in the country, wearing the uniform of Hunter wellies, a body-warmer and checked brush-cotton shirt. Marcus had thin, angular features, and a friendly expression which Ellie found encouraging.

'Here we go. Sugar?' He held out the pot, but Ellie shook her head.

'I'm good, thanks.'

A small silence settled on them as he took the seat opposite. Their circular table was in one of the windows, and Ellie took a few sips of the hot liquid, meeting Marcus's friendly look with a smile.

'Sorry. I love coffee when it's piping hot.'

'Me too.'

Marcus explained how, with the glamping site's success, he'd sought another opportunity, investing in the field above the cove when Tremayne Estates put it up for sale.

'I also saw your card for the photography and had a quick look at your website. I don't suppose you could take some for mine? It's a bit of a mess up at the site right now, though. They've not long ago finished the groundworks.'

'Could I come and see it? It would give me a better feel.'

As Ellie had no physical photos to hand, she showed him some on her phone from previous shoots. Marcus asked insightful questions, taking the time to really look at everything, and Ellie's heart, which had felt sore and battered, eased a little at his obvious admiration for her talent.

It was another hour and an additional coffee later when they both emerged onto the harbourfront, Ellie with the portfolio once more tucked under her arm and Marcus donning a cap as a few drops of rain began to fall.

They shook hands beside his mud-spattered 4x4, agreeing Ellie would visit the following day, and she waved him off before turning away.

Coming along the front, however, was a black sporty-looking Range Rover, and it slowed as it drew level with her. Ellie swallowed hard as her eyes met those of Will behind the wheel. There was a figure over in the passenger seat – a woman with long black hair, possibly the one she'd seen with him and Alex in the pub – but as her gaze returned to Will, he blanked Ellie, the car shooting along to take the turn towards the hill leading to the top of the village.

Heart hammering and throat threatening to choke her, Ellie hurried towards the bridge and the sanctuary of Westerleigh.

The sooner she lost herself in work, the better.

–

Feeling a little more optimistic after meeting with Marcus, Ellie continued with her routine, making sure Liam and Jason got to and from school, along with any after-school clubs, feeding them if Nicki was on a late shift and working hard on the Christmas collection of card packs and – for the first time – a calendar. She'd need to move swiftly to catch the market.

Both Anna and Nicki had given her a list of local emporiums, farm shops and craft outlets that might be interested in stocking them, and with the Christmas markets just a few months away, it took up most of her time.

Ellie also skimmed through the photos of Nicki. The soft evening light had highlighted her cousin's natural prettiness, the background faded out, though clearly Polkerran. Delighted with having captured exactly what she'd wanted, Ellie made a few reels ready to run once she'd shown them to Nicki.

After popping down to the post office late one morning, Ellie stopped by the harbour wall for a moment. A chill wind swept in from the sea, bringing with it a low mist that didn't look as though it would lift before nightfall, and she shivered, thankful she'd thought to wear a thicker scarf. Despite the conditions, however, she was pleased she'd slung the Canon camera round her neck, and she took some atmospheric shots before realising her hands were freezing.

She'd have a cup of something warming and whatever treat was on offer before heading back. Eschewing Karma, which looked full of yummy mummies and their offspring, the high-end buggies lined up like a row of flashy cars in a showroom, Ellie skirted down a narrow lane to where she'd found a small, old-fashioned tea shop on one of her walks.

The windows were steamed up, but a welcoming glow emanated from the Georgian-style bow windows, and Ellie pushed open the door, delighted by the tinkling of a brass bell above it.

There was a lady behind the counter sporting a spotted apron, busy placing a top on an earthenware teapot, but she looked up as Ellie closed the door.

'Come on in, my lovely. 'Tis a raw one.'

She waved her hand at an empty table by the window, and Ellie was soon studiously viewing the menu card.

The apron-clad lady ferried her laden tray to a table at the back of the cosy room, which housed four people dressed for walking.

'Well now, aren't you a proper maid?' she addressed Ellie as she came to stand by her table.

Blushing, Ellie wasn't sure what to say, so she dipped her head. 'Please could I have a pot of tea and a toasted teacake?'

'Of course, my lovely. Mek yerself comfy. Just prepping a tekkaway but will be on it dreckly.'

Fishing out her phone, Ellie skimmed through her emails, then sent a message to her mum, who was keeping an eye on the flat.

A half-hour later, happily fed, Ellie thanked the lady – busy popping the takeaway order into a large brown bag – and headed out the door, but as she reached the corner where the narrow lane joined the front, a figure came swiftly round it, his attention on his phone.

There was no way to avoid a collision, and Ellie heard the clatter of something hitting the ground as a pair of strong arms grasped hers, her nose pressed up against a broad chest and the Canon digging into her middle.

Chapter Eight

"Brief Encounter"

'Gmumph,' Ellie muttered, unsure if the pounding in her ears was emanating from her own heart or the poor person she'd cannoned into.

'Oh God! So sorry,' he began, setting her back upright. 'I'm late picking up a food order.'

Ellie froze.

Her thick, olive-green scarf, which she'd been in the process of re-winding to keep her chin warm, had bunched up as far as her eyes, but before she could free an arm to pull it down, Will raised a hand.

'Here, let me. I'm so…'

Having tugged the scarf lower, he stared at Ellie nonplussed, seemingly unaware it still covered her mouth.

She snatched an arm from his continued grasp, reaching up, but he beat her to it, giving the scarf a further yank.

'Yowch,' she howled, as a dangling earring, which had tangled with the wool, tugged at her earlobe.

'Sorry!' he exclaimed a second time. 'Stop bloody wriggling. You'll make it worse.'

How, exactly, could this get any worse?

Rubbing her ear, Ellie berated her heart for pounding away like little Emma with her toy keyboard as Will bent to retrieve his phone, and she strove to find her voice.

'It's not damaged?'

'No, it's fine.' He straightened, tucking it into his pocket.

For a moment, their eyes locked, and Ellie frantically sought a way to extend the moment. A sentence might help. Or even a word. Did she even know any?

'Never thought I'd see *you* again.' Will's tone was accusatory. 'Especially here of all places.'

Those words would have done, if I'd only thought more quickly...

'I'm not in Polkerran Point out of choice, but I made a promise, and I can't leave.'

His features tightened. 'You made a promise to me once. Broke it to follow your parents' persuasion. Chose your education over us.'

Ellie frowned. Wasn't he missing something? Several things?

'Are you following me?' he snapped suddenly, jabbing a finger towards the camera.

What?!

'No! I've got better things to do, you... you...' She sought something that wasn't massively offensive, but then she recalled Nicki's words.

'Anyway,' she straightened her shoulders, 'I thought you barely recognised me. Shouldn't take you long to forget again.'

It sounded good, but the idea of it still hurt.

Will didn't speak for a moment, then huffed out a breath. 'I remember our last meeting.'

Okay. Probably not the best memory to evoke...

Skin warming as Will's gaze raked her features, her heart pounding in time to the church clock as it sounded the hour, Ellie tried to swallow discreetly, only managing an audible gulp, which triggered the urge to giggle. Chewing frantically on the inside of her cheeks to prevent it, she decided to cut her losses. With a nod, she scurried away, shooting across the road without a thought, totally oblivious to Mrs Lovelace on her mobility scooter as she screeched to a halt that would be the envy of any grand prix driver entering the pit.

'Breathe,' Ellie intoned as she reached the harbour wall, only to look around as the mobility scooter purred into place beside her.

'How be y'on, my lovely?' The elderly lady's face expressed her concern, white curls escaping from a woolly hat bearing the words 'Alright, my 'ansum?'. 'Thought you be a goner, back along. In a right tease, you was.'

Ellie cast a wary look towards the lane, but there was no sign of Will. Then she sent the elderly lady and her daughter, who'd fetched up beside her, an apologetic look.

'Hi, Jean. I'm so sorry, Mrs Lovelace,' she said. 'Are you okay?'

'Aye. All good an' proper. 'Tis many a year since I've had to perform an emergency stop, mind.'

'All the same, I'm sorry for giving you a fright.'

'Oh, my lovely. Worse I've had in my long years. Some left scars, they did.' Mrs Lovelace leaned forward, patting Ellie on the hand. 'You can have a look-see next time.'

'Mum!' Jean sent Ellie a resigned look as she took her leave.

Once back at Westerleigh, she couldn't resist opening the laptop and searching Google images. Staring at a moody studio shot of Will, taken as promo for his last TV role, she closed her eyes, her heart responding with a resounding thump. She'd yearned to be in Will Farmer's arms once more. Imagined it, dreamt of it.

This was not *quite* how Ellie had pictured it happening.

–

Ellie had a lot of time to think as she drove back to Oxfordshire at the weekend, and none of it was to do with the wedding on the following day.

It was time for reality, and as she sped along the A30 and over the border into Devon, she gave herself a firm talking to.

She had to be in Polkerran Point for Nicki. Time to force her head to rule her heart. Long-buried emotions were draining. She'd known Will was furious when they'd split up, and his rejection of any attempt to reconcile proved it, but for some reason, his anger still lingered…

Does he have regrets, too, like the ones that have haunted me?

'Stop it,' Ellie bit out as she reached the M5 and joined the steady flow of traffic heading north. 'It's too far gone, dead in the water, and that encounter proved it.'

With the timeline currently unpredictable, it was imperative she push it aside and focus on priorities, like finding some photography assignments in Cornwall.

Hands gripping the steering wheel, she checked the satnav. She honestly didn't need it for the trip home. It was pretty simple going from the M5 to the M4 and then off at Oxford, but she'd always enjoyed seeing the miles count down and the journey time decrease.

Why was it, then, that the closer she came to home – and the further she was from Cornwall – her mood sank even lower?

–

Ellie loved her job as a photographer, and the wedding was adequate entertainment to take her mind off her worries about money and the resurgence of Will.

Once she'd completed the shots for the day, however, leaving the evening photos to family and friends and the videographer – as requested by the bride and groom – she returned to her neglected flat with a strange sense of gloom.

'You're just being a sour puss, having been surrounded by all that love and happiness,' Ellie admonished as she popped her flash and battery on charge before taking a quick shower and donning her favourite loungers.

Ellie had moved into her flat some years ago. When she'd dropped out of the MA – too distressed over the acrimonious break-up to cope – she'd taken a job as a receptionist and started an evening course on photography, with no idea where it might lead. Her new home had been a symbol of a fresh start, both in terms of life and career, and she'd wasted no time making the space her own.

But the once-cosy flat felt cold and unloved, even with the lamps lit and the comforting smell of a ready meal emanating from the oven. Missing Heathcliff's affectionate attention, she was unable to settle, despite trying to catch up on the shows she was currently streaming. Pouring herself a generous glass of Baileys over a cluster of ice cubes, Ellie sat cross-legged on the sofa, the laptop balanced on her knees as she took a sip from her glass.

'Mmmm,' she murmured, savouring the cold, creamy liquid on her tongue and resuming her study of the screen. The temptation to google Will again was fighting with a desperate desire to return him to the hole she'd managed to stuff him in for the last decade or more.

The hole was disobliging, and she devoured image after image, from Will in his earlier roles to more recent photos, some taken at awards events, but many clearly paparazzi shots – blurry and distant.

In the past, she'd shied away from looking into his life, although there had been times when it was impossible to avoid the press reports, but in recent years – as she'd discovered earlier – it was as though Will had dropped off the edge of the earth, with a paucity of information and images.

There were a couple of pictures of him with the facial hair. Ellie tilted her head to one side, studying them, trying to merge the man she'd recently encountered with the one she once knew.

Then, she found a link to an interview she'd never seen. Will's performance – in his first production after they'd split, the infamous film in Australia – as a tortured, despondent young man had won him several accolades and led to every other big thing.

Ellie swallowed hard on the lump gripping the base of her throat as she shut down the recording on his last words to the sympathetic presenter, a self-deprecating smile only enhancing his charm.

'I fear, with hindsight, that was hardly acting. It stemmed from how I felt at the time.'

'Dammit,' she groaned, flopping back on the sofa and sliding the laptop aside. 'This wasn't your best move, Arbon.' Draining her glass, she licked her lips as the last of the Baileys slipped down her throat in an icy trail.

The lowness of mood from earlier threatened to spiral further downwards, but Ellie was unable to prevent her legs from unfurling. They took her into the small bedroom, only just big enough for a double bed, a nightstand she'd found at a local antiques market and a wicker chair from her childhood, currently housing her worn teddy bear, Barney, and a rather out-of-shape bunny whose fur had seen better days. The clothes she'd worn earlier were draped over the chair too, although some had fallen to the floor.

Ellie shrugged. The closet which also doubled as a wardrobe was stuffed full, anyway, as were the hangers on the back of her bedroom door.

Crouching down, she peered under the bed, heart pounding, then stretched her arm blindly, groping around until her hand connected with the small, velvet-covered case she'd had since her grandmother passed away. Slowly, she edged it over until able to grasp it firmly.

'There,' she huffed, sinking onto the bed, placing the little case with its worn cover on her lap. Ellie eyed it warily, nerves sending a fine tremor along her fingers. 'Now what are you going to do?'

Should she just put it back, let it gather more dust under the bed? It had been there ever since she'd moved in, after all…

With a sigh, Ellie placed it on the tiny nightstand and grabbed her pyjamas.

'This is no time for looking back. You have more pressing concerns.'

Despite the sound advice, when her eyes finally closed and sleep claimed her, Ellie was helpless to resist the pull of time, a medley of scattered dreams from years past buffeting her mind much as the sea-borne breeze pummelled the rocky coastline of Polkerran Point.

Ellie slept both well and long, any remnants of her nocturnal escapades fading swiftly, as such things do, and when she woke, she passed a busy few hours, initially on her laptop, researching possible short-term pitch opportunities in the South-West, and then carefully packing up her equipment so that she had all she needed to operate her business from elsewhere. She added an extra bag of clothes and – after a moment's hesitation – shoved the little velvet case in her travel bag and fastened the zip before she could begin to question the decision.

–

Ellie's first port of call on the day after she returned to Polkerran was the village book shop and stationers, Pen & Ink, to follow up on the pitch regarding the hand-made cards and the upcoming advent calendars.

A young girl went to fetch a lady who introduced herself as Phyllida. She was dressed casually in jeans and a jumper and sported a stylish, silver-grey bob and large, hooped earrings. The enthusiastic welcome of the work by both women, and Phyllida's willingness to have the business cards in the window and on the till counter, gave Ellie a boost, and she sailed out of the door with contentment.

She looked around, then released a soft sigh of pleasure at the now-familiar sights of the cove waking up to another day, still somewhat astounded by how coming back yesterday had felt like a homecoming.

Her eye was caught by someone waving. Jean Lovelace and her mother were by the harbour wall, talking to a slightly built young woman Ellie didn't recognise.

'How are you?' Ellie warmly greeted the elderly lady perched on her mobility scooter.

'Fair to middlin', as they says.' Mrs Lovelace, her wizened face framed by silver-grey curls, grasped Ellie's hand. 'And where might you be to, my lovely?'

'Just dropping some things off at the book shop. Then I'm off up to the holiday site that's being developed to hold shepherd huts.'

Mrs Lovelace frowned. 'Well what silly old tuss came up with that piece of yarn? They shepherds, they're always in huts, up on the moor. Why would they go holidaying in one?'

Ellie met the curious gaze of the lady stood beside Jean. She had wavy, dark-blonde hair and curiously wide-spaced eyes.

'Oh, you've not met Chloe.' Jean turned to the young woman. 'This is Nicki's cousin, Ellie, who's helping out with her boys for a while.' She faced Ellie again. 'Chloe used to work up at the hotel, but she's back in the cove looking for a new job.'

Chloe shook Ellie's hand hesitantly. 'Hi. It's always hard, isn't it, starting afresh where everyone's a stranger?'

'Absolutely.' Ellie patted her bag of supplies. 'I'm lucky enough at the moment to be working for myself. I just have to make sure I don't have too many arguments with the boss.'

Chloe bade them farewell, and Ellie exchanged a few more words with Jean and her mother, before leaving them to return to the harbourside. There were a few walkers waiting for the passenger ferry to dock, someone watering the old rowing boat – now filled with autumnal blooms – and a couple of dogs walking their owners along the lane towards the tidal beach beneath Harbourwatch.

With a start, Ellie looked up as a seagull let out a piercing squeal overhead. It had started to rain again, so she tugged up the hood of her coat, wrapping her arms around her precious parcel, and turned for home.

Ellie thought she saw Chloe disappearing inside the Tremayne Estates office, and she wondered if they had a job going, but a glance at her watch was sufficient to send Ellie swiftly on her way. She'd make a light lunch and get ready for the visit to the site.

That way, she'd be too busy to dwell on a certain someone and how – much as each encounter caused the pain of loss to intensify – she longed to lay eyes on his face once more.

Chapter Nine

"Come Dine with Me"

'What do you think?'

The blatant apprehension in Marcus's voice was wholly endearing, and Ellie, who'd found the site – optimistically named The Shire – a little austere for her own taste, softened her response.

'It will be stunning when those trees become a little more established, and I think the beech hedging will fill out nicely to provide privacy, as well as blending with the natural landscape.'

'The budget didn't stretch to trees further into their life. The hedges are going to provide entirely private plots once they're established, so it's crucial to create the right – but not misleading – images for the website. I don't want to pretend it's fully enclosed yet, but I need it to look…'

'Inviting? I'll see what I can do.' Ellie looked around as Marcus dug out his keys for the cabin housing the site office. 'I'll be creative with the photos, don't worry.'

There was a track opposite the turning into The Shire, a wooden marker proclaiming it to be 'Private Property' and a slate sign bearing the word 'Peaches'.

'What's down there? Is that part of the business, too?' The Cornish climate might be mild, but she couldn't imagine it allowed the growing of such a fruit.

Pushing open the door to the cabin, Marcus shook his head. 'Peaches Cottage. It's pretty isolated; part of the Devonshire estate.'

Marcus took her coat, hanging it on a row of hooks housing various hats, a well-worn umbrella and a quilted gilet.

'Not *the* Devonshires? You know, the Chatsworth dukedom?'

He laughed. 'No. Just a local family of the same name. Quite extensive landowners, though.' Marcus indicated the small kitchen. 'Tea or coffee?'

'I'm good, thanks.' Ellie took a seat as Marcus settled behind his desk. 'Have you thought about keeping a sort of blog on your website? You know, almost like a diary of the site from conception to the first year of trading and the expansion as you move along? You could include lots of photos and links to your suppliers. Great for sharing on the socials.'

'That's a brilliant idea!' His momentary delight faded. 'The only problem is I'm not the best writer. Numbers are more my thing.'

'I'd be happy to help,' Ellie offered. 'No charge. It would help me understand the whole setup better if you share with me the challenges and rewards you've experienced along the way?'

'Perfect.' Marcus's smile reached his eyes, and Ellie returned it. He was such easy company, and she could already feel the benefit of the distraction from her thoughts, which her present lifestyle gave her far too much time to indulge.

'I don't suppose you're free Friday night, so I can talk you through the beginning of it all?'

Ellie quashed the instinctive urge to shake her head, claim a prior commitment, but as she hesitated, Marcus shook his own.

'Sorry. Pushy of me. It's just I'm over babysitting my kids this evening, and tomorrow I have to be in Truro to see the bank, but I don't want to delay getting the website sorted as I'm already running late for promoting next year's season.'

'You have children? How many? I'm experiencing all aspects just now, looking after my cousin's boys, who are at the village school, and fitting in the occasional play date with my neighbours' adorable baby twins.'

Marcus's expression softened as he reached for a photo on the desk and swung it around. 'Lucy, seven, and Poppy, five.' He released a soft sigh as he returned the framed picture to its original position. 'My wife and I split a couple of years ago. Amicable, thankfully, and they only live in Looe, not at the other end of the country, but I grab every chance to look after them that I can. Sadly, my fledgling business takes up too much time when the busy season is here. It's half-term soon, though, so I'll be taking them away for a few days.'

'Of course we can have dinner. Shall I sort it out? Would you prefer the bistro or Harbourmasters? Or there's always The Lugger? I insist we go Dutch on it.'

After all, it wasn't a date, was it?

Marcus's eager agreement was enough to reassure Ellie she'd pitched things right, and genuinely interested in the background to the business, she made a note to book a table at Harbourmasters and agreed, as she left, to meet Marcus there at seven on Friday.

–

On Friday, Oliver and Anna headed up to London for a weekend with friends, as Oliver was due to meet with his agent on the Monday. Ellie worked hard to complete two card commissions – thankful she'd managed to fit her printer into Fifi, her faithful Fiat 500 – sending them off in the post and then picking up Liam and Jason. She'd also had a call from a school over in Port Wenneth whose usual photographer had been taken ill. Would she be able to come and do the year eleven portraits for them? Agreeing to drop by to discuss the details, she added it to her pretty empty calendar, chewing on her lip as she surveyed the lack of work. She must get organised and start promoting the mini-sessions.

Ellie was just drying the last plate from their early dinner and mulling over what to wear for her meet-up with Marcus when a notification pinged on her phone.

Bella!

> I'm back in the cove! Any chance you can meet up later? xx

> I've got a business dinner in Harbourmasters at 7. Want to meet afterwards for a drink and catch up?

> Deffo! Can't wait to see you. I'll wait outside. 9 any good?

Ellie sent a thumbs-up, tidied the kitchen and headed into the cosy sitting room to check the boys were doing their homework.

Once Nicki was home, frustrated she couldn't get a sitter at short notice to join them, Ellie sped over to her room for a shower and a change, far more eager to see Bella than meet Marcus. But when she saw him, pacing nervously up and down outside the restaurant, constantly checking his watch, her heart warmed towards him, and she called his name as she scooted along the harbourfront.

'Hi. Sorry,' Ellie said breathlessly as she joined him outside Harbourmasters. 'Am I late?'

Marcus grinned. 'No. I'm just naturally angsty!'

Laughing, she entered the restaurant as he held open the door, only to hesitate by the desk. What if Will was in here, with his cronies?

Led to a table on the far side of the stylish restaurant by the manager, Ellie sank thankfully into a seat with its back to the room. A wary skim of the dining area had shown no sign of Will, but it would be kinder to Marcus, and her distraction less obvious, if she kept her attention on him and not every person who walked through the door.

Marcus, as it happened, was an entertaining dinner companion, and had plenty to say about his early steps into the new business venture, with Ellie tapping notes into her phone in between enjoying the food.

It was only as they got up to leave that Ellie recalled her trepidation over seeing Will, but a swift look around the restaurant as they left reassured her he wasn't there. She parted from Marcus with the agreement that she would draft a few suggested posts for the blog and that they would meet up again when she'd come up with some sketches for the rebranding.

'There you are!'

Ellie swung around from watching Marcus cross the road to his car.

'Bella!' They hugged in mutual delight. 'It must be a couple of years since we've managed to be in the same place at the same time!'

'Yes,' Bella said, dryly, falling into step beside Ellie. 'And of all the places.'

Ellie threw her a sidelong glance as they made their way along the front, dodging people emerging from the Three Fishes pub, amused as a couple of young men stopped in their tracks as they passed by.

Bella was incredibly striking, tall and agile, with an athlete's grace, rippling, pale gold hair, a prominent nose and incredible amber, almost hawk-like eyes, which Ellie knew missed very little.

She hadn't forgotten Bella having a fling with Alex Tremayne during that long-ago summer, but her friend had walked away about a month after they'd returned to their respective homes, head held high and claiming she hoped to never see the bastard again. She'd never said why, though, and after all this time, it felt awkward to ask.

They headed to the bistro and secured a high table by the window – Ellie having once again done a quick sweep of the clientele – as Bella fetched a bottle of wine and two glasses.

'This should keep us going.'

Ellie laughed. 'I've already had one glass with dinner. You can have the lion's share.'

Bella gave a throaty chuckle. 'My pleasure. Cheers.'

They clinked glasses, and Ellie took a sip of the red wine, savouring the flavour. 'Mmm, delish. Okay, maybe I'll help too.'

They caught up on their jobs, with Bella outlining the work she'd done lately for Oliver and how she'd come back to help him tie up the loose ends on the final book of the trilogy he'd signed up for eighteen months ago.

'Where do you stay?'

'I'm in one of Oliver's cottages. It's on the same run as Mrs L.' She sipped her wine. 'You met her yet?'

With a laugh, Ellie settled back in her seat. 'Yes. I think Jean struggles to keep her in check.'

'She's hilarious. Anna says she often mixes her words up, but Nicki reckons she does it on purpose sometimes just to wind Jean up.'

'Sounds about par for the cove.'

They chatted about Nicki for a while, and Hamish's situation, and Ellie mulled over whether to say anything about Will being in town. Would Bella even remember who he was? Although the group had splintered as they paired up, there had been days when they'd all hung out together at Tremayne Manor.

When it came time to head home, they lingered to chat a little more by the harbour wall.

'It's a shame the ferry's stopped running for the night.' Bella gestured towards the little red-and-white boat moored by the steps.

'I'll enjoy the walk. At least it's no longer raining.'

They both cast a wary glance at the dark heavens overhead, then hugged each other.

'Let's chat later about meeting up again. I have to be back in Bristol at the weekend – private student tuition.'

Bella was about to cross the street towards the lane leading up to the church, from which she could access the side road where her cottage was located, when a flashy red car came to an abrupt halt at the kerbside.

Bella placed her hands on her hips as a blond-haired man emerged into the fading light.

'Bella! You're back.'

'Shame you are too,' she drawled.

Ellie edged closer to her friend as Alex fetched up in front of Bella, wishing the recollections would stop flooding in.

'Come on, Bells. I'm trying.'

'You are. Very.'

Alex's eyes flicked to Ellie. 'Why don't you introduce me to your friend?' He flashed the gorgeous smile she remembered even to this day.

Bella's hands remained on her hips, and Ellie found it hard to read the emotions running across her face.

'Fine. Ellie, this is Scumbag. Do you remember him?'

Ellie cast a wary look at Bella, then nodded at the man by her side.

'Hi, Alex.'

He blinked. 'Sorry. Have we met?'

'It was a long time ago,' Ellie responded, touching Bella lightly on the arm. 'Are you okay if I go?'

Bella's eyes narrowed as Alex paled suddenly, his gaze fixed on Ellie.

'I— er. I'll see you another time, Bells.'

With a frown, Ellie watched as he fled back to the car and departed at a fine pace.

'What was all that about?' she mused as Bella adjusted her bag and shook her abundant tresses over her shoulder.

'I don't know. Yet. Something spooked him, and I think it's because he remembered you.'

'But why would that cause him to act like someone had just stuck a spoon up his rear?'

A spurt of laughter came from Bella. 'No idea. The man's an imbecile. I just hope it's one of his flying visits.'

They parted company, and Ellie made her way back home, deep in thought. Her friend may have buried deep the reason she and Alex had split, but right now Ellie had a suspicion the man wasn't ready to let Bella disappear from his life a second time.

As for Ellie, she'd not seen Alex in all these years, other than those early glimpses. She shuddered as she put the key in the lock at Westerleigh, closing the door with a snap. If only she could shut out the memories of the last time he'd spoken to her so easily.

Chapter Ten

"Guess Who's Coming to Dinner"

Saturday passed in a blur, and the tension in Ellie's shoulders never fully abated – somehow, every path crossed with Alex Tremayne was intrinsically linked to Will, be it the old memories, the aftermath of the split or the more recent sighting of them together here in the cove.

On Sunday, with Nicki at a bridal fair in Truro, Ellie was kept busy with Liam and Jason, coaxing them into doing their homework and promising ice cream afterwards, then tackling the ironing basket, which seemed to generate a pile of clothing every time she looked at it.

In the end, Ellie was relieved to return to Westerleigh when her cousin came home. It was strangely quiet still, with them all away, so Ellie curled up on a sofa to listen to the voice notes Marcus had sent over, sending a quick message to clarify a few things. She settled with her laptop on her knees, drafting some diary entries for him to look over, and checked all her batteries were on charge, chuckling when Heathcliff came over and tried to clamber into her lap as well.

'Much as I find a lap cat more fun than a laptop, Heathcliff, I need to get on.'

With the cat eventually curled by her side, and comforted by the purring vibrations against her leg, Ellie ploughed on, and it was gone eleven before she realised the time.

She let Dougal out for a run around the garden as she made a hot chocolate, then scampered up the steps to her attic bedroom and – for the first time since arriving in Polkerran Point – enjoyed a fairly undisturbed night's sleep, waking at dawn to the staccato pounding of rain on the roof.

Ellie walked down into the village with Nicki the next morning, where they dropped the boys at school and nabbed a quick coffee in Karma.

The rain had stopped, but the pavements were wet, puddles forming in the uneven cracks, the first fallen leaves mushy where they gathered at the kerbside.

'Here, have a look through these.'

Ellie airdropped a selection of images to her cousin's phone, and Nicki put down her mug to skim through them. 'They're fab! How have you managed to make me look content and wistful all in one go?'

Confident she'd achieved her purpose, they agreed on the best one to use. 'Can you do an Insta story, tagging me?' Ellie pocketed her phone. 'I can then do some reels and posts, give my details and so on. See if I can interest a few people in a mini-session.'

Nicki left for work shortly after, feeling much more upbeat as half-term approached because her parents' arrival for the duration of the school holidays promised some free time for Nicki.

Once Ellie's duties were done for the day, she prepped and posted a social media blast about the mini photo sessions, including a sign-up link.

Hopefully, the raw authenticity and vulnerability of Nicki's face would create just the vibe to represent Ellie's style of photography and generate some bookings.

By the time she was done, a watery blue sky – dusted with strands of wispy grey cloud – hosted a weak but determined sun as it draped its weary rays across the hillsides surrounding Polkerran. It was as though the heavy rainfall overnight had drained it of all energy.

As soon as she'd fed Dougal and Heathcliff and taken the former for a chilly walk, Ellie grabbed her Canon and Fuji cameras.

There were pools of water everywhere, the air crisp with autumn vibes, and Ellie navigated her way around a large dirty brown puddle which had formed at the bottom of the hill, before guiding Fifi into the track climbing uphill towards the field hosting the site.

Slinging both cameras across her body, she tucked a spare battery into her coat pocket and made her way carefully to the edge of the field, loving the rain drops still glistening on the uncut grass. Cobwebs hung suspended from the metal sign, droplets of water sparkling like strands of diamonds as the weak sun touched them, and Ellie took several close-ups.

Swapping to the Canon, she snapped specific portrait images of the newly installed shepherd's hut and angled photos of the site's signage, offset by the pale blue sky behind it.

Walking back to the car later, Ellie checked the time. Nicki was taking the boys over to visit Hamish that afternoon before heading into Port Wenneth on their return to go bowling. Bella was knee-deep in research at her cottage, wanting to have a certain piece finished for Oliver's return on Tuesday.

'It looks like you're in for a lonely lunch,' she warned, stamping her feet on the gravel to try and remove the mud, well aware she wasn't remotely hungry.

Perhaps a walk on the cliff top would stir her appetite? A stiff breeze blew across the exposed field, and she looked around, espying a public footpath sign. Adjusting the cameras on her body, she headed towards it.

The few remaining grey clouds had begun to dissipate, blue permeating the last fronds draped across the sky. The tarmac soon ran out, but the ground underfoot was relatively firm, being a combination of mud packed with stones and the occasional root from the thick hedgerows bordering both sides.

Ellie could hear the sea now, crashing onto invisible rocks. A bit further along, the hedgerow suddenly ended, and Ellie emerged onto a stretch of exposed path across the cliff top, a small gasp of delight escaping her parted lips.

The bracken adorning the headland had turned to burnished copper. There was no visible treeline, just the outcrops of cliffs as the land embraced the shimmering waters, the palest of blues now to reflect the heavens above and sporting a dusting of icing sugar sparkles as far as the eye could see.

And there, nestled in the embrace of the gold-tipped bracken, was a whitewashed cottage, a curl of smoke swirling upwards from one of its red-brick chimneys.

'Peaches?' Ellie essayed, softly. She could see where the name might well have come from now, with the soft, almost fuzzy haze of the colours embracing the house on all sides. She snapped away, her mouth curved upwards in appreciation at the scene, but after a while, she resumed her walk.

As she reached a particular stretch of path, however, not far beyond the cottage, her skin prickled, and she froze.

Had she walked this way before? More than once, it felt… Her curious eyes scanned the thick hedgerow bordering the edge of the cliff, which muffled the distant sound of waves pounding the rocks below. Wasn't their beach somewhere down below?

Unable to detect a gap in the hedge – much as Will had struggled the first time he'd shown it to her – and with the ground dipping away into a hollow too soggy even for Ellie's sturdy walk boots, she turned back, emotions jumbling inside like washing in a tumble drier, as she both sought and fought the memories.

She paused once more to admire the setting of the whitewashed cottage, taking a final burst of photos as the gentle sun finally glowed centre stage, bathing the scene in otherworldly light.

Reversing the car out of the parking space a few minutes later, unsettled by her recollections and uncertain if they deceived her, Ellie eased Fifi towards the gateway. As she went to turn onto the track, however, a large black car came shooting past, and she spun the wheel to avoid a collision, only for Fifi to slide into the mushy verge.

The vehicle had disappeared down the driveway with the 'Private Property' sign, and Ellie sent its disappearing back a fierce look.

'It's okay, Fifi. We had a lucky escape. Let's get home, and tomorrow I think I'd better get you cleaned!'

Except they were going nowhere. Fifi's wheels were firmly entrenched in mud, and the more Ellie tried to rev to get them out, the deeper they went.

'Great,' she muttered, tugging her scarf from her neck and tossing it onto the passenger seat before climbing out to inspect the problem.

'Can I give you a hand?'

Ellie stiffened. She couldn't move. Or turn around.

What the hell was Will doing up here?

The footsteps slowed, and Ellie spun around to face Will. Never had anyone looked more like they wished they were somewhere else.

Ellie drew in a short breath. 'I'm not sure what to do. I'm stuck in the mud.'

Will said nothing, and for a moment, she thought he was going to turn and leave. Where had he come from, anyway?

'Some stupid person forced me off the road, driving way too fast.' She glared at the 'Private Property' sign, and a faint sound came from the man who had crouched down to inspect Fifi's tyres.

Ellie tried not to stare at Will's back. He was dressed for the country, to be fair, in the usual uniform of a dark green wax jacket, cords the likes of which her dad used to wear, and was that one of those plaid flat caps poking out of his pocket?

Amused despite her jumbled emotions, Ellie stifled a small laugh, then looked away swiftly as Will glanced over his shoulder.

'I'll fetch help.' He straightened, sending Fifi a patronising look. 'It's pretty lightweight as cars go.'

If looks were weapons, Will would be staggering down the private drive now, daggers in his back, but as it was, he walked with the loping grace Ellie remembered all too well. It did nothing to improve her mood.

Barely minutes later, Will arrived with another man – sporting paint-spattered overalls – who reversed a battered truck towards Fifi, who was soon back on terra firma. Pretty certain Will had driven her off the road in the first place, Ellie ignored his closed-off expression and got into the car, determined not to look back as she drove away. Although she did look in the rear-view mirror. That was only the highway code, wasn't it? One should always check…

The other man had disappeared, but Will remained in place, staring down the lane after the car, and Ellie dragged her gaze away to negotiate a sharp bend.

–

Riddled with curiosity over why Will had been up there, Ellie called Marcus, ostensibly to discuss her draft diary entries and the initial photos, but in truth desperately seeking answers.

'So,' Ellie essayed as the conversation drew to a close. 'That Peaches place, Marcus. The one up the private driveway? Do you know who lives there? You said something about someone called Devonshire?'

'Rick Devonshire manages the estate. He lives in that big house on the cliffs. You know the one? Opposite Anna Seymour's place?'

'Yes, of course. Harbourwatch.'

'That's it. Anyway, his family are extensive landowners. The cottage is one of theirs. I know from when I acquired the fields here, as it's my boundary. It's been renovated recently, and I think there are decorators in just now.'

Ellie hesitated. How blatant would it sound to ask who lived there?

'It's a beautiful location,' she continued. 'I took a walk down the coast path when I came up to take photos and came across it. I take it someone's living there?'

Marcus shrugged. 'I've seen the odd car go past but never met who's staying there, if anyone is.'

Recalling the smoke spiralling from the chimney, Ellie knew for a fact someone was, but was it Will, or had he simply been up there looking for… something? She'd have to do some more cautious digging, but one thing was certain: Ellie wouldn't be taking a walk along that path again any time soon.

–

Ellie's heightened senses soon calmed after the unanticipated encounter, but the dull ache that had lately settled beneath her breast showed no sign of abating.

There were a few changes afoot, however, in the short term. Anna and Oliver returned from London, and Hamish's parents – who were frustrated on their son's behalf by the lack of progress in his condition – had arranged for him to be transferred to a private rehab facility in Exeter. It was further for Nicki to travel but felt like a positive step towards recovery.

Furthermore, keen to spend some time with their grandsons and give Nicki a break too, they'd booked them all into a smart hotel for the following weekend, just walking distance from where Hamish was.

On the Friday morning after they left, Ellie rummaged through an overstuffed drawer searching for her new favourite beaded earrings – a find from the little beach cafe – but as she pulled out the card on which they were fixed, it caught on something further back in the drawer.

The little velvet box.

Ellie cradled it in her hands. She hadn't looked inside since bringing it back with her, and her throat tightened as she eyed it.

'It's not like you don't remember what's in there,' Ellie murmured.

She went to open it, but her fingers froze on the zip at a tap on the bedroom door, and she shoved the box back into the drawer, beaming at Anna as she came in.

'I wondered if you fancied joining us for dinner tonight. With both Nicki and Bella away this weekend...' Anna's voice trailed off. 'Sorry. That sounds like I think you're at a loose end. You could have all sorts of plans.'

Ellie had to laugh at Anna's contrite expression. 'I could have, but I don't.'

'Then please come! We'll aim to eat around eight – it's always a bit hit and miss with the twins – but we'll be having a drink by seven. It's just us and our friends, Kate and Dev.' Anna cocked her head at the sound of a baby's plaintive wail. 'At least, that's the plan unless Bertie and Emma decide to join us.'

Scooting down to the Spar, Ellie selected a bottle of red and picked up a small bunch of flowers at the little florist which had recently opened next to the book shop.

The tantalising scent of onion and herbs hung in the air as Ellie made her way downstairs just before seven.

There was no one in the kitchen, so she placed her offering on the island before walking over to the bay window that housed the large, scrubbed pine table, laid up for dinner for five. Darkness had long swept through the cove, and lights could be seen glowing from several windows at Harbourwatch, perched on the opposite cliff.

'Sorry!' Anna came scurrying into the kitchen, refastening her apron and hurrying over to inspect a pan on the stove.

'I hope this is drinkable.' Ellie joined her, pointing at the bottle and handing the flowers to Anna. 'I tend to buy wine by how much I like the label.'

'So do I. Oliver's the expert. Thank you for these – they're beautiful.' She buried her nose in the fragrant blooms, then popped them in a vase of water.

Ellie looked over at the charming sitting area, where a fire glowed brightly in the log burner, the wall sconces dimmed low and casting a warm light over the scene. 'Where's Oliver?'

'Dougal was fussing, so he took him for a quick walk up the lane. He should be— ah, here he is.'

The door swung open and Oliver came in, rolling up Dougal's lead as the dog scampered across to Anna for a fuss before joining Heathcliff on the rug in front of the hearth.

'Can you make dinner stretch again, Anna?' Oliver walked over to drop a kiss on his wife's cheek. 'I picked up a stray when I was out.'

Ellie was on high alert, which at least gave her a moment's preparation as the last person she wanted to walk through the door... walked through the door.

Chapter Eleven

"Mission Impossible"

Anna must have spotted Ellie's rigid frame, and she bit her lip.

Oliver frowned. 'Anna?'

'Oh! Yes, of course. There's always plenty.' She sent Ellie an apologetic look, then beamed at Will, who hovered uncertainly by the door.

Ellie's skin was tingling, but she straightened her shoulders, chin held high as Will's gaze met hers briefly before his expression assumed the inscrutability with which she'd become familiar of late.

'This is Will Farmer, Ellie,' Oliver introduced them as Will came to join him. 'He's just moved in locally.'

'We've met.' Will's tone was even as he added, 'Had to dig her car out the other day.'

A light knock came on the door, and Oliver opened it, holding out his hand to shake that of a man almost as tall as his host, but a little younger and with dark red hair. He held the hand of an elegantly attired brunette, who accepted Oliver's kiss on her cheek before heading over to hug Anna.

'Ellie, this is Kate and Dev. Kate's an old friend of many years. She came to live in the cove about eighteen months ago.'

'You're here to help Nicki?' Kate's mouth curved as they shook hands. 'We both work at the hotel. She's very fond of you. Weren't you together on that holiday, back when she met Hamish?'

Ellie's mouth opened, but Kate continued. 'She told me all about that too, a while back. Said what a great summer you'd all had.'

Hoping that was all Nicki had said, Ellie didn't dare look in Will's direction as she shook Dev's hand. She cleared her throat. 'Yes, it… er, was a lot of fun.'

Well, that at least was true. The aftermath, less so.

'Wine?'

Oliver offered them a glass, then did the same for Dev and Will, who raised them.

'Cheers. I hope it's okay, my gatecrashing.'

'There's always too much food in this house,' Oliver said dryly, as they moved into the sitting room, but Ellie held back.

Anna had returned to the kitchen to inspect the pans on the stove top, and Ellie hurried over.

'Can you give me something to do?' she pleaded.

'I'm so sorry,' Anna said quietly, dropping a spoon into the sink and placing a comforting hand on Ellie's arm. 'Truly. If you want to help, I've popped some extra cutlery and a spare napkin on the table, but haven't had the chance to lay a place.'

Thankful for the respite, Ellie did as she was bid, but when she returned to the kitchen, Anna urged her to join the others.

'Go on, it'll be easier with company around. And that will help.' She gestured at Ellie's glass on the island and picked up the oven gloves, and with little choice, Ellie reluctantly walked over to the sitting area.

Dev and Kate sat next to each other on one of the sofas, Dev's arm across the back, his hand resting on Kate's shoulder. Oliver had taken one of the high-backed armchairs by the hearth, and Will the other. They were laughing about something, and Ellie scooted across to the other sofa, taking the seat furthest from Will.

'Are how's pre-production going?' Kate addressed Will. 'We've had a van parked at the hotel sporadically.'

Boyish enthusiasm spread across Will's face, and Ellie took a generous sip of wine as her heart fluttered at the flash of the man she'd once known. Without the hat pulled low over his eyes, his once oh-so-familiar features constantly drew her gaze, though she hastily withdrew it time and again.

He expounded a little on the process, but despite his obvious delight in the project, he was evasive on the details. 'I'm tying up some loose ends – need to do a bit more research of the area, carry out some interviews – but we're not filming until early next year.'

'Hoping for better weather?' Dev suggested.

'That and better light.'

'You'll get the best of that where you're staying. Will's moved into Peaches Cottage,' Dev explained to Ellie, unaware she'd already put the pieces together. 'I offered it to Oliver for his property project, but it was too remote and there were no takers.'

Then, recalling Marcus's words, Ellie blurted out, 'I thought the cottage belonged to someone called Rick Devonshire?' Damn. Would Will think she'd been asking questions, after seeing him there? She attempted a nonchalant shrug. 'Marcus – he owns the campsite up there – mentioned it, that's all.'

'That's Dev,' Oliver responded.

'I had the same confusion when I first came here.' Kate smiled kindly at Ellie, before turning to Will. 'It's very generous of you to offer an inflated rent so the extra funds can be channelled into community projects.'

Will laughed, and Ellie schooled her face to hide her delight in the sound. 'I'm keen to give back where I can, so when you mentioned not being able to use it for Oliver's scheme, it seemed the best compromise.'

Puzzled, Ellie looked to the man himself, and Oliver shrugged, saying nothing, but Anna joined them then, sharing that her husband had, for some years now, been purchasing property in the cove to offer back to locals only at affordable rents. So many residents had been forced to leave because they couldn't afford a home in the place where they'd grown up or longed to raise their families.

'That's fabulous!' Ellie turned shining eyes on Oliver, but he waved her praise away.

'I happen to be in a fortunate situation. I'm sure there are many others who'd have liked to help out.'

A suppressed snort from Dev and a shake of Kate's head was the end of the subject, though, as Anna declared the meal ready, and they made moves towards the table.

Ellie trawled behind. She knew exactly where she didn't want to be placed: next to Will, opposite Will or at any table where Will might be.

Ever.

Her eyes fell to the mat which housed Dougal and Heathcliff's feeding bowls. Perhaps they'd let her eat there instead?

During this pointless speculation, Oliver went over to help Anna ferry the dishes, and Dev and Kate took the chairs facing the window.

Assuming the hosts would sit at either end – and the wine glasses already in place confirmed it – that left the two remaining, neighbouring chairs.

Will said nothing, and stood behind one of them, but as Ellie moved round by the window, he pulled out the one nearest her, indicating she sit.

'Thank you,' she muttered, slipping into the seat, relieved to see Kate's friendly face directly opposite.

'It's a habit for me to sit facing this way,' she said with a smile. 'I used to ponder what Dev was doing over there.' She gestured out into the darkness, and the man at her side grasped her hand and pressed a kiss on it.

'Not any more.'

The food arrived then, and Oliver topped up everyone's glasses as they tucked into a sumptuous fish stew.

'This is delicious, Anna.' Ellie savoured the rich flavour of the sauce. 'Do the twins appreciate what fabulous meals they are going to enjoy as they grow up?'

Oliver gave a short laugh. 'As their current favourites are a range of Cow & Gate mush, I doubt it.'

'So, Will,' Dev addressed him across the table. 'Have you settled in? The log burner can be a bit temperamental.'

'Nothing could be as challenging as the old Rayburn we used to have at home,' Will replied. 'It was brutal in the winter. You've done a beautiful job on the renovation.'

'Mostly Kate's choices when it came to furnishings.'

Will sent the lady an appreciative look. 'You have exceptional taste.'

'She does,' quipped Dev, kissing Kate on her pink cheek, and amidst the general laughter, she turned back to Will.

'What inspired you to move away from acting? You won so many awards. Did you not want to continue?'

Will picked up the basket of garlic bread and selected a slice. 'I suppose it became a case of "been there, done that".' He shrugged. 'When I feel something's over, it's time to move on.'

He made as if to return the basket but then held it in Ellie's direction without looking at her. Reaching for a piece, Ellie willed her hand not to tremble. Was he hinting at them, or was she reading too much into it?

'I bet you'd change your mind for the right offer,' Dev said with a smile, but Will shook his head.

'I made a vow to myself many years ago to never go back over old ground.'

Ellie flinched, but Oliver nodded as he added another portion of the rich stew to his plate.

'I'm with you on that. Leave the past behind.'

Dev laughed. 'That's ripe, coming from a historian.'

With a grin, Oliver picked up his wine, saying nothing further, but Ellie sensed Will stirring in his seat.

The conversation moved to Anna and Oliver's approaching departure for America, as they continued to tuck into their food, and once everyone had finished, Anna got to her feet.

'Let's have dessert.'

'That was superb, thank you.' Ellie held up her plate as Oliver helped his wife clear. 'I can't remember the last time I had bouillabaisse.'

What sounded like a laugh turned into a cough escaped the man at her side, and Ellie's heart dipped, her face aglow as the sudden memory of meeting Will dressed as Stewie flashed through her mind.

Anna had returned to the kitchen, and Ellie grabbed the basket containing the leftover bread and shot over to join her.

'There. It's not so bad, is it?' Anna spoke softly as she opened the fridge, and Ellie stood beside her, enjoying the cool air on her overly warm skin.

'Yes!' she hissed.

Anna withdrew a cheesecake and placed it on the island, returning to remove a jug of cream.

'I wouldn't worry. The men are oblivious and Kate's a good 'un. Besides, it will get easier each time.'

'I'm hoping there won't be another one.'

'Are you?' Anna smirked, picking up the dessert.

Ellie merely rolled her eyes, following behind with some glass side plates while Oliver came over to retrieve a slate board filled with an assortment of cheeses, fruit cake, thin biscuits and grapes.

Ellie sat down, determined to make her escape as soon as was polite, but then, Dev addressed her across the table.

'What is it you do, Ellie? They must be missing you.'

Ellie placed a few slices of brie on a cracker. 'I'm a photographer. I set up my own business a few years ago.'

A sudden movement came from the man beside her, but Ellie forced her gaze to remain with Dev and Kate.

'That must be fun.' Kate reached for a celery stick. 'I saw the photos of Nicki on Insta; we shared it on the hotel's account. They were amazing, especially the black-and-white version.'

Stirring in her seat as all eyes, even Will's, turned in her direction, Ellie fixed her attention solely on Kate. 'Thank you. It's my favourite too.'

'But I thought you did history at uni, then a masters,' Will blurted out as Ellie picked up the cracker.

'I… chose a different path.'

Was Will going to challenge her on changing her mind? If only he knew the cause…

The conversation moved on to other subjects, but Ellie's concentration had been shot from the moment Will took the butter dish from her, his hand brushing against hers so unexpectedly, she almost dropped it.

Had he done it on purpose, or was it just wishful thinking?

'Ellie?'

With a start, she looked up from the hands clasped in her lap. Everyone had risen from the table. She shot to her feet, Will drawing her chair out for her.

She said another quiet thank you and hurried after Anna.

'This was lovely, but I'm going up now.'

'No coffee? Oliver's a dab hand at it.' She indicated where her husband was pushing various buttons on the state-of-the-art coffee machine.

Ellie would lie awake all night as it was.

'No, thanks. Is it okay if I take Dougal for his last walk? I just need some air before bed.'

Anna sent her an understanding look. 'Of course.' Then she lowered her voice. 'They'll all be gone in a half-hour. I'm so sorry.'

'Not at all. It was no one's fault, and you're right. Building up some immunity had to start one day. Especially as I'm stuck with it for the foreseeable.'

'Stuck where? Not your car again?'

Ellie's heart picked up its pace at Will's voice just behind her. Had he heard more than that?

'No.' She swung around, raising her chin to meet Will's dark gaze. 'I'm staying here, so I didn't need it tonight.'

Anna had gone back to the kitchen and Ellie's eyes remained locked on Will's, but then, he gave a quick nod and turned back towards the living room.

Flustered, Ellie said a quick goodbye to Dev and Kate, who'd resumed their places by the hearth, and was touched when Kate invited her for coffee at the weekend.

Will was setting mugs on a tray at the island as Oliver finished making the coffees, and she waved a casual hand before ushering Dougal into the boot room.

Stepping outside, Ellie leaned back against the wall. An autumnal chill had settled over the cove and the smell of woodsmoke wafted through the air from various chimneys.

'You did it,' she said under her breath as she pushed away and walked swiftly out into the lane, Dougal trotting companionably at her heels. 'You survived.'

No lights shone from Nicki's cottage, and Ellie could imagine the pleasure she was having in being near Hamish and not having to cook or deal with laundry for a few days.

By the time she returned to Westerleigh, the guests had gone, and Ellie helped Anna as she plumped sofa cushions and ferried mugs to the dishwasher, before bidding her and Oliver goodnight and scooting up the stairs.

Ellie flicked on the light in her room, then stared at her face in the full-length mirror as she tossed her coat on the bed.

What did Will think of her now? She tried to see the familiar reflection objectively. She favoured a more natural style, warmer colours, floaty things like full skirts and scarves, and an indulgence in statement earrings.

Ellie turned her head side to side, eyes narrowed. Would Will still consider her attractive, despite the changes the years had brought?

'Enough. It doesn't matter *what* he thinks.' She spoke firmly. 'It's been over for years, and don't forget, he rejected your attempts to mend things.'

With that, Ellie grabbed her sleepwear and headed for the bathroom. Before clambering under the covers, however, she succumbed to temptation, retrieving the velvet box. Nerves jangling, her mind in conflict over whether it was wise to do so, she slowly unzipped the lid.

Chapter Twelve

"Gone Girl"

To anyone else, there was little of value in the box, but for Ellie, every piece held poignancy. Hands trembling, she tipped the contents onto the bed, sifting through the ticket stubs, a keyring bearing a tiny stuffed shrimp, a single earring – one of a pair Will had bought her – the other having long been lost, several shells they'd picked up on their beach and a smooth, flat stone.

Will had skimmed it into the water, then charged after it to try and find it, Ellie dashing after him and shoving him, the two of them emerging dripping wet, hair plastered to their faces, bodies warm against each other as he stole a kiss before plunging his hand into the clear shallow water and raising the stone in triumph.

'It meant to be found,' he declared, holding it up against an azure-blue sky to study the intricate lines embedded in it. Then, he'd handed it to Ellie, urging her to keep it. 'It's our token,' he'd whispered. 'Years in the forming, shaped by the elements, the sea and the sand, and now it's come to us. It's a sign, Ells. Together forever.'

Heart swelling, eyes closed, Ellie had tried to hold on to the moment, the kisses they'd exchanged, pressed close to each other, only parting when the catcalls and whoops began at the other end of the beach, where they'd all pitched up for the afternoon.

Wetness clinging to her lashes, Ellie pressed a kiss to the stone, placing it back in the box and slowly adding each item, only pausing when she picked up the last two things on the bed.

Suppressing a sob, Ellie slipped the cheap ring with its bright gem onto her finger. It was still way too big, but Will had spotted it in the souvenir shop, in amongst several others of varying colours. Ellie lowered her head as a memory gripped her, as vivid as though she were watching in on a livestream.

'Keep it,' Will had murmured as he'd put it on her third finger. 'Until I can get you a proper one, only let's not tell anyone.'

Ellie had willingly agreed. It was their sweet secret, to be kept between themselves until they'd told their parents…

And look how *that* had gone.

She drew in a short, painful breath as she studied the photo clutched in her other hand. Ellie could barely see it now through the mist of her tears: a selfie taken minutes before they left Polkerran Point to head back to their homes, Will had been behind her, Ellie leaning her head against his broad chest, his tanned arm holding her close, the plastic ring on her finger and two goofy grins looking into the lens as they faced the future. Together.

For the last time…

Making no attempt to stop the tears now, Ellie switched off the lamp and sank back against the pillows, enveloped in darkness, the ring still on her finger. She felt all a-jumble, as though the contentment she had striven for in life had been made of nothing but sand, collapsing at the slightest nudge into a pool of despondency.

–

Ellie didn't see Anna when she came down the next morning as she'd taken the twins for a routine check-up before the trip away. Oliver, she assumed, was up in his den working, so she ate a hasty breakfast before heading next door to take the boys to school, giving them both a hug, with Liam shrugging out of it with an 'aww, not here, Auntie Nellie', and telling them to have a good day.

Stopping for a brief chat with Phoenix, Ellie then headed to Karma, smiling at a WhatsApp from Liam saying sorry and sending a hug emoji.

Ellie sank into her favourite seat on one of the sofas by the window, sipping an indulgent hot chocolate as she stared out into the street. She ought to go back, get on with editing the wedding photos or finishing a commission for an eightieth birthday card, but the sun had sent the early-morning cloud packing and, resplendent now against a cushion of blue sky, the outdoors beckoned.

Soon on the cliff path beyond Westerleigh, a gentle breeze stroked the tufts of long grass bordering the track, and Ellie paused to take some shots of the sea and sky, making use of the sunlight to create different shadows. Reviewing them on the screen, she smiled. This was such a gorgeous place for atmospheric images.

Footsteps came towards her as someone came up the steps from the beach below, and Anna emerged, pink in the face, Dougal at her heels.

'You're back already!' said Ellie. 'Where are the twins?'

'Gemma popped in, so she's taken them for a stroll. Thought I'd grab the opportunity to walk where I can't take a double-buggy at the moment.'

Ellie grinned. 'Thanks so much for dinner last night, by the way.'

Anna sent Ellie a contrite look. 'Do you forgive Oliver?'

'I hardly think he needs it. He wasn't to know it might be difficult.' Ellie leaned against the sturdy railings as Anna offered Dougal a biscuit from her pocket.

'True, but it wasn't the easiest evening for you.' Anna leaned next to Ellie. 'Although one thing was clear.'

Ellie sent her a questioning look.

'Will isn't indifferent to you.'

'Hah!' Ellie fished the lens cap from her pocket and replaced it on the Canon. 'No, he's not. He hates me.'

Anna began to shake her head, but Ellie continued. 'It's fine. I've got used to the idea, and ultimately it did me some good to be put in that situation, as I'm pretty much stuck here for now.'

'Talking of which, how's it going with the photography?'

They pushed away from the railing, making their way back along the track.

'It's giving me a challenge to focus on.' Ellie confirmed bookings for the mini-session were flooding in, along with a few other enquiries.

Anna was keen to book a shoot with the twins. 'It might take some time,' she warned Ellie as they scaled a stile. 'But I'd love some photos that aren't snapped by me on my phone. Nothing formal, just… you know? Ones that capture *them*.'

'You're speaking to my heart, you know. That's my purpose in life.'

They agreed to do it once the twins were back from the trip, as time was short, and Anna also put in an order for a personalised card for them at Christmas.

'Oliver will think I'm mad.' She smirked at Ellie as they approached the lane down into the village. 'He's never quite understood my sending cards to Dougal and Heathcliff.'

Ellie chuckled. 'I can do one of those too, if you like. You'd be surprised about the commissions I get.'

Anna headed home then, as she needed to get on with the packing, and Ellie continued into town. It was true she had to get back to Oxford. To her life. To her profession. But the knowledge that Will would be a Polkerran resident right through to the spring brought a wave of temptation fit to sweep her out to sea.

It wasn't a happy realisation, and Ellie crushed it. Time to focus on her business. Matters of the heart were a waste of her time.

–

Ellie enjoyed having coffee with Kate. She met her daughter, Mollie, who was fifteen and doing her GCSEs, one of which was in art, so they had a good chat about it and the career possibilities. Afterwards, they walked down to the tidal beach below the house, taking a vacant bench to watch the water and chat gently about this and that.

Kate had been with Dev for just over a year, moving into his house in the spring. He had a six-year-old son, Theo, and it was clear she was enjoying life to the full, heading off shortly to take him to a party for one of his school friends.

'Tell me more about your photography business,' Kate encouraged. 'I was blown away by what you captured in those images of Nicki. You really *got* her at this moment in her life.'

'The weddings are a staple but can be a challenge. You know, making sure everyone's happy, and as for the weather...' She rolled her eyes at Kate, laughing. 'But it gives me the opportunity to be creative, and I love capturing evocative and unexpected images. And school shoots are fun, although getting the younger ones to sit still takes all my skill and patience. I could do with finding some local assignments, if I'm honest.'

'I can imagine. I'll pop the details of your mini-session on the hotel's events page. We can host the shoots, subject to bookings, if the weather won't play ball.'

Ellie's heart swelled with gratitude. 'That's very kind of you.'

Kate glanced at her watch. 'Let's talk some more another time. I have ideas, but I'd best go and get Theo ready.'

They parted company at Harbourwatch, and Ellie walked back through the village. It was pleasing to see her cards displayed in the Spar and book-shop windows, but was there more she could do?

Tucked behind the village hall was a small building which seemed to double as a community library, tourist office and box office for local events, which Ellie had never noticed before.

She pushed open the heavy door and looked around with interest.

'Good morning.' A woman looked up from stacking leaflets into a wall-mounted shelving unit as Ellie approached.

'Hi.' Ellie summoned a bright smile. She quickly explained about her sideline of making personalised cards, and the assistant – Valerie – happily took a small stack of business cards – each side showing the dual aspects of Ellie's talents respectively – to pop into the display unit for local businesses.

Pleased, Ellie stayed to have a look around the library section. They had made good use of limited space, being a large square room with a counter supporting a till, and posters on the wall advertising events which had long passed. The opposite wall was devoted to local tourist attractions, maps and local services, and a line of tall bookcases, stuffed with a jumble of genres, ran across the centre of the room, next to a trolley of well-thumbed older books offered in exchange for a small donation.

Ellie flicked through the opening pages of a romance novel, but then Valerie called out.

'There's a section on local history, walks and the like on the back wall if you're interested.'

'Thanks,' Ellie responded, heading round the bookcase, but as soon as she espied the broad shoulders and dark hair of the man already browsing the maps, she froze.

Will must have sensed her approach, however, as he glanced over his shoulder, then turned back to resume his study of the leaflet he held.

About to back away, Ellie stalled. Why should she? The walk books interested her. So what if Will was there? He didn't own the bloody library!

Marching over, she stared unseeingly at the shelves, with no idea what she specifically sought. Will replaced the leaflet, but, typically, they both reached for the same book at the same time.

Ellie's skin was a traitor. It had not forgotten Will's touch as his hand all but landed on top of hers. She snatched it away, but he reached for the book and held it out to her.

'You got there first.'

He held her gaze for a brief moment, and Ellie took it from him, careful not to touch his fingers. Despite his closed expression, Will seemed as though he was about to say something else, but then her phone rang.

'Oh, hi Marcus.'

Ellie turned away, expecting Will to leave, and tried to focus on what Marcus was saying.

'Ellie. I love the photos! Can we get together to talk about them? I'm meeting with the website developer next week.'

She bit her lip, not so keen to return to the site, knowing now that Will lived close by. 'Where and when?'

'Are you free Monday? To come up to the site office?'

With a sigh, Ellie compromised. 'Can we make it Tuesday?'

They agreed the details, and Ellie pocketed the phone, then stalled. Was Will still behind her? She whirled about, expecting him to have somehow evaporated, but he remained where he was, clutching another walk book.

What should she say?

Nice to see you again? Hasn't this been great? Fancy a snog?

Heat gathering in her neck, ready to invade her cheeks, Ellie swallowed quickly. It didn't really matter, so long as the next words were 'goodbye'.

'Bye,' she croaked, swinging away so fast, her long metal earring slapped her in the face.

Owwww, she wailed silently, a hand to her face as she called farewell to Valerie and closed the door firmly, drawing in a deep breath of sea air.

Scurrying down the street towards the harbour, embroiled in a debate with herself over how well that had – or hadn't – gone, she was oblivious to Will emerging from the tourist-office-cum-library, or to the conflicted expression lingering in the depths of his eyes as he watched her disappear round the corner and out of sight.

Chapter Thirteen

"Location, Location, Location"

Ellie was up early the next day, the last before the Seymour family departed for their trip and was relieved to find Anna baby-free when she came into the kitchen.

'Gemma took advantage of the early high tide. She's just this minute taken the twins and Dougal out.' Anna sank onto the sofa with a soft rabbit clutched in her lap. She was flushed in the face, her ponytail escaping its clasp. 'I don't know what I'd do without her.'

She glanced at the clock. 'I didn't realise the time. Is everything okay?'

'Yes, sorry. I just…' Ellie huffed on a breath. 'I could do with a chat, and I know you tend to get a houseful around eleven.'

Anna got to her feet. 'Come on, let's have a cuppa and you can talk as much or as little as you like. Oliver won't emerge from the den until later. He and Bella are running through a fact-check of the latest book.'

Sitting at the scrubbed pine table, facing the stunning view, Ellie's gaze settled on Harbourwatch, perched on its steep cliff face.

'Kate's lovely, isn't she? We had coffee the other day.'

'We go way back. I was so happy when she moved to the cove and then decided to stay. It does that to people, you know. Be warned.'

Ellie shook her head. 'I think I might buck the trend.' She paused, then urged herself to get on with it. 'The thing is…' She lowered her mug, then sighed. 'It's a bit embarrassing. I mean, I can't leave, but—'

'Is it Will?'

Ellie sent Anna a startled look. 'No! I mean, it's not great, that he's here, but… look, it's the old money thing.'

Anna's brow furrowed. 'Didn't the mini-sessions get booked up?'

'Oh yes! It's great, and there's a second date that's slowly filling up, but it's not sustainable income, more a stopgap.'

'Ah, I see. With such a small community, the market is soon depleted.'

'Exactly. The thing is, I've no idea how long I'll be here, but I've still got bills to pay on my flat.'

As she was speaking these last words, the door opened and Bella came in.

'Hey.' Her expression quickly filled with concern, and she hurried over to join them. 'This sounds troubling. Is there anything I can do?'

Ellie looked between Anna and Bella, who had taken the seat opposite. 'It's a bit awkward.'

'Ellie's wondering if there's any work locally to supplement her income. It's a tough one in the autumn, but you could always try the hotel. It's the biggest employer in the cove, after all.'

Bella reached across the table to squeeze Ellie's hand. 'I wish I could help, but I'm running two households myself at the moment. Luckily, Oliver's not charging me rent, so I can just about manage.'

They chatted about possible places to contact about the photography, and Ellie tapped notes into her phone, looking up when the door opened, and Gemma returned.

'They've just dropped off,' she mouthed, pointing at the buggy.

She crouched down to free Dougal from his lead. 'They're all on their way, Anna. Saw Great Aunt Dee, Auntie Jay and Cleggie crossing the bridge.'

'Oh Lord,' Anna exclaimed with a laugh. 'Okay, let me take over with the twins. Who can help with the teas and coffees?'

'I'll do it,' Bella offered, heading over to fill the kettle, while Ellie retrieved plates and place mats.

Gemma returned from hanging up her coat and Dougal's lead, putting some food in his bowl and giving him a good rub before going over to wash her hands.

'I'll get some cakes out, but then I'll head back, or I'll miss the tide.'

By the time Anna had wheeled the buggy into the quiet of the snug and switched on the monitor, the locals had arrived to claim their usual seats, Old Patrick and Phoenix following in their wake, and Ellie, quietly thanking Anna for being an ear, escaped to the orangery.

It was time she followed up on some of the suggested leads.

–

Later that morning, having finished the last of the Christmas cards and put a few details on the images for June and July for the calendar, Ellie stretched her arms above her head. The murmur of conversation through the closed door was sufficient to forewarn the locals were still in situ, but keen for a hot drink, she headed inside.

Anna was now bouncing a very awake Bertie on her knee in the sitting room. Emma sat on the playmat, pounding a very cute-looking soft toy with a teether.

'Goodness. What did bunny do?'

Anna laughed as she sat Bertie next to his sister. 'Nothing. She has a penchant for beating things. I dread to think what it'll be like when she's old enough to request a set of drums! Matty says it's her inner musician trying to get out. There's fresh tea and coffee on the table if you want one?'

'I'm gasping!'

Ellie approached the table, where a discussion was in progress about someone who'd just died.

'I says to Foxy Boxey,' chuckled Old Patrick, his eyes alight, 'I says, I does, it's a surprise they was able to close the coffin on her. Not fond of lying on her back, so the word was.'

'*Pat*,' Jean admonished. 'Don't speak ill of the—'

'Aye.' Mrs Lovelace chortled. 'Bit too fond of the hanky spanky, was Iris.'

'I think you mean hanky *panky*, Mum.' Jean winked at Ellie, who grinned.

Mrs Lovelace and Mrs Clegg, however, exchanged a knowing look. 'No. Definitely spanky,' the former concluded, popping a piece of scone in her mouth and munching with satisfaction.

Ellie turned to the latter. 'Lovely to see you out, Mrs Clegg. I hear you haven't been too well?'

'Bless you, my lovely.' The old lady grasped Ellie's hand and squeezed it. She had a surprisingly firm grip.

'They various veins playing up,' Mrs Lovelace expanded.

'No Ryther today?'

Old Patrick shook his head. 'Gone up country. Some check-up or other.'

Hoping the gentleman was okay, Ellie poured a mug of tea and returned to the sitting area, taking the sofa opposite Anna.

'He adored my aunt Meg, you know,' said Anna.

Ellie's startled gaze shot to where Old Patrick was currently berating Mrs Lovelace for something, but Anna chuckled.

'Not Patrick, Ryther.'

'Meg was the lady whose house this was?'

'Yes. He gave it to her. It's so sad. They fell madly in love one summer, but something drove them apart. Neither of them ever got over it, or, as we later discovered, each other.'

Anna went on to explain the story behind her beautiful engagement ring and its connection to the story.

'That's so sad. They were never reconciled?'

'No. It was a permanent estrangement.'

Before Ellie could reflect on this, Phoenix came over to chat about the upcoming scarecrow festival.

'Liam and Jason are busy sourcing an outfit for theirs.' Ellie grinned. 'It sounds quite competitive.'

'Yes.' Anna still held Bertie, an open picture book in her hands. 'The school's heavily involved, as are most of the local clubs, but now Tremayne Manor is to be the finishing point for the competition, with scarecrows within the grounds.'

'And it's a fundraiser?'

Phoenix nodded as Ellie sipped her tea. 'Partly for the RNLI, but also for village schemes that get little or nothing from the parish council, such as the Christmas lights and some school projects.'

'Is there a prize for the best one?'

'Oh yes,' Phoenix enthused. 'And this year it's a fab offering. From that chap who's renting the whitewashed cottage on the cliffs.'

Ellie was aware of her own stillness, of how cold she suddenly felt. Rubbing her arms, she was conscious of Anna's swift look.

'Oh? That's nice.' She shook back her hair. It was. Nice. *Well, Will is nice. I haven't forgotten…*

'Yeah, he's offered some sort of holiday voucher, but it's a flexible thing, depending on whether it's a child – and their age – or a family, or team of some sort. He's very considerate.'

Towards anyone who wasn't Ellie.

–

The next day, with Oliver and Anna off on their long-awaited trip, Ellie spent the evening round at Nicki's before coming back to the empty cottage, grateful for Heathcliff's solid body against her legs as she tried to get to sleep in the empty house.

'This is it for a while, pusscat,' Ellie murmured sleepily, stroking the downy fur as Heathcliff ramped up the purring and rolled onto her back, paws aloft. 'Maybe I'll be able to leave by the time they're back, if Hamish makes some progress in Exeter?'

Heathcliff didn't really have a lot to say on this, curling into a ball around Ellie's hand, and sleep overcame her. By the time she awoke to a sunny morning, the cat sat on the stool by the dressing table having a thorough wash, one leg stuck up like a flagpole.

When she dropped Liam and Jason off at school, she bumped into Kate doing the same with Theo, and as they walked out of the school gates, Kate invited Ellie for a coffee at Karma.

'I've been meaning to talk to you,' Kate explained as they settled at a table by the window.

She revealed that, in addition to her role at the Point Hotel, she also acted in an advisory capacity at Tremayne Manor, mainly in connection with a newly created event space.

'Hey, are you free this morning?'

As they emerged from the cafe onto the harbourfront, Ellie tried not to think about the state of the orangery, where she'd been editing photos and had several cards drying in racks.

'Yes,' she replied carefully.

'Tell you what then – come with me.'

Ellie hurried after Kate, as she walked with purpose along the harbourfront.

'Where are we going, exactly?'

'Mrs Tremayne saw the photos you shared on Instagram.'

Ellie had been doing reels and stories for over a week, promoting the mini-sessions by using the photos of Nicki, along with images from around the village and harbour.

She cast Kate a curious look. 'The lady doesn't sound like someone who goes on the socials.'

'Nor does she, but I showed them to her. The images seem to have given Mrs Tremayne an idea. She mentioned wanting to meet you to talk it through.'

'What, now? Where?'

'Here.' Kate waved a hand at the castellated roofline of Tremayne Manor, as they approached the rear of the church. 'This is the local stately pile. Tremaynes have lived there for over three hundred years and haven't been particularly approachable as lords of the manor. Until now.'

She led the way up a path towards a wrought-iron gate set into stone and flint walls, pushing it open. Ellie almost caved and ran as memories flooded her mind.

'Come on,' Kate called over her shoulder, and reluctantly, Ellie followed her across a vast courtyard, bordered on one side by a stable block, with green lawns stretching away towards a bank of trees, the glistening waters of the bay below.

Wrapping her arms around her middle, Ellie forced away an unanticipated swirl of emotion. All her previous visits to this manor house had been filled with delight: love and laughter. She couldn't help but feel things wouldn't be quite the same this time around.

Chapter Fourteen

"The Beach"

Trying to pull herself together, Ellie glanced at Kate as she grasped the heavy iron ring set into the stone architrave and tugged. The faint jangling of an old-fashioned bell could be heard through the thick wood of the door, and as the heavy door swung aside, Kate smiled warmly at a lady in a smart, grey dress, her salt-and-pepper hair tied in a neat bun.

'Good morning, Kate. Mrs Tremayne is waiting for you in the office.'

'Thank you, Norma.'

Ellie, her curiosity vying with her memories, followed Kate along a stone-flagged hallway, the walls adorned with portraits of long-gone Tremaynes.

'Ah, Kate, come on in.'

They entered a room Ellie hadn't seen before, and to her surprise, Kate walked over to the lady by the desk and gave her a warm hug. 'How are you, Arabella?'

'All the better for seeing your welcome face. I feel like I've been in solitary confinement.' Mrs Tremayne turned to Ellie. 'This must be your photographer friend.'

'Yes, this is Ellie Arbon.'

They shook hands, and the lady continued. 'I've been recovering from a nasty bout of flu, and visitors were banned. I've seen nothing but staff for a week.'

'I'm so sorry to hear it,' Ellie said with sympathy. 'There are always such awful bugs going around at this time of year.'

She couldn't help but reflect, however, glancing discreetly around the opulent room – a stunning library with a solitary desk by the window, which probably accounted for its demotion to the sad title of 'office' – that Mrs Tremayne's version of solitary confinement might well have been more inaccurate than most.

They settled on a couple of sofas, an elegant low table between them, and as if by magic a young man appeared bearing a tray of tea things.

Feeling as though she'd somehow stepped into an episode of *Downton Abbey*, Ellie half expected an elderly butler to emerge from the woodwork, offering to pour for them.

As they sipped weak tea from fine china cups, Mrs Tremayne explained – with occasional interjections from Kate – how her son, Alex, now managed Tremayne Estates, which included the family home.

Ellie tried not to react at yet another mention of Alex.

'My son is based in London,' the lady continued, pride evident in her voice. 'He therefore prefers to have a local team here running things, but he's very commercially focused, being such a successful financier.'

'I've reduced my hours at the hotel recently so that I can oversee the implementation of a new scheme,' Kate continued. 'The manor will soon be licensed for ceremonies. One of the outbuildings is currently under conversion into a beautiful, barn-style space for receptions and other celebrations.'

A slightly disapproving look had settled on Mrs Tremayne's features.

'I am not entirely comfortable with the notion, but Alex says we must make the house pay its way if we are to continue to keep it. However,' she brightened, 'thanks to Kate, who ran a vastly successful village fayre in our grounds the last two summers, there has been a compromise. Alex has agreed I may occasionally allow the grounds to be used gratis for community events.'

'That's lovely,' Ellie enthused, not entirely sure where this was going.

Kate leaned forward. 'Perhaps mention to Ellie the idea you had, Arabella? It makes perfect sense.'

'Yes, of course.' The lady turned to Ellie, her expression more engaged. 'I saw your beautiful photos, and I wondered if you had time to come here and take the pictures for our launch. We would need a full brochure, covering weddings, of course, but also other things we can offer, such as business gatherings, family celebrations and so on.'

Her imagination quickly fired, Ellie nodded eagerly. 'I'd be delighted. I have done brochure work before, and I'd be happy to send you some samples.'

'Excellent.' Mrs Tremayne turned to Kate. 'Would you ring the bell, Kate, to save me getting up? I think this calls for more tea as we discuss the details.'

It was an hour later before they emerged back into the daylight, and as they walked down into the village, Ellie's mind spun on the conversation. Then, her brow furrowed.

'Wait, how long has Mrs Tremayne been widowed?'

To her surprise, Kate laughed. 'She isn't. I've discovered she always speaks as though she's alone. They seem to live totally separate lives. Laurence is a keen golfer and spends weeks on end away having fun on various courses.'

'Oh!' Ellie grinned at Kate as they reached the harbour. 'Good job I didn't say anything, then.'

It was relatively quiet at this time of the morning, aside from the drone of an electric street cleaner trundling along the front and a few shouts from a fishing vessel moored in the harbour. A couple sat outside Karma as they passed, enjoying the final days of mild temperatures as they indulged in coffee and cake and, inhaling the pleasing aroma of freshly baked goods, Ellie made a mental note to pick something up before heading home.

They settled on a vacant bench by the water.

'What do you think?' Kate crossed her legs, shod in elegant dog-tooth patterned trousers, and Ellie briefly admired her stylish designer pumps before shifting round to face her.

'It was lovely of you to suggest my services to Mrs Tremayne. Are you sure she's not just being kind?'

An impish smile appeared. 'Not at all. Arabella's not the most clued-in person, but she's started to come into her own this last year. Besides, we need a high-calibre photographer. Interiors and exteriors. Bridal and celebration mock-ups and so on. It will be invaluable with the marketing we need to do. In reality, Mrs Tremayne needs Alex's sign-off on any hiring, but not when it's ad hoc like this.'

'It would help massively,' Ellie beamed.

'I'll send you the details.' Kate smiled at Ellie's evident enthusiasm. 'You can do the promo shots for the scarecrow festival too. Shame they dropped plans for an Oktoberfest.'

'In *Cornwall*?'

Kate merely laughed, waving a hand as she turned for home, and Ellie speeded up as she crossed the bridge. She had a video call in a half-hour to talk through some invitations with a prospective client and needed to get her head back into the proposed designs.

Fetching up outside Westerleigh, she rummaged for her keys, her head a jumble of scarecrows and vast tankards of beer. Surely Old Patrick hadn't been planning to don some lederhosen?

With a huffed laugh, Ellie let herself in.

This was the cove. Anything could happen!

–

The days spiralled through October, much as the leaves eddied and swirled, falling from the fond grasp of the trees that had nurtured them since the spring until they were embraced by the crisp and golden bed below.

With half-term rapidly approaching, Ellie finalised the details for the first mini-session, which was due to take place during the holidays, relieved to see the second date now almost full.

Nicki was busy with her parents' imminent arrival, doing a major deep clean with Ellie's help and chivvying the boys to finish their scarecrow. Their grandparents had opted to do something similar to Nicki's in-laws and had booked a few nights in a cottage near Hamish.

Busy with continuing her before- and after-school duties, Ellie applied herself to finishing the photography commission for Marcus, who insisted on making a date to have dinner as a thank-you, despite his already having settled her invoice. There was also a one-off job for a connection of Valerie at the tourist office. She spent every spare moment outside of that up at Tremayne Manor, haunted at every corner by memories of long ago, but determined to erase them with new ones.

The scarecrow festival was due to take place on the last weekend of the autumn half-term break for the local schools, which would also bring in a welcome – from the traders' perspective, at least – return of emmet families intent on a break before winter descended.

Nicki's parents soon arrived – greeting their niece, Ellie, warmly and gushing with thanks for all she was doing to help out – and a day later, they all headed off to the cottage in Devon.

She had the first mini-shoot coming up, and the scarecrows to photograph for the local paper. Thankful she had seen nothing of Will for a week, other than a few glimpses from a distance, Ellie looked forward to the festival, reassured that, despite his offering a prize, the man himself was unlikely to be in attendance. But before that, she had the dinner with Marcus.

Walking into the centre of Polkerran, Ellie found herself to be early. All the shops had closed for the night, other than the Spar, but there were plenty of people about, many of whom she could tell were visitors. There were groups of people outside the Three Fishes opposite the harbour, which was likewise busy, and all the benches were filled, mainly with those tucking into their takeaways from the fish and chip shop.

A queue had formed beside the steps, waiting for the last passenger ferry across to the other side of the bay, and the little red boat could be seen chugging its way towards them. Children shouted and squealed down on the tiny expanse of sand which exposed itself at low tide, and sea birds hovered overhead as a fishing boat approached.

'Hello, Ryther. I didn't expect to see you down here in the evening.' Ellie took a seat beside the elderly gentleman on a bench looking out across the water towards where the sea rolled into the bay.

'I am waiting on my grandson. He's in there with Theo.' He pointed towards Thai Dai. 'We're having a takeaway for supper as a treat.'

They chatted amiably for a few minutes, but then Ryther shifted in his seat, his keen blue eyes raking Ellie's face.

'Anna says you came here many years ago?'

'Yes. Had an amazing summer after graduating. Far too much fun to ever be the same again. Not sure I'll ever quite get over it.'

A soft smile lit Ryther's features for a moment, but it quickly faded. 'I share your sentiment, my dear. I too once had the most wonderful summer of my life in the cove. I never fully recovered from it, or the aftermath.'

'I'm sorry.' Ellie touched him on the arm, and he patted her hand.

'As am I. But your story isn't over, is it? Mine, sadly, had no possible happy conclusion, but where there is hope, Ellie… Never give up on it.'

He eased onto his feet, raised a hand and headed to where Dev and Theo could be seen emerging from the takeaway, and Ellie shivered. Had she given up? Was she just accepting that this was the way it was with Will? The way it always would be? That there could be no other outcome?

She looked around, then crossed the cobbles, returning a wave from Old Patrick, who sat with some men of a similar age outside the harbourfront pub, before turning to browse the window of Pen & Ink.

'Hey, Ellie!'

Spinning around, she waved at Marcus, walking towards the bistro where he waited.

Dinner was fun. Marcus reminded Ellie of her brother, though clearly older, and they'd had a good laugh.

Despite Nicki's kissing noises and that old thing you do to your mates of turning your back and caressing your own shoulders as she'd left, Ellie was somewhat relieved when Marcus opened up about a current dilemma. He'd been trying to date for over a year – he was lonely, he admitted – but out of the blue, he'd realised there were feelings buried deep for someone he'd known for years.

Ellie sat back in her seat as a beautifully presented dish of crispy chicken was placed before her, and she leaned forward to inhale the scents of yummy Thai spices. 'Gosh, that smells good. So, is this lady aware of how you feel?'

Marcus paled. 'Lord, I hope not!'

Chuckling, Ellie sipped her wine. 'Well, you might have to drop some hints, then.'

They tucked into their food, jokingly coming up with ways to discover if a person likes someone else without making it obvious what they were about. Ellie struggled to contain her laughter as Marcus recalled how a local friend – not renowned for his love of theatre – had once tried to impress a woman he fancied – known for her rather prim views on life – by taking her to what he thought was a classy magician's show at the London Hippodrome, only for it to turn out to be Magic Mike. The humour fled, however, as Ellie's eye caught a party entering the bistro.

Will, dammit.

Pretend it's a stranger.

Fine. Obviously. That's easy.

'Are you okay?' Marcus sobered, eyeing Ellie across the table. 'You've gone awfully red. Here, have some water.'

He filled her glass, and Ellie snatched it up and took a gulp.

'Yes, thanks. Sorry. Think the sauce was too hot and spicy.'

'A bit like the show.'

Marcus waggled his brows, and Ellie began laughing again. It was successful, at least momentarily, in blotting out Will, who happened to be on the opposite side of the cosy bistro, but in her direct line of sight. The same couldn't be said for the gentleman, who frowned fiercely.

Thankfully, Marcus didn't have a sweet tooth, so once they'd finished their bottle of wine, they left the bistro. Ellie deliberately didn't look towards Will's table, which was fortunate, because if she had, she'd have found his gaze fixed hungrily on her as they passed by.

–

Fastening her camera strap over her favourite plum-coloured jumper, Ellie stuffed her feet into her walk boots and headed into the town and along the lane down past Harbourwatch, taking the coast path from where it led from the tidal beach up through a dense coppice of trees. With no particular route in mind, she let her feet guide her, but with her head down, mulling on the upcoming shoot and Mrs Tremayne's demands, she barely heeded the path's direction until she detected the smell of woodsmoke and looked up, puzzled.

'Great,' she muttered as she crested the brow of the hill, pausing to draw breath, hands on hips.

Ellie emerged onto the track outside Marcus's site, chewing on her lip as her eyes fell on the sign for Peaches Cottage.

She turned back, but just then a shaft of sunlight pierced the thin layer of cloud overhead, sending a golden pathway across the sea, and her breath caught. Removing her lens cap and stuffing it in her jeans pocket, she scooted onto the coast path again, heading for where she knew there would be an unrestricted view of the water.

The whitewashed cottage remained much as she'd last seen it, nestled in its russet blanket, smoke billowing from the chimney. Ellie glanced around, then turned her back to the building to face the sea, clicking away in delight, tilting the camera now and again for an unusual angle, stepping further down the path than she'd gone when she'd first come across Peaches.

'Beautiful,' Ellie murmured, lowering her camera and simply enjoying the view for a moment. She reached for the lens cap, but as she fastened it in place, her gaze straying further down the path, a strange sensation took hold.

Memories coalesced in her mind, wrapped precious tendrils around her heart as Ellie was drawn further along as though tugged by an invisible cord.

And then she saw it, the overgrown opening beside a stretch of wooden fencing, partially concealed by the hedgerow, and emotion came from out of the blue, gripping her rib cage, closing in on her throat. Squeezing through, she stared at the steps and, down below, the beach. *Their* beach.

Ellie forced a few more branches aside and peered down. It looked passable, and before she could change her mind, she was through the gap, the branches snatching at her jumper, as though objecting to her passing through.

Stepping carefully, one hand grasping the handrail – which hadn't existed last time – and the other her camera, she slowly made her way down the roughly hewn steps.

Someone had certainly done a good job of making the beach more accessible from the cliff top, though it clearly hadn't been used since the summer, autumn debris liberally scattered on each step.

Reaching the sands, Ellie jumped down the last deep step, then looked around, assailed by the sweetest of memories. The breeze was less kind on the shore, whipping her hair from inside the scarf, tendrils slapping her in the face, the salty sea air caressing her lips.

She licked them, relishing the familiar taste, then shivered. With a faint laugh, she brushed the hair from her eyes. The taste was a memory, indeed, but it had been preferable when her bare skin was kissed by the summer sun's rays.

A faint sound came from the left, and she glanced over as a figure emerged from behind an outcrop of rocks.

Really? Again?

Chapter Fifteen

"Match of the Day"

'What are you doing here?'

The words were out before Ellie could think straight, and she wished them immediately unsaid – or, at the very least, that the wind would be so obliging as to whip them away across the water.

'I could ask you the same thing,' Will drawled.

No such luck, then.

Will had fetched up in front of her, and Ellie stared up at him. Where were the words now? Fine time to desert her...

A chilly breeze brushed between them, lifting the hair from Will's forehead, and Ellie strove to conceal a shudder as he held her gaze.

The silence stretched, the dim sound of waves crashing against the rocks, of sea birds calling, faded. Then, typically, they both found their voices in unison.

'I'm walking.'

'I live near here.'

'Yes, yes I know,' Ellie spoke quickly, edging backwards. 'Sorry.'

Will looked puzzled, the habitual inscrutability diminishing. 'Why are you sorry?'

'For intruding.'

'Weren't you looking for solitude too?' He glanced around, then met Ellie's gaze with an enquiring look. 'This seems like the perfect place. It's a bit off the beaten track. You did well to find it.'

Had he *forgotten*? Ellie drew in a sharp breath.

Ouch. No, seriously. *Ouch!*

'I've seen enough, thank you.' She turned away, head bowed in embarrassment at the foolish hope that had so easily taken hold, that he was on the beach as she was, drawn there by memories of a happier time…

'Liar.'

Excuse me?

Swinging back, Ellie glared at Will. 'I am not!'

'You just got here. I saw you arrive, so you can hardly have explored the beach.'

'Well, that's the sort of mistake that happens when you make assumptions,' she retorted. 'I said I'd seen enough, not that I'd seen everything.'

'That changeable mind at play again, Ellie?'

It was the first time he'd used her name, and heat shot up Ellie's neck and into her cheeks even as her eyes flashed at the comment.

'Sometimes,' she declared, raising her chin and looking Will firmly in his oh-so gorgeous eyes – damn him. 'It's the best way. You should try it some time.'

About to go, something took hold of Ellie, roared in her ears, and if it hadn't been for the camera across her body, she swore she'd have squared up to him.

Except she wasn't tall enough.

'Maybe,' she bit out, 'if you'd replied to my olive branch, we could talk civilly. It would be nicer for everyone while we're both stuck here.'

Will raised a mocking brow. 'No branches came my way.'

'It's called an email,' Ellie snapped. 'I could hardly message; you'd blocked me on every app we ever used, including your phone number.'

Will glared at her. 'I think I'd remember something like that arriving in my inbox.'

'Well your inbox kindly sent me a "read receipt", so perhaps you two can have a chat sometime?'

A sound escaped him, but Ellie had had enough, and she strode away as fast as she could without breaking into a very indecorous run.

Will's incredulous laugh swept past her on the breeze, but she willed herself to keep moving. All the heartache built up over the years, the unanswered questions of *why*, steamed through her head. If he'd truly loved her, why hadn't he responded to her overture? And how could he have moved on so quickly?

'Stupid beach,' she muttered as she fled up the steps with little respect for the danger, or her breathing, which came in painful rasps as she reached the top.

The sands weren't visible from the path, and – heart pounding painfully from the encounter – Ellie made her way back to Polkerran as fast as she could.

So much for thinking the day couldn't get any worse!

–

The encounter with Will had shaken Ellie, not because of its rancour, but because of seeing him. There. On their beach as though it was anywhere, not important. He hadn't been wearing that stupid hat, either, his face fully visible, as were those dark eyes that had once looked so lovingly into her own.

Keen to keep busy and desperate to shut out such traitorous thoughts – and unaided by her responsibilities at Little Cott and Westerleigh – Ellie started going down into the village each morning to photograph daily life in Polkerran Point.

After downloading the card onto her hard drive, she scanned through the images on the screen, delighted with how they were coming out.

The light was in her favour, with the low sun, the golden backdrop of the wooded hillsides around the cove and the steely reflection of the water. Viewing the images in black and white, she made a few tweaks, leaning back in her seat to better assess the results.

The locals were a generally friendly bunch, full of curiosity, but more than willing to let her click away. She'd amassed striking, evocative images of fishermen mending nets, leaning against the weathered harbour wall, welders in the boat yard, working on a rusty hull, the WI ladies chuckling over something naughty during a talk at the village hall, an artist in the lane capturing the view, the tea shop lady – whom she now knew to be Morwenna – in her pinny, cleaning tables.

There was an endless stream of opportunities, and Ellie's talent for capturing an essence, a flavour, a moment, would, she hoped, resonate with the locals.

Despite keeping busy, however, a niggling doubt kept resurfacing: why had Will claimed he'd never seen the email? It didn't make any sense…

–

On the Wednesday morning, before the initial mini-session took place, Kate invited her over to Harbour-watch to catch up. Ellie looked around with interest as she followed her down a stone-paved hallway to a room she hadn't seen before.

'I thought this would be more comfortable than meeting at the manor. Arabella does her best to make you feel welcome...' Kate hesitated. 'She struggles sometimes to let go of a fascination with her superiority, but she's definitely trying to embrace the change.'

They entered a wonderful space, and despite the grey day outside, the room was flooded with light from a vast glass roof, Victorian in design.

'What a gorgeous room!' Ellie exclaimed, surveying her surroundings with delight. There were squashy leather sofas either side of a low table before the vast hearth and a well-polished wooden table in the centre supporting a vase of copper-coloured roses, berries and greenery. A long side table against the far wall housed a smaller vase of similar blooms, as well as a glittering array of decanters and glasses.

'It's the hub of the house, to be honest, though there is a stunning drawing room and a beautiful panelled library-cum-office.'

Kate, however, didn't stop there, heading for a door in the far wall, and Ellie cast a reluctant glance over her shoulder before they emerged into a large, square kitchen with an equally square scrubbed wood table at its centre.

'I've just made coffee. Come and take a seat.'

Furnished with a mug, Ellie wrapped her hands around it as Kate opened her laptop.

'The scarecrows are top of the agenda.' She grinned at Ellie. 'If only they knew they were so popular! Entries are looking solid. Phee has designed a map a bit like she does for the trails, so people pay a nominal fee for one to participate. The backup bad–weather plan is we move them inside the barn in the manor grounds.'

'When will the map be available?'

'It's being printed now, but I'll let you have a list of locations so you can get on with your side of things.'

Ellie listened intently as Kate ran through the groups already lined up to get involved, from the church, the village school, youth club, kayak club, rowing club and so on, all of which would mean her moving around the village, up and down the hills and visiting several places she'd not yet seen.

'Even the WI are wanting in.' Kate took a sip of coffee. 'They come up with some hilarious offerings. The local press love it too. I'm hoping they'll want some of your images.' She smiled encouragingly at Ellie, who felt warmed by her enthusiasm. 'Make sure you charge; don't give them away. Oh, and we've printed flyers to pop through letterboxes. Mollie and her mates have been roped in. At cost, of course. Teenagers!'

Kate rolled her eyes, but was clearly amused, and Ellie leaned forward as she swung the laptop round to show the list of locations.

'I'll whizz this over to you. What would be really great is if you could also get a couple of shots of the one we've put in the window of the tourist info place.'

Ellie tapped into her Notes app, welcoming the distraction as Kate's requests continued. One she needed. Desperately.

'It sounds very full on.'

Kate topped up their mugs. 'Story of my life. Dev's always telling me to simplify, but I love it!'

The conversation turned to the manor's role in the festival, and once they'd finished their drinks, they walked along the lane into the village, Kate intent on calling on Arabella Tremayne.

As they approached the harbour, however, they paused outside Pen & Ink, just as a slightly familiar young woman emerged from the shop.

'Hi, Chloe.' Brow furrowing, Kate eyed her former work colleague. 'What job did you decide to go for in the end?'

A flash of discomfort zipped across Chloe's features, before she smiled hesitantly at Kate.

'Something just came up, and I think it's going to be ideal. For now, at least.'

'I'm keen to drum up some business, too,' Ellie said encouragingly, as Chloe seemed so nervous. 'I've got cards in several places, so I'm hoping things come up too.'

They parted ways, with Kate continuing on her way to the manor, and Ellie turned back along the front just as Jean arrived, but she didn't seem her usual smiling self.

'Hey, you okay?' Ellie fell into step with her as they approached the Spar.

There was no response at first, but then Jean nodded. 'Yes. Yes, fine, thanks.' The smile she summoned seemed a bit of an effort. 'Just tracking down Mother.'

Jean gestured towards a pair of mobility scooters, but before they could enter the shop, the door swung open and both Mrs Lovelace and Mrs Clegg emerged, the former clutching a bulging crochet shopping bag, the latter wielding her sticks as she made her way over to where the scooters had been haphazardly parked.

When Jean and Ellie reached them, Mrs Lovelace looked up from stowing the bag in the appropriate compartment.

'How be y'on, young'un? Missing that maid, Anna, I'll be betting.'

'I am indeed, Mrs Lovelace. It's very lonely without the family there.'

'Bless you. Word is, you'm sorted for work, my lovely.'

Ellie glanced at Jean, but her attention was on helping Mrs Clegg onto her scooter and storing the sticks.

'S'right,' Mrs Lovelace continued. 'Old Patrick, he was down yonder, by the gate to yon manor, and all they staff comes pouring out. Forced to ejaculate, they was.'

'The fire alarm went off,' Jean elucidated as she straightened, and Ellie's eyes twinkled.

'So Pat stayed to natter, and according to Albert, the garden boy – been at the manor these sixty years, mind – *he* said word was, you'd been to see Lady T, and then—' Mrs Lovelace broke off to fish a tissue from up her sleeve, noisily blowing her nose. 'When Christie the Post called with a signed-for the day a-fore, she stopped for a while, and Albert said Lady T was talking to that housekeeper woman of hers—'

'Norma,' Jean supplied.

'And said the mistress was right teasy about getting some photos done drekkly, and said it was good young Ellie was on board.'

Wow. Impressive.

Ellie conceded with a smile. 'Yes, I've manged to secure a few photo assignments, which is lovely. Well, I'll leave you to get on.'

Ellie continued on her way, but then a flashy red sports car came speeding along the street, pulling to a halt outside Tremayne Estates.

Was that Alex? Trying not to stare, Ellie walked slowly on, but then she looked back again.

It was Alex. He stood by the car now, parked on double yellows outside the Tremayne Estates office, talking to Chloe, who still clasped her bag of purchases to her chest.

Every sighting of Alex brought bad associations, and Ellie tried to push them away. She'd pop back to the Spar, get something simple for dinner.

By the time she came out, it had begun to rain in earnest. The wind wheeling in across a steely grey sea, whipping white caps into the entrance to the bay, made a brolly pointless. Pulling her scarf over her hair, Ellie shot along the front, head down, eager to get into the warm.

Then, she needed to find something to do. Keep busy. Anything to shut out the lingering hurt of those painful moments with Will on a beach he didn't remember…

Chapter Sixteen

"Pulp Fiction"

'Why have I done this to myself,' Ellie muttered as she burrowed through the mess on the table the following day. 'Where are you?'

She looked around. When had she last had her phone?

Ellie shot into the house, tying her hair out of the way and pulling the camera straps over her head.

The cottage still had a landline, a throwback to its bed and breakfast days, and she hurried down the hallway to grab the handset, dialling her own number.

'There you are,' she exclaimed with relief as a pile of blank greetings cards began to ring. 'Damn, only two bars of battery.'

Despite her obsession with keeping her camera batteries fully charged, Ellie had never quite mastered the same elsewhere. Phones, iPads, laptops, toothbrushes… all fell victim from time to time.

Ellie fled out of the boot room and was soon dashing along hedge-bound lanes in her car, a chorus of russet leaves cascading in the air behind Fifi as they sped past. Thankfully, the weather had delivered a beautiful early autumn day, with wistful blue skies dusted with tendrils of fine cloud and a gentle breeze.

Once she reached the waterside at Polwelyn, she was relieved to find the small car park full of people waiting for her.

It took her a few minutes to set up on the grassy play area beside the creek, but then the mini-sessions began, fifteen minutes each, three per hour, and taking a deep breath, Ellie turned around, camera at the ready, to welcome the first people.

'Hi,' Ellie exclaimed warmly as one of the mums she recognised from the school drop-off came up, shepherding a little boy.

'This is Rupert,' the lady explained. 'He's a bit nervous, aren't you darling?'

Rupert didn't respond, merely ducking behind his mother's coat.

'That's okay.' Ellie settled back in her folding chair. 'We can just chat for a bit.'

Ellie's patience and gentle voice encouraged Rupert sufficiently for him to settle beside his mum on a bench. As she rambled on about the upcoming scarecrow festival, Ellie managed to capture some adorable photos of the little boy, both solo and looking up at his mum as he whispered something to her.

The next few sessions were a bit livelier, with parents who wanted active shots of their children running across the lawn or jumping from the bottom of the slide, arms spread out to catch the air, and the morning sped by.

Taking a slug of water, Ellie checked her phone. Barely alive. She was vaguely aware of people on the periphery of her vision, walking dogs and parking up to lunch at the quaint pub overlooking the creek.

Another couple of hours passed, with Ellie pleased with what she could see on her screen. She changed the camera battery again, trying not to think about how hungry she was as she paused to take another swig of water.

One of her bookings hadn't turned up, and Ellie grabbed the moment to pick up the Fuji, soon lost in the imagery as she took shot after shot of the incoming tide, slowly lifting the small boats resting on their sides, as though they enjoyed a moment's kip before bobbing back into action.

A sound behind Ellie made her start, and she lowered the Fuji and glanced over her shoulder as she capped the lens.

'Oh!'

Staring at Will, she couldn't think of another word. He said nothing, hat low over his eyes, merely held out a brown paper bag.

Ellie attempted to clear her throat. 'I— for me?'

Will stepped forward and took her hand, placing the bag in it before turning away.

'Wait!'

He stopped, and she eyed his rigid shoulders, her mind fizzing with confusion, skin tingling from the unanticipated touch.

Slowly, Will moved round to face her.

'What?'

Ellie gave the bag a hopeful squeeze, then peered inside at the roll, from which thick slices of ham and tomato protruded. An old favourite.

'You… you brought me lunch? How did you know I'd be here?'

An impatient sigh emanated from Will as he whipped off his hat and ran a hand through his thick hair.

'Haven't you been advertising your shoot?'

Yes. Of course I have.

'I met someone for lunch,' he gestured back towards the pub. 'You didn't look as though you were going to get a break.'

Will's tone was begrudging, as if he couldn't quite believe he'd done what he had, and if Ellie hadn't been quite so hungry, she might have thrust it back at him.

'How… kind.'

'It's nothing,' Will bit out, replacing the hat. 'They were giving them away.'

With that, he left, and Ellie watched him go, a myriad of thoughts churning through her head, but a protesting growl from her tummy persuaded her to tuck into the surprise offering. It didn't take long to consume, but as she realised the roll had been spread with mustard, not butter, the puzzlement intensified.

Giving them away, were they? Funny how they knew she preferred mustard with ham over butter. Or at least, funny *someone* remembered it, but couldn't quite manage to recall their special beach…

The arrival of her next booking, a group of four women celebrating one of the group's fiftieth, put paid to any further speculation. It was a hilarious shoot, and Ellie half-wished it could have lasted longer, the women so enthusiastic, posing on the roundabout, see-saw and swings and all rushing over to peer over her shoulder to have a quick look at the images.

'We come down every year at this time,' one of them said as they made to leave. 'We love it when it's quiet.'

With the final session was over, Ellie safely secured all her equipment in her bag and packed up for the day, trying not to think about the anomaly of Will and his behaviour. Once up in her room, Ellie sat cross-legged against the pillows, laptop open as she downloaded the photos. When the battery was on its last legs, she headed down to the orangery to plug it in next to the already-charging camera batteries, then viewed a message on her phone.

Marcus.

> Sorry, Ellie, but can you spare time for a
> coffee? Need to talk to you. Bit delicate,
> would rather not do it on the phone.

Sinking onto the sofa in the sitting room, Ellie's mouth curved upwards as she tapped a brief reply, agreeing to meet him for drinks the following week. She might be lacking in company generally, but she and Marcus had fallen into one of those swift friendships that happen out of the blue sometimes and then endure forever.

With a sigh, Ellie pushed up off the sofa and walked over to the kitchen. Her own heart seemed impervious to anything else, as though having once been pierced by love, it wasn't prepared to open up again.

–

Nicki and the boys were due home later on the Friday, with Ellie's aunt and uncle staying up at the Point Hotel until they had to return home to start work again, and Ellie passed the morning walking Dougal and spending far too much time staring out to sea, consumed by the memory of meeting Will again on their beach.

Did he *truly* not remember? Or was he simply trying to hurt her? But why, after all this time? If Will was over her, if he'd relegated her to the past, why did he even care? And even more contradictory, what had driven him to bring her lunch at the shoot?

Ellie hadn't a clue what drove Will's behaviour. It would be ridiculous for him to still be resentful of her ending the engagement when he'd roundly refused her efforts to reconcile… unless he was telling the truth and never saw the email? But how could that be?

'Pointless,' Ellie exclaimed in frustration as her phone rang. 'There is no answer. Stop damn speculating.'

Nicki was full of excitement. Hamish had started to experience sporadic pins and needles in his legs, which had given them all a burst of hope. If it continued, they would instigate an increased programme of rehabilitative therapy to help him regain muscle control.

Inspired by the positive news, Ellie made the most of the peace of Westerleigh to finish the designs for the calendar, adding pearly ink dots to several cards, and stacking them to dry so they'd be ready to be made up into packs later.

She then opened the laptop to update some images on her socials, only to find a negative comment about her designs on both Instagram and Facebook.

Aside from the hurt, Ellie was puzzled, not recognising the names as existing customers. Even more oddly, when she went onto the respective profiles, the accounts had no followers, and the profile image in both cases was an avatar.

Was she being trolled? But why, and by whom?

Disgruntled and not a little saddened, Ellie called to Dougal and marched into the boot room. Time to blow away some cobwebs.

Eschewing the cliff path, Ellie and Dougal headed into the village and up to the field where dogs could be exercised and socialise with others. Dusk was falling by the time they came back down into the centre of town, and Ellie toyed with picking up a takeaway.

Her diet had not been very healthy lately. It would be a relief when Anna was back and putting tempting but better-balanced meals on the table!

At the bottom of the hill, the lane split, branching off towards both the church and down to the front, and Ellie's brow furrowed as she saw a man huddled into a doorway near the corner. She threw him a piercing glance as she passed. He had his head ducked, clutching something to his front, and if she was not mistaken, it was a camera.

As she emerged onto the street bordering the harbour, however, she fetched up short, Dougal at her feet.

Alex was back in town, and stood outside the bistro talking to Bella, who'd appeared from who knew where, and there, lurking behind his friend, was Will, the habitual hat pulled low over his eyes. Unwilling to interrupt, and certain Will wouldn't appreciate her presence, Ellie made to cross over, but Bella looked round, relief flooding her features.

'Ellie, wait!'

She could detect the uneasiness in her friend's eyes as she strode towards her.

'When did you get back, Bells? Are you okay?'

'Yes, just stay with me, promise?'

Thoroughly muddled by this uncharacteristic behaviour, Ellie nodded. 'Of course.'

Bella linked arms with Ellie, and she cast a glance over at the men. To her surprise, Will's gaze was fixed on her, and he made a movement, as though he intended to walk over, but Alex restrained him.

What was going on?

'Come on,' Bella urged, her pace increasing, and Ellie all but skipped to keep up as they hurried towards the bridge, Dougal trotting happily at her heels, as though being chased by Daphne du Maurier's infamous flock of birds.

'Are you going to tell me why we're speeding like we're competing in a 10k run?' Ellie managed to blurt as they passed The Lugger.

'There's nothing to tell. I just don't want to be around that man.'

Chapter Seventeen

"Blankety Blank"

Nicki and the boys returned to Little Cott the following day, and Ellie spent a rowdy evening there, along with Nicki's parents, as they all enjoyed pizza and took it in turns to play games with the boys.

The following morning, Ellie viewed her calendar with surprise. Anna and Oliver would be back in a few days. Where had the time gone?

Ellie was relieved Bella had decided to stick around for the weekend, and they both followed Matt – who'd been roped in to help in Oliver's absence – as he wheeled Liam and Jason's scarecrow down the lane in a barrow, accompanied by two over-excited boys.

Bella finished tapping into her phone and shoved it in her pocket. 'What time does Nicki's shift end?'

'Five, I think. I'm doing a chilli for dinner, if you fancy joining us? Nicki's parents are dining at the hotel. Think they needed a break!' Ellie smirked up at Bella, striding by her side, her glorious hair jostling with the breeze sweeping in across the bay. 'There will be wine.'

'Count me in. So, are you actually earning anything on this one?' Bella indicated the camera slung across Ellie's body as they reached the bridge over the River Polwey and took the lane to the right, leading uphill towards the manor.

Ellie mulled over the best way to answer as she realised Matt and the boys were already out of sight.

'No. But—'

'Elinor Arbon!' Bella exclaimed, flicking her abundant tresses over her shoulder and flashing a pretend glare.

'But if I can get the images in the local freebie, where they've promised me a photo credit, there's a chance one of the regional papers will come across them.'

A faint sound emanated from Bella. It could have been a ladylike snort.

'What, wrapped around their chips?' Bella's smile was sceptical as they followed the others through the wrought-iron gates into the grounds, and Ellie had to laugh.

'You never know. Stranger things have happened.'

'True,' Bella agreed as they all headed to the converted stables.

'I'm fine,' Ellie insisted as Matt began hoisting the scarecrow onto its allocated stand and the boys buzzed around him, piping out instructions. 'Now I've got some paid work from Mrs Tremayne, along with the few local shoots, I can tick over, so long as I don't get tempted to splash out on something madly expensive.'

'Good. Let's save the yacht shopping for now.'

Bella headed over to straighten the hat on the scare-crow, and Ellie was about to replace her lens cap when she was hailed from behind.

'Hey, Ellie!'

She waved at Kate as she came through the archway, Dev following behind with a scarecrow flung across his shoulders, Mollie filming on her phone as Theo skipped alongside him.

Perching on a low wall next to some thick hedging, Ellie watched the proceedings, holding up her camera to assess possible photo angles for when all the figures were in place, but suddenly her skin prickled as a rustling came from the bushes behind her.

Before she could look around, Matt came striding across.

'Hey, you!'

Startled, Ellie jumped off the wall as a man dressed in dark colours, camera aloft, appeared through a gap in the hedging.

'Get out!' Matt shouted, his dark eyes flashing as he approached, Dev hurrying over to join him.

'These are private grounds,' the latter said in more measured tones. 'I suggest you do as you've been asked.'

Partially concealed by his hood, the man shrugged. 'You'll do.'

Before anyone could prevent it, he clicked madly away, the camera aimed at Matt, who would have flown at him had Dev not held him back.

'Let him go. Stupid pap.'

Kate joined them, out of breath. 'What's going on?'

'Nothing to worry about,' Dev reassured her, an arm on Matt's shoulder. 'Some idiot trying to get an exclusive on the scarecrows, I expect.'

He guided a reluctant Matt back to the display, and Kate joined Ellie as she resumed her position on the wall.

It sounded like the man had been looking for an opportunity, but if wasn't to bag a snap of Matt – who was known to rigidly protect his privacy – then had he been looking for Will? Had word got out he was offering the prize, leading people to expect him to be around?

'Never a dull moment in the cove.' Kate sounded amused, and thankful for the distraction. Ellie fell into a discussion with her about the upcoming shoot at the manor house, and as the men continued their work with the questionable help of the children, Ellie reflected on how bizarrely her stay was going.

Did she wish she'd never come back to Polkerran Point, or was it turning into an adventure that had, perhaps, only just begun?

After the exhibits were all in place and suitably labelled, Ellie worked around the grounds taking photos. The manor and the grounds were a fabulous backdrop for the scarecrows, which had certainly brought out the inventiveness of the villagers. They ranged from a dapper gent in period dress via a stormtrooper to a seated fisherman, complete with rod and line. There was even a group of presumably elderly scarecrows clustered together, one on a mobility scooter, and it didn't take too much of a leap to realise they depicted Mrs Lovelace and her cronies.

Not wanting to speculate on whose scooter had been confiscated for the purpose, Ellie continued clicking away, the light in her favour as it reflected off the old stone walls of the stables and gatehouse.

Bella had gone back to her cottage to change, saying she'd message Nicki and walk up with her later, and Ellie strolled through the archway to the lawned area in front of the main entrance.

'Hey.' Kate greeted her as she emerged from the house, only to stumble slightly on the low step and drop her bag. 'Whoops.'

Dev, who'd been on her heels, stooped down to scoop it up, sending Kate a look of affectionate amusement as they joined Ellie, who lowered her camera and fished the lens cap out of her bra strap. She really did have enough images, but knew that, without the interruption, she'd have just kept going.

'I've got some great shots.' She smiled at them both as they turned back towards the archway. 'I'll get the standard ones up as soon as I'm home so the locals can start to vote. Will there be a box for voting papers for those using the flyers instead?'

'Over by the gate.' Dev pointed to where Dickie the Chippie, the local carpenter, could be seen bolting a wooden box to a stand, watched by Theo, whose hand was clasped by Ryther.

'Gosh,' Ellie laughed. 'He's taking it very seriously.'

Ryther patted Dickie on his shoulder and turned away, Theo by his side, and Ellie eyed the elderly gentleman with concern.

'Is your grandfather okay?'

Dev's expression sobered as Kate sent him a sympathetic look, winding her arm around his. 'He's been for more treatment. It always tires him. We wanted him to rest before coming back—'

'But he insists nothing restores his health better than being in the cove of late.'

Dev's look was contemplative as he watched his grandfather walk over to a bench to sit with Theo.

'He's not got long,' Kate added softly, squeezing Dev's arm. 'But this is where he wants to be when—' Her eyes filled with tears, and this time, Dev wrapped an arm around her shoulders, holding her close.

'He's moved back into Harbourwatch until the time comes. Grandy grew up in the house, and there's a long history that binds him to it and… other places in the cove.'

Moved, Ellie squeezed Kate's hand gently. As they went to join the others, a notification pinged on her phone. A comment on her website. Ellie idly loaded the page.

'What the hell!'

Usually, comments were compliments on the imagery, sometimes grateful customers saying thank you for a particular job. This was…

'Hateful.'

Something leaden formed in the pit of Ellie's middle. It wasn't even a negative but constructive comment, such as 'I don't think the light worked well in this photo'. It was an attack on the person who'd taken the photo. On Ellie.

Going into the dashboard, Ellie studied the associated email address, which turned out to be as indiscernible as the ones used lately on her socials. Were they connected?

Marking the comment and deleting it, she shoved the phone into her pocket and drew in a short breath, trying not to let the hurt surface.

Someone had it in for Ellie. But who? And why?

–

With Liam and Jason fed and happily watching TV in the snug at Westerleigh, Ellie, Nicki and Bella settled round the scrubbed pine table to enjoy their dinner.

Although there was no further news on Hamish beyond the initial tingling, which had soon faded, Nicki was full of plans for when he returned and how soon she could get her old life back.

Bella regaled them with anecdotes from her teaching life in Bristol as they tucked into the chilli and rice, but remained evasive about Alex, and Ellie and Nicki exchanged a puzzled glance when Bella nipped to the loo.

'Do you get the feeling she's hiding something?'

'Definitely, but it's Bella. Getting something out of her when she doesn't want to give it is like…' Ellie floundered, trying to think of a good metaphor.

'Being constipated?' Nicki offered, and they both dissolved into laughter.

When Bella returned, and they'd cleared the plates and carried over a shop-bought cheesecake and cream, the conversation turned to Ellie.

'Managed to make any income yet?' Bella questioned, slicing the cheesecake into quarters and sliding a piece onto each plate.

'As a matter of fact,' Ellie said proudly as she picked up the cream carton, 'the feedback from the mini-sessions, which were all paid for in advance, has been excellent, and the second one is fully booked.'

The memory of the negative comments intruded for a moment, but she shook it aside.

'Hmm.' Bella sent Ellie a sceptical look. 'Just make sure you focus on those money-spinning things, not the crowd-pleasing freebies.'

By the time they'd finished, stacked the dishwasher and gravitated to the sofas in front of the empty hearth, the conversation had returned to past relationships.

'What about you, Ellie? Did you ever think you'd found "the one"?' Nicki leaned forward to claim her glass from the table. 'I know you dated someone for a long time. Weren't you with that Gareth until last summer?'

'Yep. He was nice, but just not…'

The one. Since Will, it had all seemed pointless. But then, no one – not even Nicki – knew quite how serious it had become back then…

Ellie sipped her wine, cradling her glass in both hands in her lap. 'I dated this one other guy for a bit, a few years back, but fortunately it didn't go beyond the dinner table.'

'Why fortunately? Did he turn out to be a bit of an idiot?'

'No, he's lovely, actually. Just not for me.' She grinned at Bella. Nicki knew the outcome of this one. 'He ended up marrying my sister.'

Bella lowered her glass, amber eyes wide. 'Ew, that could've been a bit… ick!'

Grinning, Ellie tucked her legs up on the sofa. 'Tell me about it! Thankfully, the most intimate thing Robin ever learned about me before he met Sara was that I'm not keen on anchovies.'

'Hey.' Bella leaned forward suddenly, brow creasing. 'That chap the other day – the one with Alex, in the cap. I thought I knew him from somewhere. Wasn't he that one you had a thing for, all those years ago?'

'Will Farmer is old history,' Nicki declared. 'And Ellie's well shot of him.' An impish look formed. 'So, Bella. What gives with you and Alex Tremayne? Why did you split up back then? And why is he sniffing around again?'

Bella drew in a short breath. 'Let's just say he wasn't who I thought he was. Now, who's up for another drink?'

Trying not to think about Nicki's earlier metaphor, Ellie hid her smile as they moved the conversation on to more mundane things.

Whatever was in Alex and Bella's past, it clearly wasn't about to come out.

Chapter Eighteen

"Line of Duty"

With Nicki's parents returning home, the village school back in session and the scarecrow festival prizes awarded – including Will's generous voucher for a family of four to spend an all-expenses-covered weekend at a popular waterpark on the north coast – Polkerran Point moved on to the next thing: Hallowe'en. The eating and drinking venues were going to town with their seasonal menus and decor, the shops all dressing their windows with cobwebs, hanging bats, skeleton bunting and more.

Carved pumpkins, some looking as though they'd seen better days and probably leftovers from the earlier trail, began to appear on doorsteps, and crisp bronze leaves began to gather at their bases as though they'd known exactly where the breeze should send them.

Ellie encountered neither sight nor sound of Will for days, but her relief seemed shadowed by the desperate urge to lay eyes on him again. It had occurred to her, after their clash, that she ought to try and find the email and shove it under his nose to remind him, but it turned out to be a Herculean task.

Although she'd had the Outlook account since she'd been a teenager, a search for any combination of Will's name brought nothing up. Confused, Ellie put it aside to get on with some work, but the niggling doubt had begun: had she *dreamt* sending that email? She'd certainly gone through it in her mind often enough…

The second mini-session was full, but a third – as anticipated – wasn't really getting much traction, and knowing the local market had probably been depleted for the foreseeable, Ellie mulled over casting her net wider across the region or pushing her business in other ways.

Still deep in speculation on which direction to go, she stayed in the village on the Tuesday after the schools reopened, heading to Karma for coffee and some inspiration, bumping into Gemma as she emerged from the lane leading up to the church.

They chatted about Matt and how the composition was progressing, Gemma full of the news that an artist at Secret Gem Records had taken to some lyrics she'd written and was presently in the studio making demos.

'It'll be so much fun if she wants to use it.' Gemma's eyes shone with delight as they drew to a halt on the corner. 'Hey, there's Ryther.' She waved energetically as a beautiful, well cared for, dark green Jag purred past, her gaze following its sedate progress as it turned up the hill out of Polkerran. 'That's the Lady Margarethe.' She turned back to face Ellie. 'I love Ryther. He really helped me when I first came to the cove to stay.'

Recalling Kate's sadness over Ryther's fate, Ellie hoped being in Polkerran brought the solace the elderly man sought.

'Have you been in yet?' Gemma gestured at the stone building behind them, and Ellie's skin prickled, her heart skipping a beat as she eyed the tiny aquarium.

I knew someone who worked there, once upon a time…

Ellie shrugged. 'What, so I can pay a fiver to kill all of five minutes?'

Gemma grinned. 'It's very cute, well maintained and ever so popular with the village kids – and the adults, who find the names hilarious.'

She pointed to the blackboard sign propped by the entrance to the aquarium. Ellie skimmed it and started to chuckle.

'Bernard the Gurnard?'

'A particular favourite.'

'Oh! I love Veronique the Sole. Didn't someone mention Charlie the Crab once?'

Gemma fell into step beside Ellie as they moved further along the street.

'Ah, now he's a human. He's known for walking sideways.' She mimed taking a slug from a bottle, and Ellie giggled.

'I love it here.'

The words fell into a deep silence, and Gemma smirked.

'Do you, now?'

'Yes. I suppose. Maybe.'

Gemma said no more, but as they parted ways, Ellie reflected on how sometimes, words have a way of saying it like it is.

Deep in thought, she turned her steps along the front, but as she passed the ice cream shop, she stalled. Jean stood inside, mopping her face with a disintegrating piece of paper cloth.

Ellie pushed open the door. 'Jean? Can I help? Here.' She fished in her bag for a packet of tissues and handed one over.

'Sorry,' Jean hiccupped. 'Just not in a good place right now.'

Ellie shut the door to the shop and turned the sign round to 'Closed'.

'Want to talk, or shall I just keep my nose out? It's not your mum?'

Patting her cheeks, Jean sniffed, then shook her head. 'No. Mum's fine. I'll be good. Think something needed to come out.' Her phone pinged and she snatched it up, eyes racing to and fro. Then, she placed it back on the counter with an unsteady hand and the tears started again.

'Okay, take the packet.' Ellie thrust the tissues at Jean, who took them and sank onto a stool behind the serving counter.

Ellie fidgeted from foot to foot, twisting the tendrils of her scarf in her hand. She felt so helpless, but Jean had calmed now, and summoned a weak smile.

'Lord, what a mess I am! So sorry.'

Shaking her head, Ellie leaned over the counter. 'Do you need an ear? I'm a pretty good listener, if it would help?'

Five minutes later, the shop locked for the night, Jean and Ellie headed into the Three Fishes. It was quiet at this time of night, mainly because it didn't serve food, and they selected a booth tucked away in the back of the bar, each clutching a glass of wine.

Ellie looked around with interest as Jean popped to the ladies' to do something to her face. It was typical of a seventeenth-century fishermen's pub, with uneven beams, blackened with age, supporting a low, bowed ceiling. The supporting uprights were festooned with random rusty implements, the ceiling above the bar plastered with an array of beer mats.

A large circular mirror, framed with what looked like an old porthole, adorned one wall. The others bore prints, fading with age, of ancient ships rolling on unrealistic seas, of wizened men working on nets, and opposite the mirror, a large case containing every type of knot or hitch known to man – and several that possibly weren't.

'Phew. That's better.' Jean sank into the booth – made of similar dark wood and with a red velvet curtain separating it from the adjacent one.

'Don't feel you have to talk if you'd rather not.'

'I don't say a lot about what's going on in my life, to be honest. To anyone. It's just…' Jean released an unhappy sigh, her gaze drifting to the latticed windows looking out over the harbour. 'I feel trapped. Here. In the cove.'

Not wanting to put her foot in it, Ellie said gently, 'Because of your mum?'

Jean nodded. 'I hate myself for saying it, for even thinking it, but since Dad died, she's needed me, and the older she's getting, I can see it'll never get any easier. At first, it didn't matter, but then…' Voice wobbling, Jean grabbed her wine and took a slug.

'You met someone?' Ellie essayed.

This time, a soft smile touched Jean's mouth, and her eyes misted over as she stared into space. 'We met at university. Dated for a time. Then went our separate ways. As you do.'

Her eyes met Ellie's, and she shrugged. 'We reconnected a few years back. Fell in love again. Properly this time. Adult love, not the silly crush type. Greg—' She broke off, wetness gathering on her lashes again. 'We… he bought me the ice cream van.' She emitted a watery laugh. 'A silly promise, and yet there it was.'

'And now?' Ellie prompted.

'He asked me to marry him.'

'Oh my God! Jean, that's wonderful.' Ellie's heart, so battered of late by her own troubles, swelled with delight, but Jean's face told the story. 'You didn't refuse?'

'I had no choice.' Jean's voice wavered. 'His life – work – the kids from his first marriage – they're all up near Newcastle. I can't leave Mum, and there's no way I can take her away from the cove. It's been her life. It would break her.'

Lord, what a mess.

'And how's Greg with all of this?'

'Devastated. Although I don't know how he ever thought it might work.' She sent Ellie a mournful look. 'I'm in my early fifties and only just had my first proposal, fallen truly in love.'

Ellie reached across the slightly sticky table to pat Jean comfortingly on the arm. She didn't really know what to say, other than 'want to join the lonely-hearts club I'm thinking of setting up?' It felt a bit flippant in the circumstances.

'Can't Greg work from home down here most of the time, and then go north for...'

Jean shook her head. 'He's a surgeon.'

Oh.

'How old are the children?'

'His daughter's graduating next summer, but it's his son that's the issue. Bless the boy, he's fifteen but was born with learning difficulties. Severe ones. He needs constant care, and Greg wants to do his share, despite the split household. He won't move away.' She lowered her head. 'And I can't leave here.'

'Gosh, that's complicated.'

'Isn't it just?'

Ellie did her best to cheer her up as they drank their wine, and when they parted an hour later, Jean thanked Ellie profusely for listening, claiming it had helped.

Walking back to Westerleigh, Ellie reflected on Anna's sun-shiney view of life in the cove, of how people came and never left. For Jean, perhaps that wasn't such a happy ending.

Chapter Nineteen

"I'm a Celebrity… Get Me Out of Here"

Drinks with Marcus had been fun, but also bittersweet, not least because the delicate matter he'd mentioned was him finally explaining who he had, as he described it, a bit of a schoolboy crush on.

'Phyllida? As in the friendly redhead in the book shop?'

Marcus stirred in his seat, colour rushing into his cheeks, and Ellie's heart went out to him.

'She's lovely. Why won't you ask her out? I'm assuming she's single.'

'Of course!' A hand shot to his mouth. 'Oh my God. What if she's not? She's not wearing a ring, but these days does that mean anything?'

It meant she probably wasn't married or engaged, but didn't mean she wasn't seeing someone…

'It could hardly be a health and safety at work issue,' Ellie mused out loud, and Marcus chuckled.

'Oh, I don't know. Some of those books are tightly packed together. Might get in the way.'

Ellie desperately wanted to reassure Marcus but not mislead him.

She tugged open her packet of crisps. 'Want one?' He shook his head, and she popped one in her mouth, savouring its saltiness. 'Right, so how is she when you go in the shop?'

'Usually sitting behind the counter.'

Ellie shook her head, laughing. 'Pillock, you know what I mean.'

'She's friendly. But then, you called her that too.'

'What sort of things do you talk about?'

'Books,' Marcus essayed, then seeing Ellie's warning look, raised his hands. 'Okay. Sorry. I'll be serious. We talk about lots. She's an incomer like me, been here a few years, and loves it. She co-owns the shop with her brother, but he doesn't work there. It's one of his investments, and he leaves Phyllida to run it, manage the stock and so on. She's started taking some evening classes locally, mainly to try and meet people, as she gets lonely.'

'Hold on, hold on. Phyllida told you she gets lonely? Then she's single.'

'Unless he – or she – works on an oil rig.'

'Marcus!'

'Sorry.'

Ellie dipped into the crisps again, munching as quietly as she could as he continued to outline the things they discussed, which seemed to cover pretty much everything. Except each other.

'It sounds to me like she'd really enjoy a dinner out, or even just a coffee. Why don't you ask her? Then you'll know.'

'Easy for you to say,' Marcus grumbled, picking up his pint of Guiness 0.0% and draining the glass before tapping his phone. 'Heck, I'd best go. Didn't realise the time. Shall I give you a lift back?'

Ellie grinned. 'It's about a fifteen-minute walk. I think I'll cope, thanks.'

They parted on the harbourfront, and as Marcus drove away into the darkness, Ellie looked over at the Spar. The lights had just gone off, so it must be gone ten.

She strolled past Pen & Ink, mulling on the conversation about Phyllida, pausing to peer through the window. Light from the lamppost directly outside shone on the area around the main desk, and Ellie peered more intently through the window.

The stack of hand-made cards she'd left with Phyllida was no longer on the display stand and, if she craned her neck, nor did her business cards appear to be on the counter. Had they all been sold or picked up? Phyllida hadn't been in touch, but she'd contact her tomorrow to see if she needed more supplies.

–

Nicki had a long-overdue day off on the Friday, as she had to work all weekend, so Ellie left her to enjoy a rare chance to drop the boys at school and go for a leisurely coffee with some school-gate friends. Ellie stepped out onto the patio after an early breakfast, hugging her favourite thick cardigan around her body.

There seemed to have been an almost constant breeze lately, and it scampered mischievously across the undulating waters of the bay towards her, toying with her hair, tempting her to follow it up into the trees and out on to the cliff path.

'Wait for us,' she called to the soft gusts buffeting the coastline. 'Walkies, Dougal. Let's go and enjoy ourselves.'

An hour later, they headed back down the hill from the coast path, but as Ellie went to turn left up the lane to Westerleigh – intent on settling the pets before heading down to see if the book shop needed a restock – Phoenix appeared from her right.

'It's that time of day.' She grinned at Ellie. 'You ready?'

She pointed back along the lane to where the usual elderly crew could be seen.

'Oh Lord!'

Phoenix chuckled. 'Come on, I'll help. Jean's gone up country to see Greg – he's her… I'm not quite sure. I just saw Nicki sitting outside Karma with friends. You'll need someone sane to talk to.'

Laughing, Ellie fell into step with her. She'd pop into town afterwards.

The morning proceeded much as they usually did, and Phoenix had a point. Although Ryther managed to maintain a slightly more demure group, a debate soon arose over how suitable Mrs Clegg's cottage was for her now her mobility was so compromised.

'And that there stove don't work no more, Cleggie,' Mrs Lovelace admonished as she slathered jam on a scone.

Ryther looked up from staring at his mug of tea. 'I would be happy to buy a replacement for you, but I would not wish to step on Oliver's toes.'

'I'll be rights,' Mrs Clegg said firmly, folding her arms across her chest, and nodding, as if that sealed the matter.

'Aye, for now,' mumbled Old Patrick through his biscuit, crumbs all down his front. 'But winter waits on no man, nor woman. 'Ow you be going on then without hot food, you silly mare?'

'Jeannie says as she'll get her one of they hair fryers,' Mrs Lovelace offered, picking up her scone.

Phoenix smirked. 'Mum had one of them in the eighties. Her hair used to resemble corrugated cardboard by the time she'd finished.'

'Why don't you tell Oliver about the oven, Mrs Clegg?' Ellie queried as she offered more tea to Mrs Lovelace. 'Or that you're struggling with stairs. I'm sure he'd be happy to help you.'

'I'm not troubling the big man,' Mrs Clegg stated, the arms across her chest tightening. 'Master Oliver has enough on his plate, he has, bless 'im.'

Another hour, and they went on their way, Ryther stopping to thank Ellie, apologising for stopping her working, and leaving her aglow from his praise of the photos she'd taken of Theo recently.

The mention of work, however, reminded Ellie about the book shop, and selecting some more cards, she added envelopes, scooped up a few more business cards and headed into the village.

Phyllida was thoroughly confused, however. Although some of the cards had sold, she'd come in after her day off to hear Ellie had phoned asking for the remainder to be taken off sale, and for her business cards to be removed, as she'd had a change of plan.

With nothing more to offer other than to restock the cards, Phyllida promised to call the assistant to see if she could find out more.

A quick check of the board displaying ads in the Spar window only added to the confusion. Yet again, no sign of Ellie's business cards.

Luckily, the man who'd taken them and put it in the window was stacking shelves. He spoke to a couple of staff, and one of them said there'd been a phone call saying to please remove it as Ellie was no longer making cards or doing photography.

What on earth was going on? And why?

She really ought to get back and do some work, but Ellie felt demotivated and not a little hurt. Why would anyone want to harm her fledgling businesses?

Ellie's mobile pinged. It was Kate, asking if she had time to pop over to Tremayne Manor to go through a few things. Grateful for something to take her mind off things, she was soon at the house and being led down the grand hallway to the room where she'd first met Mrs Tremayne.

'It's the damn media team. I can't get anyone to call me back.'

The hair on Ellie's neck shot to attention as Will's voice drifted out of an open doorway, and she almost stumbled. A man answered, but she wasn't sure if it was Alex. It would hardly be a surprise. This was the family home, after all.

Pulling herself together, Ellie smiled warmly at Kate as she was shown into the library – she refused to call it the office, such a beautiful room that it was.

'Hey, sorry to nab you at short notice.'

'No worries. I was in the village anyway.' Ellie pushed away her dissatisfaction over the missing cards. The hurt was a little harder to ignore.

Kate, however, had a list to get through, and soon Ellie's head was engaged, her imagination taking flight on possible images.

'Let's go and look at the layout outside.'

Ellie followed Kate, relieved to see the door to the room where she'd heard Will's voice firmly closed. Once they'd sorted the details, they headed back cross the stone-paved former stable yard, only to be greeted by Mrs Tremayne.

'Yoo hoo!' she trilled as she waited for them in the archway leading to the house.

They exchanged pleasantries, but then she said, 'You will join me for luncheon.'

It wasn't an invitation, and Ellie sent Kate a curious look, but she merely shrugged. They fell into step behind the lady, following her back into the house to a smaller wood-panelled room, and Ellie drew in a sharp breath. This was where she and Will had hidden away to talk at the party...

'Do take a seat.'

Mrs Tremayne waved a manicured hand towards a circular table, laid as though for fine dining, beside an arched bay window.

Kate sent Ellie an amused look, leading the way over, and Ellie sat down, thankful there were only three places laid. She took a discreet look around, her gaze landing on an alcove partially concealed by a heavily draped curtain fastened to one side by a thick rope tie.

Sadness swept through her. The alcove had become a secret place, the curtain drawn to shut out the world. It was where she and Will had shared their first kiss. Then another, and another, as though it was all that was left in the world to keep them both alive.

Ellie's breath caught in her throat as memories encased her.

I have to get out of here...

With a start, Ellie stared at the glass of water in Kate's hand.

'Here,' she urged, her expression indicative of her concern. 'Take a sip. You look like you're about to keel over.'

'Thank you,' Ellie whispered, emitting a shudder as the cold liquid trickled down her throat. 'Sorry.'

'You okay?' Kate glanced over to where Mrs Tremayne was talking to a member of her staff by the door. 'We can make our excuses if you feel unwell.'

Ellie took another sip of water. 'I'm fine, truly. It's been a bit of a wild morning, that's all.'

Mrs Tremayne had disappeared, but as Kate chatted to Ellie about her daughter's progress on a history project, the member of staff came over and began rearranging the settings.

'Sorry, ma'am,' she said. 'Would you mind?' She gestured to a sofa. 'Mrs Tremayne wishes the table set for five.'

Heart leaping like a gazelle scaling a fence, Ellie grabbed the water and joined Kate on the indicated seating.

Okay. Now, she needed to make her excuses, and—

The door opened, and a smiling Mrs Tremayne returned, and in her wake, deep in conversation and oblivious to the company already in the room, Will and Alex.

Damn. Things were clearly about to get wilder.

At least having a few moments of awareness gave Ellie a modicum of composure. Not that Will was likely to care. She no longer had the ability to evoke a—

'*Hell.*'

Chapter Twenty

"Forget Paris"

The muttered word seemed to pass unnoticed by anyone but Ellie, and Will diverted his gaze as soon as hers flicked upwards.

What she wasn't expecting was another wary glance in her direction from Alex, before his fled to Will.

'This is nice,' declared Mrs Tremayne, accepting her son's kiss on her cheek as the gentlemen reached the table.

Ellie took another slug of water, conscious of a flicker of alarm on Alex's face as Will took the chair between Kate and Ellie.

'Why do we have guests?' Alex turned to his mother, who waved an airy hand.

'Kate, as you know, is here regularly. We're making excellent progress, and Ellie is a professional photographer. She is going to handle all the promotional photos for our brochure and the new website.'

Alex faked a yawn. 'We need to go, Will.'

'Alex! Sit!'

Ellie blinked at the stern voice emanating from Mrs Tremayne, then exchanged a look with a clearly amused Kate as Alex slunk into the seat beside his mother.

There was an awkward silence as a young man brought warm bread rolls and a dish of carefully shaped pats of butter. Ellie – despite being on high alert to the silent man sat beside her – struggled to contain her amusement at the formality of the meal. Seriously. Did people really still live like this?

She didn't dare glance at Kate either, who'd nudged her in the arm as the server moved around, laying each person's napkin across their laps.

Alex seemed resigned to his temporary fate, and the conversation turned to other estate matters, but despite being thankful she wasn't opposite Will – and thus having to avoid his gaze every time she raised her head – Ellie found herself restricting every move she made. Even though there was ample room for five around the table, his closeness was all-consuming. The faint wisps of his cologne toyed with her senses, the low throb of his voice caressed her heart. Her fascinated gaze lingered as his hand touched his glass or simply rested on the fine linen cloth…

'Ma'am?'

Ellie started, sitting back in her seat as the young man placed a bowl of watercress soup before her. Then she grasped her spoon, thankful to have something else to focus on.

By the time the main course of cured sea trout with side salad was served, Ellie had relaxed, though that could have been down to the refreshingly light wine being liberally poured by Alex, waving away the server with obvious irritation.

'Honestly, Mother. Is this level of staffing quite necessary?'

The young man had frozen by the door, and Mrs Tremayne fixed her son with a stern eye. 'You live your life as you will, Alex, and leave us to do the same.'

When the plates were cleared, everyone refused dessert except Mrs Tremayne, opting for coffee instead, and the conversation moved to the upcoming community events to be hosted at Tremayne Manor. Alex's boredom became evident, and he urged Will to drink up.

'Come on, I want to go upriver. That new bar opened last week – the one on the waterfront at Polwelyn.'

Will, however, ignored him and accepted a coffee refill from Mrs Tremayne with a smile.

'Now, why is there no ring on your finger?' she enquired in the way only parents of friends can. 'My husband and I have given up on our son. He shows no sign of settling down and presenting us with the next generation to inherit. But what can be your excuse, Will? You must be in constant demand from the ladies.'

Ellie suspected Will would quite like the floor to open up and offer him a secret passage of escape, and she all but held her breath, flashing a glance at Kate, who tried to hide her smile behind her coffee cup.

'It's precisely why I've stepped behind the camera,' Will confessed.

Alex yawned. 'When do you go to Paris, Mother?'

'Next week, dear. It's only for a few days, of course. I cannot be away for long.'

'For heaven's sake,' he bit out. 'There are enough staff on hand to run the house. You're hardly needed.'

Ellie doubted he detected Mrs Tremayne's wince at his cavalier comment, so she smiled warmly at her.

'Have you been before?'

The lady waxed lyrical about going there on honeymoon many years ago, but not having been since, and just as Ellie was wondering how she could escape, her phone pinged.

'Excuse me,' she said quietly, but no one seemed to notice, chatting as the men now were about the upcoming production and the difficulties Will was having nailing down the necessary permissions from both the local council and the National Trust, who owned much of the coastline thereabouts and, significantly, at Polridmouth beach, where they wanted to film one of the dramatised scenes from *Rebecca*.

'I'm so sorry – I have to dash.' Ellie waved her phone, never so grateful in her life for a text informing her the latest mobile bill was available.

Agreeing to chat later to Kate, she thanked Mrs Tremayne for her kindness in inviting her to lunch, and was touched by the lady taking her hands, telling her she was welcome any time.

The men were on their feet too, though neither acknowledged her departure, and she sped through the doorway, along the hallway and out into the fresh air. Leaning back against ancient stone walls which had no doubt seen their share of turmoil, Ellie gulped in a breath.

'Bloody hell,' she whispered, breathing more steadily. 'It never rains but it pours…'

Casting her eyes heavenwards, she glared at the brooding clouds overhead.

'Don't take that literally. I didn't bring a hat.'

As she pushed away from the wall, the door opened, and her senses leapt to attention as Will came out. With no coherent words coming to mind, Ellie headed down the driveway, puzzled to find he followed.

'I wanted to leave too.' Will's tone was matter-of-fact. 'My phone was less obliging.'

Ellie didn't feel this needed a response, and they walked under the stone gateway in silence. As they reached the lane, however, Will spoke.

'You always wanted to go to Paris.'

And you said you'd take me...

Was he recalling that too?

'I went. With a boyfriend.'

'Oh.'

They were at the corner of the lane now, where it joined the street running parallel with the harbour.

Ellie released a huff of breath. Why was he still there? She turned to face him.

'Spent all my time walking away from the Eiffel Tower.'

Will's brow furrowed, but she set off across the cobbles, only to find him on her heels. 'Why?'

'I was worried he might try and propose.'

That should shut him up. Stepping onto the pavement on the front, Ellie increased her pace.

'And did he?'

With a heavy sigh, she stopped and faced Will.

'Yes. A week later. In the drive-thru at Costa.'

Will's gaze dropped briefly to Ellie's hand on her bag strap.

'Sorry it didn't work out.'

'It did,' she said firmly. 'I said no, we split up. Best thing we ever did, as we're good friends now.'

'Unlike us.'

Eyes flashing, Ellie was out of patience. 'And we all know whose fault that is!'

Silence descended on them both, green eyes locked with unflinching brown, and Ellie's spurt of anger fizzled out. What was the point? Why was Will even talking to her, when acknowledging the acquaintance was clearly the last thing he wanted?

Heart aching for what might have been, Ellie summoned a forced smile. 'Well, this has been fun. Bye.'

She shot back across the street, then realised someone was waving at her through the window of Karma.

'Hey.' Ellie greeted Marcus more warmly than she would've if she wasn't so relieved to be away from Will's disturbing presence.

He gestured at the sofas by the window.

'Join me in a sandwich?'

'Sounds a bit suggestive,' Ellie quipped as she removed her coat, and then laughed at Marcus's appalled expression before he too chuckled.

'Sorry. That didn't quite come out right.'

'I've just had lunch, but could use the company.'

They chatted across the low table about the new website, which incorporated not only Ellie's photography but also a tab linking to the diary notes she'd compiled for him.

'I'm so pleased you liked how the interior shots came out. Those beds looked so comfortable. I think going high-end on the bedding was worth it,' Ellie said, nestling more comfortably into her corner. Marcus's company was the perfect balm to her disturbed thoughts. 'I'd love a sneak peek.'

Marcus waggled his brows, and she giggled.

'Of the website, you pillock.'

'I know. I'll ping you the link.'

They chatted a bit longer while Marcus finished his late lunch, before emerging into an afternoon that had brightened considerably, along with Ellie's mood.

The curtain of cloud from earlier had lifted, revealing the palest of blue skies, streaked with wispy slashes of pale grey and white. Gulls wheeled overhead as a fishing boat landed its catch, the plastic crates sliding across the cobbles and into the waiting hands of the man loading a nearby van bearing the signage 'Port Wenneth Fisheries'.

'I'm just popping to the book shop.' Ellie narrowed her gaze. Uncharacteristic colour swept into Marcus's cheeks as he hesitated beside a flower display on the harbourfront. 'Is anything wrong?'

'No, no,' he reassured her, placing a hand on her arm. 'It's just…' He looked around to his left and right, then stepped closer, and Ellie leaned towards him as he spoke quietly. 'I haven't tried to talk to Phyllida about… you know.'

Ellie held his gaze for a moment, then slipped her arm through his. 'You don't have to confess your feelings! Just see if she's up for a coffee some time. Come on, you'd best come with me.'

Eyes wide, Marcus remained stock still, and she tugged at his arm, an impish smile forming. 'She doesn't know, Marcus. Remember? I have to go anyway, so you can just *happen* to be there.'

He drew in a breath, then nodded vigorously. 'You're right. Time to man up.'

'By hiding behind a long-retired rowing boat stuffed with seasonal flowers?'

Despite his obvious agitation, Marcus chuckled, this time towing her along with him. 'Fine. Just promise me your reason for going in is brief so I don't have to say anything.'

'Wow.' Ellie grinned as they reached Pen & Ink. 'I suggest you go to the dictionaries section and look up the meaning of manning up! Come on – just pretend, as we go in, I've just said something really funny.'

Before Marcus could change his mind, Ellie pushed him inside, their laughter drifting out into the autumnal air.

She was oblivious to a pair of dark brown eyes, narrowed and far from amused, on the opposite side of the street.

–

'Are you okay picking the boys up? They're arguing endlessly about what costume they want for Hallowe'en, so put your referee cap on.'

Ellie saw Nicki on her way for her afternoon shift. She had plenty to keep her occupied, what with suggesting some tweaks to the website to Marcus, editing photos, making more card sets for the Christmas market and handling a call from someone who wanted to know if she could 'just pop round and take one photo of their pet rabbit'.

After explaining her costs for the time involved – travel, setup, taking 'one' photo (Ellie rolled her eyes), editing – she fully expected the prospective client to decide it wasn't worth it, but apparently, Flopsy Wopsy Buttontail *was* worth it, and she pencilled it into her calendar.

Surveying the orangery after the call, Ellie sighed. Anna and Oliver would be back straight after Hallowe'en. They really didn't deserve to come home to a mess like this.

Setting to, she busied herself tidying stacks of blank cards and envelopes, delighted to find a missing earring under a pack of unused inks and a mislaid memory card tucked inside an open packet of paper sitting on top of the printer.

All the time, though – as she scurried to and fro, in some cases merely moving one pile of mess to another place – Ellie's mind puzzled over what Will's email addy could have been back then. Was her only recourse going to be sitting for however long it took, scrolling back through all her sent items until she reached the month and year in question?

Was it worth it, when it might not even be there and would only prove Will right? Ellie shuddered as a tremor unease rippled through her. It would explain the depth of his resentment, if he knew nothing of it... but how could that be?

Chapter Twenty-One

"The Sound of Music"

Ellie eyed the grey skies on Saturday with a dubious eye. It wasn't a day for walking, with mist hovering over the hills surrounding the cove, shrouding the shedding trees with a ghostly mantle. The sea heaved in a seething dull mass between Westerleigh and Harbourwatch.

Dougal, however, had other ideas, and Ellie bent down to pat him as he circled round her legs then trotted pointedly over to the boot room door.

'Okay, okay. Don't worry, I've not forgotten my duties.'

She gave Heathcliff a fuss, where she lay curled up in her usual place on the window seat and, five minutes later, warmly dressed in her favourite cord skirt and a thick burgundy jumper under a quilted gilet, Ellie plonked a knitted beret on her head and followed Dougal out onto the lane.

'What's it to be today? Up to the cliff path? A run on the beach? Or the grassy park?' She waved a hand across the water to the other side of the cove.

Tugging on the lead, Dougal veered to the right and, laughing, Ellie followed.

'The beach it is, then.'

After a good run, Ellie went back down the hill, but remembering she was low on milk, headed into the village to pick some up, bumping into Old Patrick on the corner of the lane leading up to the village hall.

'Alright, my lover?' he asked, bending down to pat Dougal.

'All good, thank you. And you, Pat?'

'Aye, nay so bad.' He straightened with a groan, putting a hand to his back, then pointed at a blackboard propped against the wall advertising a coffee and cake morning. 'Thought I'd pop along. T'will be full of they ole coffin dodgers, mind.'

Once back at the cottage, with Dougal settled in his basket by the hearth and Heathcliff fed and preening on the window seat, Ellie entered the orangery, surveying her efforts from earlier.

'Could be worse,' she whispered, heading upstairs to change. A weak shaft of sunlight had pierced the cloud above the sea and a gold ripple spread across the water. Ellie glanced at her watch. Lunchtime.

She set her phone to play the radio from her portable speaker, turning it up so she could hear it in the kitchen, humming as she boiled the kettle and wishing her heart would accept the reality of her prosaic life and stop leaping around as though something exciting could happen at any minute.

Sitting beside the now-sleeping Heathcliff as she debated between a sandwich or a jacket potato, Ellie stroked the soft, black fur. Then a favourite tune came on, and Ellie returned to the kitchen, singing under her breath as she inspected the bread bin, then opened the fridge.

Once her plate was laden, she turned to head back to the window seat, still carolling along to the music, only to fetch up short opposite the door to the boot room as it swung open to reveal Will.

Heat flooding her skin, Ellie's mood sank like an anchor plunging into the watery depths of the harbour as she placed the plate on the island.

'Don't you know it's polite to knock first?'

'I did. You were making such a racket you didn't hear me.'

Rude.

Regardless of the full mug of tea on the table, Ellie busied herself with the coffee machine, topping up the water and retrieving the bag of beans. She'd be blowed if she'd offer him one.

'Why are you here?' It was a lot easier addressing the beans as they tumbled into the container, the heady aroma of coffee in the air, than looking at Will. His dark hair was less smooth than usual, no doubt due to the mist which continued to cling to the land. But was it… had there been a *smile* tugging at that firm mouth when she'd first spotted him in the open doorway?

'I would have thought that was obvious. I may be an animal lover, but I'm not given to paying social calls on them.'

This was a *social* call? On *her*? Fine words, but the tone implied the contrary.

Ellie risked a look over her shoulder. Despite his claim, Will had walked over to crouch down by Dougal's basket, giving him a good rub. The traitorous hound writhed in ecstasy as Will's hand firmly stroked his belly, and Ellie fiercely shut down her mind.

Don't go there. Whatever you do.

Then, Will straightened and faced her. 'I wanted to—'

Ellie hit the espresso symbol, quickly remembering to shove a cup under the nozzle, and the machine whirred into action, noisily grinding the beans. Will pressed his lips together, eyes flashing.

She stirred the cup vigorously when the machine stopped pouring – a pointless exercise when it was nothing but coffee – but as Will started to speak again, she decided a double would be rather nice and hit the symbol again.

Turning around, she folded her arms, meeting his frustrated gaze as the machine did its thing. Then, clutching a drink she didn't even want, Ellie leaned against the island, chin raised and ready for battle.

'Done now?'

Ellie took a sip of espresso – which she hated – clamping her jaws tight so as not to indicate how much she disliked the bitter taste.

'I wanted to ask you something. About that day on the beach.' He waved a vague hand, which she assumed summed up their encounter. 'You said something that made no sense.'

Just the one thing? That must be a record for me.

'It all seemed straightforward,' Ellie countered. 'The truth's like that, you know.'

Will winced, and Ellie's heart skipped hopefully. Had he had time to think, then?

'Look, can we sit down?' He ran a hand round the back of his neck. 'Something's bugging me.'

Willingly abandoning the espresso, Ellie gestured towards the sitting room, taking a seat on the sofa. Will tossed his coat onto the opposite one before settling into Oliver's generously proportioned armchair.

Silence spun through the air for a moment, the only sounds being a faint snore from Dougal and the muted call of seabirds from the orangery, where Ellie had opened a window. Their eyes met and held, but this time one held curiosity and the other confusion.

'It's a long time since we... talked. Properly.'

Unsure what to say, Ellie opted for saying nothing. After all, the ball was in Will's court right now.

He leaned forward, elbows on his knees, fixing her with a keen look. Ellie had no clue where this was going, but a more open Will, with no negativity fizzing in the air between them was so welcome, she'd have sat in silence for however long it took for him to get to the point.

His expectant look became a frown.

'Oh, sorry.' This time, Ellie's brow furrowed. 'Er, what did you say?'

'You said something about sending an email, but it never happened.'

So he keeps saying...

Despite her recent doubts, Ellie levelled her shoulders. 'Yes, it did. And it was read. I told you.' Will held her gaze steadily and she tried – oh so hard – not to want him. 'And if I didn't send it, prove it.'

Will got to his feet. 'Easily done. You never had my email address. We only ever used message apps or spoke on the phone.'

Ellie rose to face him. 'Oh, but I did. Those tickets, remember? For the beer festival over in Looe? You asked me to send them to you in case my phone was dead.'

It was galling to realise she was no better at charging her phone than she had been all those years ago, but satisfaction came from the stunned expression on Will's face.

'I'd forgotten.'

'Clearly.' An idea popped into Ellie's head. 'Do you still use it, that email account? What was the address again?'

Will's dark eyes flashed. 'Nice try.' He glared at Ellie. 'I never heard from you, and I don't understand why you keep saying it. You were never a liar. Besides, there's no credit in changing your mind when I'd found success.'

'I agree,' Ellie stated firmly. 'But I realised my mistake about two hours after you left, and wrote to you the following morning. Get your facts right, Will.'

Will blanched. 'That's not possible.'

Ellie merely raised her chin, staring him out until he straightened his shoulders, the distrust returning to his features.

'So what was in it, this supposed email? What was its point?'

'I—'

Ellie faltered. It was impossible to recall every detail of the War-and-Peace-length outpouring, but even if he'd skimmed it, it didn't take an idiot to get the gist... assuming she *had* sent it...

'I told you I regretted everything. Immediately. That my parents' words had given me pause. Whether it was the right advice or not, my heart won out over my head. When the "read receipt" arrived, I waited. Minute after minute, hour after hour, constantly refreshing my inbox. Then days, and soon weeks, had passed, but nothing came. In the end, I came up to London, called at your flat, but I was told you'd already gone abroad. And,' despite the many years that had passed, Ellie's voice wobbled, 'and that you'd got someone else.'

Will's eyes flashed, his whole air disbelieving. She really ought to take a step back, but would that look like acquiescing? Giving in? Admitting defeat?

She released a shaky breath. They were so close, Will's cologne was all around her in an invisible embrace, though his arms remained rigidly by his side, as did hers. She wasn't mistaken, was she? There was sadness in his gaze, albeit briefly before it once again assumed the hardness she'd become familiar with.

Unable to face his stoicism any more, Ellie spun towards the orangery.

'Wait.'

She stiffened.

'This is ridiculous. We're just going round in circles. I don't understand why—'

'Yoo hoo!'

Cheeks flushed at the sudden interruption, Ellie stepped away from Will, then followed his frustrated gaze to the boot room door, through which came the usual crowd.

'I'd better go.'

He grabbed his coat and then he was gone, and all that was left was the radio blaring out a song Ellie barely heard and the low mutter of speculation as the locals settled around the table.

Chapter Twenty-Two

"Halloween"

By the time the end of October arrived, Ellie had sorted things out over the new cards with both the Spar and Phyllida, but nothing could assuage the unhappiness caused by knowing someone wanted to harm her business. There had been no further comments on the socials, thank goodness, but two people had phoned to cancel their mini-session slot, claiming they'd changed their minds, and she'd had to delete yet more negative comments on posts on her website.

None of her friends in Polkerran – old or new – seemed to have any idea what was going on, and with little option, Ellie poured her efforts into expanding her range of cards, finishing the calendar and ramping up her efforts on social media.

There had been neither sight nor sound of Will, even when Ellie's treacherous feet had taken her along the cliff path past Peaches that morning. No smoke billowed from the chimney, there was no car in the driveway and the wooden gate was fastened shut.

Ellie, in the meantime, had doubled her efforts to find any trace of an email in her sent items, the only recourse being a painful scroll back through the years until she reached the summer in question. As this took an inordinate amount of time, and had to constantly be abandoned because of this or that – and the damn thing kept defaulting back to the most recent sent email every time she tried again – she wasn't making much progress.

Ellie was sure Will had gone back to London, and this was confirmed by Mrs Tremayne, who'd lamented the fact when Ellie and Kate met her in Harbourmasters for lunch one day, telling them he'd gone to see his researcher and carry out some preliminary interviews.

As they were crossing the restaurant to leave, however, Chloe came in with someone Ellie didn't recognise.

She and Kate exchanged greetings, but Ellie couldn't help but notice Chloe's avid attention being fixed on Mrs Tremayne, who remained oblivious.

'I'm organising a guided walk,' she explained to Kate. 'For the man running the show on the documentary. I'm working closely with him now.'

Ears on alert, Ellie attempted nonchalance as Mrs Tremayne turned to speak to her about the wedding brochure. As a result, she couldn't hear the rest of the dialogue between Kate and Chloe. Once they were outside and had said their farewells to the lady, Kate ushered Ellie along the front.

'What time is Anna due home?'

'Quite early. They're flying overnight, get into Heathrow around seven, so hopefully by the time the locals have landed!'

Kate chuckled as they leaned on the harbour wall.

The waters were quieter now, as November hovered in the wings, with many of the pleasure craft returned to their home ports or lifted out of the water into storage for the winter months. It was a cloudy day, noticeably chillier, and Ellie was grateful for her thick scarf and fingerless gloves.

'I'm not bad at baking, but I think they'll be relieved to have Anna home.'

'I expect you will too. Isn't it a bit lonely up there?'

'Sometimes. I spend a lot of my evenings with Nicki, of course, and Heathcliff's a great comfort. She's still sleeping on the bed. I hope Anna doesn't mind.'

'I doubt it. Anna loves her pets. I remember her finding Heathcliff as a stray, and I know for a fact she used to sleep with her. She probably only got ousted when Oliver moved in.'

Reflecting on the fact that there wasn't much likelihood of Heathcliff getting ousted from Ellie's bed in the near future, she left Kate to go back to the hotel and headed for the little library. She'd work on her laptop for an hour, by which time she could make her way to the school to meet the boys.

Settled at a table, Ellie began once again to scroll down through her sent items, searching and searching for the all-important year.

Yet again, it wasn't to be. Her phone started to ring, and she sent Valerie an apologetic look as she took the call, speaking as quietly as possible.

Nicki, on her tea break, was in a panic about the boys' costumes and what she'd forgotten to get, leaving Ellie no choice but to hop in the car and grab a few things from the party store in Port Wenneth, only just making it back to Polkerran in time for the school to turn out.

–

Ellie prepared an early tea for Liam and Jason, then sat at Nicki's kitchen table to work through the images from the previous week's shoots while the boys ran upstairs to don their costumes. Surely Hamish's progress would become more established? Otherwise, she'd be here until Christmas! She really needed to get home…

Except I don't really want to, do I?

'Of course I do,' Ellie snapped at the recalcitrant thought.

She strove to focus on some of the scarecrow images, improving the colour on one and cropping another to remove a glimpse of stone wall from one edge, then sat back with a huff.

'But it's true,' she whispered, her heart picking up its beat.

The sheer notion of those crossing paths was sufficient to stir feelings – long suppressed, but never forgotten – for a man she never expected to see again. It was as though Will was her last supper, a moment in time where they both existed in the same place, but never would again, and the hunger to see him again showed no sign of abating.

'How strange,' Ellie murmured after Nicki had come home from work and she had returned to Westerleigh to deal with Dougal and Heathcliff. She'd been in such dread of her and Will meeting in those early days and weeks, and yet now…

Chest aching, Ellie put a hand to it, but then a demanding growl emanated from her middle. She'd forgotten to have lunch, and it was now nearly six. With Nicki out with the boys trick or treating, then joining all the children at the village hall for a suitably ghoulish buffet, she'd been left to her own devices.

She may have a hunger for Will, but it wasn't going to satisfy her stomach!

Ellie opened the fridge and pulled out some leftover frittata from the previous day. It looked wholly unappetising, and she headed for the drawer housing the takeaway menus, just as the doorbell rang.

Heart bounding against her rib cage, Ellie scooted down the hall, casting a swift look in the mirror and tucking a loose strand of hair behind her ear. Could she have manifested Will, simply through her longing?

There were three small witches on the doorstep, each one endearingly attired in black, with suitably made-up faces and pointy hats.

'Trick or treat,' they trilled, and Ellie smiled at the young woman accompanying them.

'Well now, don't you all look scary!'

She reached for the cauldron of sweets.

'That's enough,' the lady cautioned as eager hands dug in, and off they went.

The next caller was Nicki with Liam and Jason, superbly dressed as a skeleton and a bat.

'Excellent make-up,' she praised her cousin, as the boys excitedly burrowed into the cauldron.

'It took a while,' Nicki laughed. 'Not sure we'll be able to get it all off before tomorrow.'

Ellie closed the door, returning to the kitchen and picking up the leaflet, but then the bell went again.

This time it was Phoenix with Verity Blue, who looked very pretty in a fairy costume and seemed to be having a disagreement with her mum about wearing a coat on such a chilly evening.

'She must be frozen,' Phoenix exclaimed as Ellie offered the cauldron to Verity Blue, who, from her pink cheeks and excited eyes, didn't look as if she cared.

The interruptions continued for the next hour, but Ellie managed to phone an order through to Thai Dai's in between the visiting ghouls, zombies and wizard folk.

'Does it ever quiet down?' she asked, amused, as Kate appeared with Theo.

'About now. It's only really the little ones that do the door to door. Molls has gone to the teen event organised by the youth club. To say she changed her mind over her costume every day this week wouldn't be an exaggeration.'

Ellie chuckled. 'I used to be like that.'

It seemed Kate was right, as the doorbell soon fell quiet, and Ellie dashed upstairs to don her favourite loungewear and unfasten her hair, leaving her chunky earrings on the dresser in her room and almost falling down the stairs in her enthusiasm to respond to the next ring of the bell.

'Thank goodness you're here!' she exclaimed with a beaming smile, only for it to falter.

It was, indeed, her takeaway, but holding the carrier was Will.

'Thanks.' Without waiting for an invitation, he walked past her into the hallway. 'Someone just handed me this.'

Ellie's heart sprang into action as she recalled the last time Will had called and how it had ended.

'And you just happened to be outside?' Proud of her attempt at nonchalance as they reached the kitchen, Ellie took the bag from him, placing it on the island. There was probably enough for two, but she doubted Will had called in expectation of being fed. 'What can I do for you?'

'Something, I hope. I've been trying to find a freelance photographer who would be available to shadow some of the pre-production.'

'And you weren't prepared to ask the one currently living on-site. Charming.'

'Look, Ellie, I'm sorry, okay? With things how they were – are – it didn't naturally suggest itself as an ideal partnership. But you *are* a photographer.'

Ten out of ten…

'And I need one,' he continued.

Tempted to say 'good luck' and tell him to go away, Ellie reined in the words.

'You only have to put a shout out on the socials, and you'll be inundated,' she suggested.

'I hate social media, and I don't want a stranger on the team.'

Ellie held his gaze, unblinking. Was he implying they *weren't*? Estranged, but not strangers… it was a questionable concept.

Will ran a hand through his neat hair, leaving it charmingly tousled, and Ellie sighed inwardly. Why didn't he look like Chewbacca having just rolled out of his cave instead of being even more drop-dead gorgeous?

'There's to be a making-of programme. They want it to run after the documentary has gone out, about how the production came about, evolved and so on. The magazine wants behind-the-scenes stills.'

Questions racing through her mind, Ellie stared at Will in disbelief. 'Are you…' Was she being stupid asking? Wasn't this just a trap where she'd think he needed her ability, and he would just shoot her down by asking if she had any fellow photographers she could recommend, put him in touch with?

'Do you have time?' he asked.

'I— I mean, yes, but… Sorry.' She shook her head. 'Are you asking *me* to do this?'

Will looked around the empty room.

'Can you see anyone else?'

This time Ellie let out a genuine laugh. 'No! But it's… unexpected. In the circumstances.'

'Great. So you're on board. You'd better give me your number.'

It was the same as it had always been… but then, he'd probably still got her blocked.

Ellie fished in her bag, hanging off the kitchen chair, and went to hand him a business card, but then retracted it.

'Hold on.' She grabbed a pen, then scribbled something on the card.

Will took it from her, then raised his gaze to Ellie.

'Missyellycinderelly@outlook.com. You surely don't use that for business.'

Ellie huffed. 'Obviously. The business one is printed, see?' She pointed to it. 'That's a personal one; I've had it since sixth form college. You should try searching for it in your account. You might be surprised by what you find.'

Skin paling, Will said nothing as he tucked the card in his pocket. Then he nodded and turned for the door, heading down the hall with his long stride.

'Wait!' Ellie hurried after him.

'What?' He swung around and she all but crashed into him, righting herself with difficulty.

'Why? Why me?'

Will held her frantic, confused gaze, and she tried not to care, to not want him to like her, *love* her still.

He shrugged. 'I'm desperate. Not many photographers of your calibre in the area.'

Blunt, but at least he was being honest. To Ellie's surprise, however, he continued.

'I've been studying your recent work. This ability you have of bringing out vulnerability, naturalness. Even the images of the scarecrow festival in the local rag... And as for those incredible stills of life and locals in the cove, they—'

'How did you know about those?'

'Ah.' He ran a hand round the back of his neck. 'You left a portfolio up at the manor. I went for dinner the other night. Arabella Tremayne was full of them. Said she felt they were worthy of an exhibition. Look, your style is thought-provoking, evocative, layered and exactly what I'm looking for.'

Will shoved his hands in his pockets, and Ellie all but held her breath as his words washed over her like honey, despite his deliberately offhand tone.

'But most of all, I want to hire you because I need someone who doesn't have their own agenda. Someone who I trust to respect my privacy and not share anything without my approval. The magazine is an exclusive-or-nothing deal.'

With that, he was gone, and Ellie sank back against the wall, her mind in tatters and her heart acting like it had just discovered the joys of trampolining.

Chapter Twenty-Three

"Would I Lie to You?"

'How's the jet lag?' Ellie's tone was sympathetic as a yawning Anna trudged over to the coffee machine the following afternoon.

They'd arrived back in good time around ten in the morning, but exhaustion had knocked them sideways after lunch and they'd all retired for a siesta, the twins included.

'Quite as bad as expected.' Anna smiled nonetheless, before topping up the beans in the machine and heading to the fridge. 'Both the twins are still asleep, thankfully, and Oliver's spark out.'

'But it was worth it?' Ellie took the milk off Anna. 'Go and sit, I'll do the coffee.'

'Almost beyond words,' Anna gushed, sinking into a chair, her hand playing mindlessly with a table mat. 'Lauren and Daniel are blissfully happy, Ellie. And Mia is growing up so fast. I can't wait until they get here next month.'

Ellie placed mugs on the island and walked over to stand by the table while the coffee machine did its thing.

'Is it a honeymoon of sorts?'

Anna's tired features lit up. 'I thought so. They never said until after the small ceremony, but they're moving back to the cove.'

'Wow. How come? Isn't Lauren high-flying through the corporate world?' Ellie took a seat beside her, placing Anna's mug of coffee on the mat.

'There's been a bit of role reversal. They're having a baby, so Lauren's taking a backseat from work, picking up on the consultancy she set up during the last pregnancy, and Daniel's been offered a role as financial director at a company in Plymouth.'

They chatted for a while about the trip to the US, the wedding and Anna's excitement over her best friend's imminent return, and Ellie was grateful for the distraction from the constantly wheeling emotions whirring through her head.

'What about you? What's been happening since we left?' Anna's voice became gentle. 'How's it been, you know, around…'

Not sure where to begin, they were interrupted by a wail from the baby monitor.

'Let's catch up later,' Ellie reassured Anna when she got wearily to her feet. 'I'd better get on with some work.'

–

Some hours later, Ellie stretched her back, leaving the computer to complete its download of the latest card. She needed to get to the post office with some of her completed card commissions, but before that she'd upload some of the Christmas designs to her website.

Scrolling through the latest reviews on Facebook an hour later, Ellie's heart dipped suddenly, then lurched almost into her throat.

What the hell was going *on*? Not more?

A notification pinged on her phone: Anna, asking her if she wanted to join her on a walk with the twins and Dougal.

Desperate for company, Ellie poked her head around the door into the house.

Anna was wrestling Emma into the stroller beside her brother. 'Sorry. Didn't want to knock and disturb if you were head-down in something.'

'It's perfect timing. The boys have an after-school club, so I'm desperate for another excuse to down tools. I'll grab my things.'

Ellie shoved the packaged cards into a tote. She'd worry about what she'd just seen later.

They emerged into late-afternoon sunshine, although the sun was already dipping towards the distant horizon as it headed for bed.

Ellie took hold of Dougal's lead as they walked down the lane and across the bridge into town, and Anna waited outside while she popped into the Spar to post her packages before resuming their walk, taking the lane parallel with the water out past Harbourwatch and down to the charming tidal beach.

Bertie and Emma were obliging, sleeping contentedly, and Anna positioned the double buggy by one of the benches as Ellie went into the little shop to pick up two hot chocolates and a biscuit for Dougal.

'Thanks.' Anna took the cup, inhaling deeply. 'I'd forgotten how much I loved these.' Then, she turned her hazel eyes on Ellie. 'So, tell me why you look so haunted. And don't deny it.'

Ellie puffed out a breath, placing her takeaway cup on the ground beside the bench. It helped to talk, didn't it?

'Someone is actively trying to destroy my businesses. Both of them. They've posted one-star reviews on the Facebook page and left negative comments on my Instagram posts. It's the same account, but I can't work out where it's coming from.' She dropped her head into her hands. 'I don't understand. Who would do this?'

She felt Anna's hand on her back, rubbing it consolingly, probably much as she did when the twins needed winding.

If only a good burp could clear this obstacle.

'And Will?' Anna prompted gently.

Ellie sat up. 'I have no idea what's going on with him. One minute we're each barely acknowledging the other exists, the next he turns up with a ham roll for my lunch or engages my services as a photographer, as if there's no history between us. He messaged earlier. He's hired a local guide who's leading a walk from Fowey to Polridmouth. Will said I need to be there to capture some footage and identify the best spots for when he's doing pieces to camera, you know, just explaining things directly. I told him I was going for a walk with Kate,' Ellie continued. 'But his response was, "bring her along". Honestly. I can't fathom the man out.'

'And this history. There's more to it than you're saying, isn't there?'

Leaning back against the bench, Ellie watched the waves slide across the wet sand before retreating. It was a bit like her and Will, performing some sort of catch-me-if-you-can dance.

'Yes,' she said softly, the word floating away on the breeze.

A lot more…

On the morning of the walk, Ellie threw back the curtains and leaned on the sill, her chin resting in her hands.

She'd slept better than expected, and she opened one of the windows to inhale deeply. The autumn air was crisp and laden with a heady combination of woodsmoke and gentle gusts of wind, enticing her to be outside. The glimmering water rippled in its endless flow towards the harbour, and crows gathered in the bare branches of the trees clinging to the steep hillsides, their rasping caws accompanied by hammering from the boat yard.

There had been no further contact from Will, beyond telling her to meet him and the guide in the car park at Readymoney in Fowey.

Time to get ready.

It took a stupid amount of time to decide what to wear, how to do her hair, what footwear to use and the most suitable bag that wouldn't be too onerous to carry on a long walk.

'Come on,' Kate called out to her as Ellie came out of the cottage. 'They'll leave without us.'

'I wish they would,' she muttered.

Kate sent her an amused look. 'Do you?'

'Sorry. I'm grateful you could come along.'

'It's fine. We were going to walk anyway, weren't we, and this isn't one I've done before. I was going to bring Bayley – he's Dev's lab – but he's got a poorly paw just now.'

Ellie settled into Kate's car, but as they reached the harbour, she spotted a woman she didn't recognise, walking a dog, and she frowned, unhappy with the way the lead was being tugged.

'What's the purpose of the walk?' Kate glanced at Ellie as they turned onto the main road to Fowey.

'It's Will's idea, wanting the full experience of approaching the beach from that direction, before heading up towards Menabilly. It should deliver some great photo ops for the feature.'

Soon parked up, Ellie emerged from the car, her expression indicative of her apprehension. Every encounter with Will had proved unpredictable so far. What would today bring?

'Are you okay?'

Ellie summoned a smile for Kate as she retrieved her backpack and cameras from the boot.

'I'm fine. Sorry our plans got hijacked. They can take the lead; that way, we still get our walk.'

'Hello there!'

Ellie exchanged a look with Kate, and they both waved at Chloe, who looked far too excited, as Will emerged from his car.

'Too much time in Will's company,' Kate said quietly as they made their way across the car park to join them.

Ellie hefted the bag more comfortably onto her shoulder, adjusting both camera straps so they wouldn't jostle with each other, trying to quash a flutter of jealousy as she followed the others down the path. Had Chloe and Will been spending time together then?

Chloe led them to the right, skirting Readymoney Cove and following a Saints' Way marker, ascending a steep, rock-strewn path up through some woods.

Will barely looked in Ellie's direction, and she paused, out of puff, as they reached a flatter, leaf-strewn lane stretching from left to right. Clearly, today was to be a not-so-friendly encounter.

'It's this way, but you might like to visit St Catherine's Castle first. There are stunning views back towards Fowey, and you can even see Daphne du Maurier's home at Ferryside if you use binoculars. Or a zoom,' she added to Ellie.

They followed her out to the ruins, perched on a cliff opposite the entrance to Fowey, a wide expanse of water separating it from the smaller settlement of Polruan on the opposite side of the river.

Chloe chattered on about block houses, Henry VIII, American soldiers stationed there in World War II and more. Ellie shut her voice out. She was, after all, talking expressly to Will, all but ignoring Kate too.

Picking up the Fuji with the wide-angle lens, Ellie clicked almost continuously, checking the viewfinder, moving around to establish the best light, conscious Kate had perched on a rocky outcrop as Chloe led Will up some steep stone steps to a higher viewpoint.

Ellie's phone rang, and she tugged it from her jeans pocket. Marcus.

'I did it!'

Laughing, Ellie walked over to sit on a low stone wall overlooking the water. 'Details, Marcus. Did what?'

'Oh! I asked Phyllida out. Well, I said would she like to go for something to eat, and she said yes, so then I had to explain I meant with me.'

Still grinning, her gaze roamed up to the castle ruins. Chloe seemed to be talking non-stop – much like Marcus at the moment – but then she realised Will was staring down at Ellie, that assessing look on his features again, and she stood up and turned her back.

Ending the call, Ellie's mind dwelled on what might have got Will's goat today. She was soon to have an answer.

Regrouping and ready to take up the Saints' Way again, he dropped back as Ellie replaced her lens cap, and she raised her head to find him staring at her as if he couldn't quite make her out.

Feeling the habitual tension building in her shoulders, she held his gaze.

'What?'

'I checked. No email from that address you gave me. So that's the end of the matter.'

Ellie's throat tightened momentarily. How could that be? But hold on... he didn't exactly sound triumphant...

She skipped ahead of him as he walked away.

'But you looked,' she threw over her shoulder.

She wasn't sure why, but the fact Will had made the effort, felt it was worth considering – even though it had proved him right – lifted her spirits, and Ellie bounded along the path with renewed energy, determined to double her efforts to search back in her own sent items.

It didn't occur to Ellie that if she *did* find the email, then what might *that* imply?

Chapter Twenty-Four

"Star Trek"

The walk continued, with them climbing steadily uphill again, soon emerging into an open field, the sounds of the surf breaking against the invisible cliffs below them.

'Will wants to follow the cliff path,' Chloe called back to Kate and Ellie. 'This way.'

She fell into step with Will as they picked up a dirt track running along the edge of the field next to coarse hedging, beyond which the sea stretched towards the horizon, but as the walkway narrowed, permitting single file only, Chloe edged in front of Will, sending him a coy look. Ellie's heart twanged in envy over the warm smile in response.

'Is he likely to be taken in by someone like this?' Kate mused as she stepped ahead of Ellie to lead the way in the wake of the others.

Ellie didn't honestly know what Will wanted in a woman these days, but she answered nonetheless.

'I suspect all men are prone to enjoying a bit of obvious attention.'

'Discreet,' Kate laughed over her shoulder at Ellie.

They deliberately walked several paces behind Will and Chloe, chatting about Ryther and how much he was enjoying being back in the cove, and Theo, Dev's son, who had a fascination for lighthouses.

'They have an open day at the Gribbin every year.' Kate pointed towards the red-and-white-banded daymark perched on a headland in the distance. 'We went this year, and I swear the little cutie was positively quivering in anticipation!'

Ellie smiled affectionately at Kate's back. Her voice throbbed with the love she clearly held for the little boy.

Will and Chloe had reached a stile, and again, Ellie tried not to notice the twinge within her chest as he held out a hand to help Chloe over. Was it her imagination, or did he hold on to it longer than necessary? Were the girl's cheeks pink from exercise, or something else?

They both clambered over the stile, but Ellie – protective of the cameras – landed awkwardly.

'You okay?' Kate grasped her arm. 'It's normally me stumbling. Don't do that when we're out on the exposed cliff path, will you?'

Ellie rubbed her ankle. 'I'll try not to.'

She was all too aware of Will's impassive face staring back down the path at them, but she straightened her shoulders and followed Kate, using her as an effective visual block to hide the two in front.

After a while, they reached a small beach. The light was stunning, and Ellie clicked away, conscious that Will had bent down to collect some pebbles, and before long he was skimming them with precision across the water, accompanied by Chloe's cries of delight.

An unbidden memory flashed into Ellie's mind as emotion caught at her throat – the day Will had found the flat, smooth stone still sitting in the small velvet box, and for a second, she couldn't breathe for the pain.

'Stop it,' she intoned silently, pushing the memory ruthlessly aside to resume her clicking, swapping from the Canon to the Fuji and back again, depending on whether she was snapping scenery or people.

She pretended not to notice how many were actually of Will: his profile as he stared out across the water, the breeze lifting the hair from his forehead; the silhouette of his figure standing on the rocks, the sun full behind him; Will laughing as a seagull swooped low and snatched a crisp from Chloe's hand.

There was another small cove after that before they finally approached Polridmouth, and Ellie took a moment to absorb the scene.

Using the widescreen lens, she clicked speedily, the light perfect at that moment, then took copious shots on both cameras of the little cottage nestled at the back of the cove – the alleged inspiration for the boat house in *Rebecca* – before turning her attention to capturing the reflections in the small, magical lagoon formed by the retreat of the tide.

'It's like having a walking Siri with us,' Kate muttered as Chloe waxed lyrical about the location.

Ellie merely smiled, desperately trying to catch a few images of the ever-changing beach as the waves rolled in and out, shifting shells and seaweed on their retreat. There were ample places for Will to do his pieces to camera. The main difficulty would be choosing one.

'Beautiful,' she sighed, carefully wiping the camera lens.

After a while, and when Ellie confirmed she had all the shots she needed for now, Will suggested they head back.

'The way we came?' Chloe asked, pointing towards the cliff path. 'Or we can go across the fields via Coombe

Farm? They both join above Readymoney Cove, but the field route is a bit quicker.'

'Let's do that.'

Will set off with Chloe at a brisk pace, and Ellie adjusted the camera straps again and shouldered the backpack before following Kate up the track.

Ellie tried not to hear Will and Chloe's conversation, but the breeze was disobliging, drawing their words across the crisp, autumnal air towards her, as Will outlined some diary entries he'd recently been studying.

'It's alleged her parents were not inspired by Daphne's decision to marry; they had no confidence in the match at first. She was determined, though, ignoring any naysaying. She wanted little fuss, taking the boat early in the morning from Ferryside up Pont Pill and walking up through the woods to Lanteglos Church.'

Chloe gave a gasp of delight. 'We must do that too, follow in her footsteps.' She clapped her hands. 'It's *sooo* romantic. Oh, to be so in love that you allow nothing and no one to part you. I long for such a love, such a simple ceremony. No fuss, just me and...' Her words faded, and Ellie all but held her breath, then let it out in a rush as Chloe continued. '...the person I loved.'

'That's all very noble,' Will said dryly. 'But you need witnesses. Daphne and her beau had to resort to using the gravedigger.'

Kate did her best to conceal a splutter of laughter, but Will looked over as though he'd only just realised they were there.

'Yes, well.' Chloe hurriedly moved them along. 'Come on, this is a steep bit.'

She wasn't wrong, and when they reached the top of the incline by the farm, Ellie paused to draw breath, shifting the backpack a little in an attempt to ease the strain on her shoulders, which had begun to ache.

Will had stopped to take a call, and Ellie grabbed the moment to perch on a tree stump, fishing out her own phone and skimming through her inbox.

'It's been fabulous, hasn't it?' Chloe joined her and Kate. 'Will wants to do the walk from Bodinnick to Lanteglos next week.'

'It's part of the Hall Walk,' Kate offered.

Ellie looked up from studying her phone. 'I picked up a good walk book from the tourist place not long ago. Covers a good few walks over the top there, if you'd like to borrow it to plan a route?'

Chloe beamed, but as Will ended his call and beckoned, she scurried across the field to join him.

Relieved the ordeal would soon be over, Ellie rose wearily to her feet as they resumed the walk, scaling stiles and kissing gates, trailing ever further behind. They entered a copse of trees with a more even path underfoot, and almost out of breath, Ellie paused for a second, reassuring Kate she was fine, merely needing to remove a stone from her boot.

At Ellie's insistence, Kate continued on, but as Ellie bent to retie her lace, she heard footsteps and straightened to meet Will's solemn gaze.

'Give that to me.'

He gestured at the cumbersome pack, which remained on Ellie's back.

Unimpressed with his resigned air, and out of patience with her heart, which dipped as she took in the windraked hair and those dark, intense eyes, Ellie sought for words that wouldn't come.

'Ellie? Did you hear me?'

She rolled her eyes. 'Obviously. I'm a bit tired, Will, not deaf.'

Will's countenance reflected uncertainty, and Ellie tore her gaze away before she could throw herself into his arms, begging him to never let go.

Cameras might get in the way… could be awks…

Despite the now-careering heartbeat, unable to prevent her lips from twitching, Ellie calmly removed the backpack and handed it over.

'Give me the cameras, too. I'll wear them for the rest of the way.'

'No. The cameras are my lifeblood. The tools of my profession. I will protect them fiercely.' Ellie folded her arms over the cameras. 'Nice little dig at parental influence back there, by the way, and the alleged merits of being as stubborn as an ox.'

'It's a mule.' Will's eyes flashed. 'And I was simply explaining how parents aren't always right.'

'And they don't always win their point, like with Daphne.'

Will hefted the backpack onto his shoulder, his dark, brooding gaze lingering on Ellie's flushed countenance.

As a reel spun through Ellie's mind, snapshots of them falling in love that summer, her eyes scanned Will's conflicted features. Could he be recalling the same?

'Will!'

They both started at Chloe's call.

'Come on, you said you needed to be back by four, remember?'

Will hesitated, the expression on his face hard to read, then turned on his heel, and Ellie followed him across the last field before the descent back down to Readymoney Cove.

'Well, that was fun,' she mused to herself as Kate fell into step beside her.

For some reason, she could feel a laugh bubbling up, but where it came from, she had no idea. She didn't feel remotely amused at all.

–

As soon as she got home, Ellie put the camera batteries on charge and retrieved the memory cards, inserting them in the reader before ensuring the cameras were carefully stored for when she next needed them.

Setting up the laptop on the island – and thankful for the quiet, with Anna out at baby and toddler group and Oliver at work – Ellie plugged in the hard drive and created a folder for the day's shots. Heavens, she must have taken hundreds!

Dragging the shoot to the drive, she checked the download notification. Two hours.

'You'd better not take that long,' she warned the screen, heading for the kettle.

After a snack of tea and biscuits, Ellie brushed her fingers against her jeans, checking on the progress with the photos, which were speeding along now.

'Oh, no, cutie.' She scooped Heathcliff into her arms as she jumped onto the island to see what Ellie was up to. 'You can come with me. Cats and keyboards during a download do not mix well.'

Heading upstairs with Heathcliff, Ellie deposited her on the bed and released her hair from its scarf, before going to shower and donning her loungewear.

By the time she'd returned to the kitchen, and she'd fed both Heathcliff and Dougal, the download was almost complete. After making another cup of tea, Ellie perched on a stool and stared across to the window, reflecting on Will's words.

A double-edged sword, she acknowledged. On one side, at least he'd been curious enough to look for the elusive email; on the other, he'd proved it wasn't in his inbox.

Eventually, the download completed, but the images were slow to load, an occupational hazard for Ellie, as she always took so many. Gradually, she began working through them, her heart lurching every time a headshot of Will appeared on the screen.

Sticking to the spec for the job, Ellie had kept her focus mainly on shooting wide-angle pictures, making the most of the landscape and backdrop while also showcasing the figures – suitably distant and anonymous, almost Lowry-like shadows on the canvas. Her love of portraits, however, had taken over now and again, and she'd switched to the other camera, clicking continuously on closer shots of Will, stood on the firm sand, staring out to sea, or head down, deep in thought; of Chloe pointing here and there, laughing at something Will had said.

Had Kate's speculations been on point? Chloe's manner towards him was definitely on the flirtatious side, but what about Will?

Ellie swallowed hard and shot out of her seat. She couldn't bear thinking about it…

Chapter Twenty-Five

"Clueless"

Ellie gulped down a welcome glass of water, gave herself a good talking to, and settled back at the island. She had to keep things in perspective, get on with the job she'd been given.

The pictures were natural and atmospheric, and Ellie became lost in her delight over the overriding mood of them, but as the next images became more landscapes, Ellie clicked back to the ones of Will.

Trying to quell rising emotion, she was nonetheless powerless to stop herself reaching out to rest a gentle finger on his face, but then she started as the doorbell rang out.

'Hi. I hope it's okay – I thought I'd drop by to pick up the walk book you mentioned?'

Ellie stared blankly at Chloe for a second, then shook her head slightly. 'Yes. Sorry, come on in.'

Chloe followed her back to the kitchen.

'Take a seat.' She gestured to one of the stools tucked under the island. 'I'll just go and fetch it.'

'Sorry, am I interrupting?' Chloe pointed to the open laptop.

Ellie shook her head. 'No, it's fine. I won't be a sec.'

She hurried into the orangery. Where the hell had she put the damn thing? She hadn't even taken it out of the paper bag.

She moved a stack of cards from by the printer, lifted a discarded scarf and got on her knees to shuffle through some papers. Nothing. Turning on her heel, she looked around the room. There was nothing on the small sofa beside the doors to the terrace other than a jumper, two throws, some spare camera leads and a half-read novel.

'Aha!'

Ellie shot over to the small bookcase, where she'd stacked her boxes of inks. Underneath the top box was the bag.

'Sorry. I'm such a clutter box; I never can find anything!'

Chloe started as Ellie returned to the room, shoving her phone into her pocket and taking the paper bag.

'Thanks so much.'

'Are you alright? You look a bit flushed.'

'Oh yes,' Chloe said in her breathy voice. 'Just distracted. I swear I ought to switch the phone off, sometimes. There's no peace from them, is there?'

Ellie grinned. 'I'd say I occasionally turn mine off, but in truth, it's usually dead because I forgot to charge it. Oh!' She went to retrieve her bag, which she'd dropped onto the island on returning home. 'As shown by Exhibit A.' She waved the evidence as she popped it on charge.

Chloe had edged towards the door, the book clutched to her chest, still flushed pink. 'I'll leave you to it. I can let myself out.'

She was gone, and Ellie resumed her seat and her study of Will's silent image.

'She's still a bit odd, that one,' Ellie mused, soon lost in flicking between the images of Will. 'Now, which of these shall I give top stars to?'

Marcus phoned just as Ellie finished some more edits to her favourite shots.

'She's asked if it's okay to bring a friend!'

Frowning, Ellie stood and walked over to admire the view from the tall windows. 'Phyllida? Well, that's okay. People sometimes do these days, on first dates.'

'But does it mean it's not a date? If she's bringing another man?'

'A man?'

'Yes. Look, Ellie, will you come with me? To balance out this Clifford bloke?'

'Oh, I'm not sure that's a—'

'Pleeeease,' Marcus pleaded. 'She said it was okay.'

'You've already asked her?'

'Sorry. I panicked!'

Trying not to laugh, Ellie conceded, jotting the date and time down before ending the call, reassuring Marcus it would all be fine.

'Come and join us.' Anna greeted Ellie when she entered the sitting room, patting the rug where she sat with the twins who were gnawing on carrot sticks.

'I'd love to, but I need to drop a fresh stock of cards in at the book shop, and I want to grab a sandwich when I'm out. I'll catch you later.' Ellie tickled Emma, who giggled and held on to Bertie's hand for a moment. 'Bless them – I'd far rather stay and feed these two.'

'Oh, that reminds me.' Anna got to her feet. 'Fancy joining us for dinner? No,' she added, laughing at Ellie's wide eyes. 'No surprises. Oliver needs to talk to Nicki. She can bring Liam and Jason too.'

'Fab, see you later.'

Ellie said a quick goodbye as she passed the table, but Oliver, who had made his coffee and was heading out as well, followed her.

'How's it going with the book?'

'All done, thanks to Bella.'

They emerged into the garden, making their way along the path, but pausing where it divided.

'Oliver, you don't have any of your other properties available, do you?'

He said nothing for a moment, his steely blue eyes on Ellie, who found looking up at him quite the challenge. Had she spoken out of line? He was a bit of a closed book, after all.

'Are you not happy here?'

'No! I love it. It's Mrs Clegg. I shouldn't poke my nose in, I realise, but she's having a few problems now she can't manage stairs very well, and it seems her stove has stopped working too.'

Oliver blinked. 'Why on earth didn't she say?'

'I think she feels so grateful to you for giving her a home it feels wrong to her to say anything.'

Rolling his eyes, Oliver took a sip of his coffee. 'Sounds very like her. She was in service, you know, all her life, until she came to housekeep for me in her retirement. Always believes everyone else's needs come before her own. Thank you.'

–

Marcus sent a WhatsApp just as Ellie sat down to dinner with Anna, Oliver and Nicki. As it consisted of one word – help! – and a frantic-faced emoji, she excused herself and hurried into the hall.

The poor man was becoming increasingly nervous about meeting up with Phyllida the following evening, obsessing over her wish to bring the faceless Clifford.

'Does he sound tall?' Marcus asked, as Ellie giggled.

'Why would he be tall because he's called Clifford?'

'I don't know,' he exclaimed. 'Isn't there a Clifford Tower somewhere?'

'Yes, it's in York, Marcus, and it's short and round. Now stop worrying. I'm your plus one.'

'At least Phyllida's met you before.'

Shaking her head, Ellie repeated her belief that it was perfectly understandable in this day and age for taking a backup. Fairly confident there was a mutual attraction, Ellie didn't hold the same trepidation for her friend, but she did her best to reassure him, and he promised he wouldn't message again. At least, not for an hour...

Ellie pocketed her phone and returned to the kitchen.

'And you say Phyllida's assistant doesn't know who made the call?'

Resuming her seat at the table, Ellie looked from Anna to Oliver and then Nicki. 'No, although unlike the Spar, she said the caller was female.'

Oliver picked up the breadbasket, offering it round a second time, and Ellie selected a small white dinner roll. 'What were the cards about?'

'My business ones, only on the back there's an ad for the greeting cards. You know the sort of thing, what I can offer, such as personalised cards for occasions, packs of invitations, illustrations and so on, and contact details. I'd left some with several places in town, so they could display both sides for me.'

'It doesn't sound like something that's treading on anyone else's toes in the cove,' Anna mused as she dished aromatic curry out onto a plate and handed it across to Nicki.

'Phee's our local artist,' Nicki added, 'and she's not only well aware of but has also been really supportive of Ellie's work.'

Ellie still nursed a lingering hurt. 'Phee's talents lie in watercolours or pen and ink drawings. We've talked about doing some combined projects, but you could hardly say we're in competition.'

'Phee wouldn't hold back if she had a problem with it,' Oliver stated as he passed the bowl of rice around.

'It's bothering you, isn't it?' Anna asked kindly, placing a comforting hand on Ellie's arm.

'I wish it wasn't, but I've clearly upset someone. I just can't work out who or how. After all, I'm only here short term. How much damage can you do in a few months? It's almost as though even that is too long and they'd prefer me to disappear ASAP.'

There seemed no logical answer, and the conversation moved to Bella, who'd finished her work for Oliver and was therefore spending time back in Bristol.

'She's giving up the cottage in the village centre,' Oliver said. 'Nicki, I wondered if you'd like to have it for a while? Rent-free, of course.'

Nicki – who had been about to take a sip of wine – lowered her glass, her puzzled gaze moving from Oliver to Anna and back. 'Why would I want to take it?'

'It's got a ground-floor bathroom,' Anna said.

'And there are two sitting rooms, so one could easily be made into a bedroom. Hamish would be able to come home to the cove sooner and finish his rehab with his family around him.'

'Oh,' Nicki gulped, a small sob suddenly escaping. She dashed a hand across her eyes, which did little to prevent the torrent of tears pouring down her cheeks.

Ellie scooted her chair over to pull Nicki into a hug. 'I think that means "yes, please,"' she said to Oliver, whose puzzled gaze had flown to Anna.

'It's okay,' she reassured her husband, and came round to sit on Nicki's other side, joining in on the one-armed hug.

'I'm such an idiot,' Nicki exclaimed a few minutes later. Ellie and Anna sat back, and she straightened, accepting a paper napkin from the latter and dabbing underneath her eyes. 'I just didn't expect it, and—'

'Despite his philanthropic venture, Oliver never quite gets how significant a lifeline he's offering,' Anna interjected. 'It happens a lot when he manages to give someone a hand with their housing needs. Come on, this needs a celebration. Oliver—' She looked over at him, a twinkle in her eye. 'Let's open that champagne Matty brought last time they came to dinner.'

Nicki hurried to the cloakroom to repair her make-up while Anna went in search of champagne flutes, and Ellie walked over to the window to stare out into the black night. The windows of Harbourwatch glowed across the bay, casting golden patches of light over the water, which glimmered in the darkness.

There was no sign of the lighthouse which stood on its stretch of rocks somewhere out there. Nor was there any glimpse of what lay beyond the headland: Will's white-washed cottage, where no doubt he was reclining in front of the log burner, smoke spiralling from the chimney, relishing his solitude – unless Chloe was with him…

The pop of a cork and a burst of laughter from Nicki reclaimed Ellie's attention, as Oliver poured the foaming liquid into sparkling crystal. This was such a wonderful moment for Nicki, great news.

If Hamish could come home, even if he couldn't be as active as normal, he'd be there for Liam and Jason outside school hours. And then there would be no reason to stay... would there?

There was no need for anyone to try and drive Ellie away. Her days in Polkerran Point were already numbered.

Chapter Twenty-Six

"The Apprentice"

Nicki phoned early the next morning.

'I'll take the boys down. I don't need to start until ten; had a cancellation. Fancy a quick coffee in Karma when I'm done?'

Ellie grabbed her bag and the Canon and headed into town, her head still mired in the thoughts that had taken up residence overnight and the conflict they presented over leaving Polkerran Point.

'Snap out of it,' she scolded herself as she approached the stone bridge over the River Polwey. 'Just weeks ago, you were worried sick about meeting your household bills. Now you can go home and life will revert to normal.'

Except it wouldn't.

Ellie leaned on the parapet. It was mild for early November, and a hazy sun caressed her cheeks. A pale, cloudless sky became a misty blue as it merged with the distant ocean. They were as one, the sea and the sky at that moment, and Ellie closed her eyes, relishing the sounds of early-morning Polkerran: the chug of a fishing boat leaving the harbour for the day, the clunk-clunk-thud of the gig rowers going out for a practice, the continuous tap-tap of a mallet from the boat yard and the constant mewling and cawing of seabirds soaring across the water and then upwards towards the trees, which continued to turn all shades of brown and gold.

The cove had taken its hold, much as it had twelve years ago. She'd fallen in love with it all over again.

And Will? her mind whispered.

'No,' she enunciated clearly into the soft autumn air as she set off across the bridge again. 'I didn't need to.'

Ellie had come to realise a profound truth: she'd never stopped loving him. It had been buried deep, but it had shaped every relationship since, because there was no one but Will. *He* was the real reason she didn't want to leave. They may no longer be lovers – they weren't even friends – but just being able to see him, hear his voice after all this time, brought some form of solace to her bruised heart.

She didn't care any more about what he had or hadn't done. They may never be together, but she wanted Will to be happy…

'Hey, how's it going?'

Ellie looked up as Matt joined her by the wall. 'Good, thanks. I—'

'Hold on,' he cautioned, a warning hand on Ellie's arm. He'd narrowed his dark eyes as the woman Ellie had spotted the other day strolled along the street in front of Karma, still trailing a reluctant dog, stopping to talk to the people sat outside.

'What's up?'

He huffed out a breath. 'Just a nagging suspicion. Leave it with me.' He flashed his attractive smile at Ellie and set off along the front towards where she could see Mrs Lovelace and Old Patrick chatting to one of the fishermen unloading his catch.

'There you are!' Nicki waved as Ellie approached the cafe, the woman and the dog now much further up the street, talking to Phyllida as she cleaned the windowsill of the book shop.

'I stopped to admire the view.'

'Hard not to,' Nicki said dryly. They walked up to the counter and ordered their drinks. 'So. I'm calling at the rehab centre as soon as my shift is over to find out the discharge process for Hamish, and what needs doing to set up his continued physio. Oliver says Bella's handing the keys back end of next week, and once the cleaners have been in, he'll set up the downstairs bedroom for us.'

'I'm so happy for you, Nicki.' Ellie hugged her cousin before they took their favourite squashy leather sofa by the window.

'It leaves you free to go home. I'll never be able to thank you enough for what you've done.'

Ellie's brow furrowed. 'But you still have your shifts, and Hamish isn't mobile enough to take the boys to school.'

'I think Liam's old enough to take himself; he's heading to big school in September next year. If I can't drop Jason off, Anna has said she can do it short term. Hamish will be able to get around a bit on his crutches, too. We'll be fine.'

Nicki's pretty eyes scanned Ellie's features.

'You look… unhappy. I thought you'd be keen to escape. You know, especially with Will in town.'

'I thought so too.' Ellie stirred in her seat, skin warming at every mention of him. 'Before I came back here, I assumed I'd hate the place… associate it with the despair that followed on from such intense happiness. It took me a while to work it out, but I think it's because the unhappiness didn't happen here, did it?'

At least, not until now…

Ellie drew in a short breath. 'Besides, I'm committed to completing the photography for Tremayne Manor.'

Which is almost done…

'Will it set you right for money, with the extra from that job?'

'Yes, I'll be fine,' Ellie reassured her.

'Right.' Nicki drained her mug. 'I need to get to work.'

So did Ellie. Time to forget the past and focus on the future, and that meant dedicating herself to her business.

Pointless dreams would have to take a back seat.

—

That evening, Ellie met Marcus by the harbourmaster's office, where he'd managed to find a parking space, and she sent him an encouraging smile as he emerged from the car.

'Come on,' she said, linking arms with him as they made their way down the narrow street towards the harbour itself. 'Let's get this lovely wind whipping some colour into those cheeks. Otherwise, she's going to think she's dating a ghost.'

'It's not a date when there's four of us! Is it?'

Trying not to chuckle at Marcus's petrified countenance, Ellie urged him along, talking as soothingly as she did to Dougal and Heathcliff, pleased when she managed to elicit a laugh from him just as they came to a halt opposite the bistro.

'Good pitch, not going for Harbourmasters. A pub would be too casual, as if it didn't matter, and the formality of the restaurant might feel a bit too pressured.'

Marcus drew in a slow breath and turned to look out across the water. 'You do know it was your suggestion? I don't think I've held a sensible thought in my head since we set this up.'

'It'll be *fine*. Besides, Phyllida's the one who suggested you both take a friend. She's at least as nervous as you, if not doubly so.'

Marcus stuffed his hands into his jacket pockets. Then he took them out again. 'So… *is* it a date, or isn't it?'

'It's a date.' Ellie checked the time. 'Come on. It'll look better if you're there first. Shows you're keen.'

Marcus's skin paled further, but at least he joined Ellie as they crossed the cobbled street. The last thing she needed was having to herd him like a nervous sheep!

'Hello. Do you have a booking?' A smiling young woman came to greet them as the glass door swished to a close behind them, and Ellie gave Marcus a nudge.

'Oh, er, yes. Marcus. Table for four.'

'Lovely.' She fished out a couple of menus. 'Just one of you to come, then. Follow me.'

Marcus shot a fraught look at Ellie as they entered the bistro. 'What if the friend's here first?' he hissed out of the side of his mouth.

'He isn't. Phyllida's already at the table.' Ellie lowered her voice as they approached. 'Because she's *keen*.'

Marcus came to a stumbling halt at the table as the lady laid the menus by two of the places and disappeared.

Phyllida's puzzled gaze moved from Marcus to Ellie and back. 'Is there some sort of misunderstanding? I thought we—' She broke off, a hand going to her face as colour shot up her neck.

Confused, Ellie glanced at Marcus, but he seemed frozen in place, hands gripping the back of his chair, so she smiled at Phyllida.

'Marcus said you were bringing a friend, so he asked me to come along too. I hope it's okay?'

Blinking, Phyllida lowered her hand, swallowing visibly.

'Oh dear. I must have… maybe I wasn't clear.' She glanced down, under the table, and after exchanging a confounded look, Marcus and Ellie peered round to see what she was looking at.

A gorgeous spaniel with wide, soulful eyes and the silkiest-looking ears Ellie had ever seen gazed back up at them.

'This is my best friend, Clifford.' Phyllida's colour faded as she looked between the two of them, then fastened onto Marcus. 'I thought you had a dog too.'

Ellie started to laugh, even though Marcus seemed unable to say or do anything. Then Phyllida joined in, and Ellie gave the man a meaningful nudge in the arm.

'You said you'd told Phyllida you were bringing me!'

'I— er.' Marcus looked down, then up again, his face awash with embarrassment. 'I didn't mention your name; I just said could I bring my friend, too.'

He looked from Ellie to Phyllida, but then, thankfully, his mouth began to turn upwards, and he shook his head.

'I'm an imbecile. I'm so sorry, Phyllida.'

'Look, guys, I'll leave you to it.'

They both made to protest, but Ellie knew when she was surplus to requirements.

Heading back out, she informed the lady on the front desk that the full party was now in, emerging onto the street beaming.

Sometimes, life turned out just right.

The day ended badly.

Ellie had done her best to keep her spirits up, concentrating on work, finalising the last slots for the next mini-session, thankful no one else had withdrawn. It hadn't helped that someone had shared the image of Nicki to an Instagram story, with a caption of 'AI Generated' plastered across it and tagging Ellie's photography business account.

Luckily, it had been the same account as before, which had reached a dizzying three followers somehow, but not so luckily, one of them had been one of the mums from the school, who'd taken some persuading that there was nothing fake about Ellie's photography.

Reporting it to Instagram, but with little faith in any retribution, Ellie tried to put it aside. Bella had been strangely evasive in a recent message about her return, despite the alleged handing over of the keys to her cottage the following week. She'd been reluctant to confirm at all when she'd next be in Polkerran, and Ellie had gone to bed unsettled.

She'd also made the mistake, before switching off the light, of checking her websites, only to find another negative rating, which again in no way related to actual customers. She fired off an email to the support desk but didn't hold out much hope of finding out how something that couldn't happen was happening.

If her mind was troubled, it was nothing to the ache in Ellie's breast, which had felt like a permanent fixture when it had taken possession twelve years ago, and had returned with all the familiarity of an old friend, taking up residence as though it had no intention of moving out any time soon.

Ellie's waking thought each day was of Will, and it had become impossible not to recall those heady summer nights where a new dawn had meant lifting her eyelids to the sight of his face – sometimes in repose, often simply facing her on the pillow, his gaze infused with love…

Will had become her bedtime solace too. Ellie curled into a ball, her back to the side of the bed he used to occupy when they'd been able to stay in his room at the manor, closing her eyes tightly, imagining he was simply there, that the weight of the duvet was really his body, nestled up against hers.

The following morning, however, Ellie woke to find her pillow wet with tears she'd shed in her sleep, and wiping her damp cheeks on the backs of her hands, she shuffled upright, blinking as the bright light seared through a gap in the curtains.

Whatever had caused the upset had dissipated, as dreams do, and determined to face the day with positivity, Ellie settled in the orangery after breakfast with the family and began working on the commission for Anna, but her attempt at normality was interrupted when her phone rang.

Will.

Ellie's heart careered round her ribcage like an untrained puppy let off a lead.

Getting up, she walked over to the window overlooking the terrace, the phone pressed to her ear.

'Hi?' she said, warily. The small sliver of hope it might be a friendly day was shot to dust immediately.

'I thought I'd made it plain.' Will's voice was edged with steel. 'None of those photos are to be released without my approval, and definitely not before the programme is finished!'

Ellie held the phone away, giving it a confused look, then put it back to her ear. 'You did make it plain. Abundantly so.'

'So what the hell are you playing at?'

'I have no idea what you're talking about. And stop shouting!' she all but yelled back.

Ellie turned her back on the gorgeous view, folding an arm across her waist as Will sucked in an audible breath.

'Get a copy of the *Daily Recorder*. You'll see your handiwork. Oh, and you're fired.'

Chapter Twenty-Seven

"Crazy, Stupid, Love"

The line went dead, and Ellie sank onto the small sofa, a leaden weight forming in her stomach while her mind cantered around in confusion.

Then she shoved the phone in her pocket, closed the doors with a fierce snap, snatched up her bag and a thick shawl and shot over to the boot room.

'Sorry, Dougal,' she called, as the dog raised its head in hopeful expectation. 'I'll take you out as soon as I'm back.'

Ellie strode quickly out of the drive. 'That's assuming I'm still alive by then,' she muttered, speeding down the lane, over the bridge and into the Spar to grab a copy of the paper.

Taking a bench by the harbour, oblivious to the cold stabbing her arms through the ineffectual shawl, she flicked through the pages with shaking hands until she reached the Showbiz News section.

'Damn it,' she hissed through her teeth.

How the devil had they got hold of those? And how come her photography business was credited?

Slumping back against the bench, the paper crumpled in her lap, Ellie stared across the water to the trees rising up the steep hillside on the quieter side of the cove. A few bare branches stretched upwards towards the pale blue sky, surrounded by clusters of gold, copper and russet, with the occasional tall evergreen punctuating the leafy canvas.

Crows caw-cackled in black covens as sea birds soared overhead, but Ellie was oblivious, the sound drowned out by Will's cutting accusation.

'How be y'on, my lover?'

With a start, Ellie looked up, then dug deep for a smile as someone emerged from the small chemist shop. 'Hi, Patrick. How are you?'

'I's on me way to visit Cleggie.' He waved a net bag containing what looked like prescription medication. Then his wizened features sobered, his flint-grey eyes scanning Ellie's face. 'You tek care, young'un.'

Ellie watched him go, emotion catching in her throat at his kindness hard on the heels of Will's anger, but then she became aware of the crunched-up newspaper, and she stuffed it into a nearby recycling bin.

'Right,' she said through gritted teeth. 'Enough, Will Farmer. It's about time I proved one thing: I can give as good as I get.'

Ellie wrapped her shawl more firmly around her shoulders and marched along the lane leading to the tidal beach and up the track to top.

There were no cars outside Marcus's cabin when she passed by, and Ellie sped through the gates marked 'Private', squelching through muddy puddles until the grassy track became a gravel driveway. The aroma of woodsmoke reached her, a pale grey spiral of smoke drifting from one of the cottage chimneys, swept aside by the stiff breeze on the clifftop.

Warm now from the exercise, Ellie tied the shawl around her waist, glaring at Will's filthy black car, parked at an angle by the woodshed. She stalked past it, determined to keep the fire inside burning and stoked, ready for a blazing row.

Ellie had never come this close to Peaches before, having merely skirted past on the path which pierced its way through the bracken-covered hillsides. It was a pretty building, whitewashed and with a slate roof. For all its obvious age, the windows looked new and the exterior well maintained.

Fetching up outside a stable door, the top half of which was hooked open, Ellie was suddenly uncertain of what to do next.

What now? Tap politely, as if she were a neighbour asking for a cup of sugar? Call 'cooee'?

Ellie suppressed a very unladylike snort. That would simply dilute her arrival. Banging the door with her fist three times, she unlatched the bottom half and stepped into the quarry-tiled porch. There were several timber-latch doors and a staircase winding upwards.

'Will!' she shouted. 'We need to talk!'

A clatter came from somewhere the other side of the far door, and Ellie stepped over, ready to hammer on that one too, but as she raised her fist, it swung open to reveal an ashen-faced Will.

'Why?' he barked, his glare pretty indicative of his present feelings.

'Because,' Ellie retorted, 'your tendency to assume the worst of me is continuing to lead you astray, and someone needs to help you see the truth.'

A fraught silence gripped the air between them for a moment, Ellie's body all but quivering with a combination of dread, anger and desire. Much as Will roused her ire at that moment, the love she bore for him yet again overrode every emotion and there was nothing she wanted more than to throw herself into his arms.

Except he'd probably stand aside and let her fall flat on her face.

Ellie suppressed the sudden urge to laugh, straightening her shoulders and fixing Will with a stern eye.

'Fine,' he bit out, standing back. 'You'd better come in.'

Ellie brushed past him, trying not to inhale his cologne. It almost worked.

The clatter appeared to be a poker, which lay across the hearth of a deep, inglenook fireplace. Logs crackled merrily and a warm glow emanated from several lamps. A laptop lay open on a coffee table which also accommodated a trug of autumn foliage and a stack of magazines. A squashy leather sofa was placed opposite the hearth, with two armchairs either side, and bookshelves lined both alcoves.

Turning her back on the cosy scene, Ellie tried to hold on to her annoyance.

'You can't fire me. I'm a self-employed contractor.'

Will glared at her, closing the door to the hallway and retrieving the poker to stoke the fire.

'Then our verbal agreement is at an end.' He shoved a few logs aside, reaching into a basket and tossing a new one on the top.

'But I haven't done anything!'

Will swung around, eyes flashing. 'Yet more lies.' He flung a newspaper down on the table, the same edition Ellie had just disposed of. 'Your photos,' he rasped, hitting the first image with the end of the poker. 'Taken on your camera.' He tapped the second. 'And the article quotes the locations they were taken. Who else has access to them?'

Ellie's mouth opened, then closed.

'Exactly!' Will snapped, folding his arms, the poker now sticking upwards like a sword, unaware he now had soot streaked across his shirt.

'Just because they are mine, from my camera, doesn't mean I sold them to the damn paper!' Ellie retaliated, leaning towards him. 'Why are you obsessed with assuming the worst of me?'

The last word was, to be fair, a tad high-pitched, and Ellie let out a huff of breath.

Damn him for riling her.

'Oh, I don't know,' he essayed, raising a mocking brow. 'Past experience, perhaps?'

'All of which is untrue! Why won't you believe me? You're prepared to accept anyone's word but mine. Seems like I'm not the one with the problem, Will!'

A growl escaped him as he unfolded his arms, but then Will noticed his soiled shirt. Ellie eyed the poker warily as it waved in the air between them as he inspected the damage.

'Sorry.' Putting the poker once more in its place, he gestured at the sofa. 'You may as well sit down. I'm sure we can shout at each other just as well in comfort.'

Will brushed ineffectually at the smear of soot, then dropped into one of the armchairs across the table from Ellie as she perched on the sofa's edge.

'Tell me what you *do* know,' he said firmly.

'I'm not blind to the fact they look like my photos, and the paper has me as the photo credit, but I have never been approached by any publication. Nor have I contacted anyone in the press.'

'And the fact they came from the walk the other day?'

Ellie was flummoxed. 'I honestly can't explain it. The laptop is password protected, with fingerprint sign in, two-factor authentication. I've been working in there for days, constantly editing and marking up the best ones for you to consider.' The anger was spent. She had no desire to argue with Will, and much as she hated his constant doubts about her honesty, as much as it pained her, she simply didn't want the fight to defend her business integrity. 'Why? What would I gain from doing this?'

Will raised a mocking brow. 'Money?'

'Don't be ridiculous,' Ellie bit out. Then, a thought slid into place. 'I wonder if this is all part of the same game…'

Will's dark eyes scanned Ellie's features, his brow furrowed, and he leaned forward, elbows on his knees, curiosity replacing the earlier anger. 'What game?'

Ellie got up. It was easier to think if she wasn't looking at Will, so she walked over to the sash window, which afforded a stunning view of the ocean above the sea of bracken. Wrapping her arms around her middle, she swung around, surprised to find Will had risen to his feet too.

'Things keep happening. Odd things. I started to wonder if someone was simply being mean, but the pieces suggest the puzzle is more complex. It's as though my small businesses are being attacked by an invisible hand. Nasty comments, negative reviews, but not from any known customer. Thwarting my attempts to promote. But why?' She held up both hands, palms up, then lowered them. 'I'm a photographer. I do weddings, events, portraits and school photos. I'm making the most innocent of personalised cards, celebrating a baby's birth, milestone events, Christmas cards. And now this. Someone, somehow, has managed to steal some images they can't possibly have had access to and sold them to a paper in my name.'

Ellie's voice cracked on the last word. It hurt, it truly did, that there was enough hatred out there somewhere for this to be happening. Emotion was rising in her chest, and her throat had all but closed. Will thought she was a liar, that she'd done this to him. Believed it without question. Struggling for breath, she shot towards the door.

'Got to go,' she managed to gasp out, dashing from the room and almost running down the driveway, ears stretched in the hope Will would call her back, or follow, but when she reached the gate, she glanced over her shoulder.

There was no one in sight, no movement beyond the seagulls wheeling against a vivid blue sky and a plume of smoke drifting into the air before fading away.

-

Friday rolled around, and Ellie was torn over whether she felt relief or despair Will hadn't made any further attempt at contact.

As this led her down a frustrating path of delusion she'd travelled before, she resolutely turned her back on thoughts of the man, determined instead to look forward to a girly evening at Kate's. With Bella finally back, ready to pack up her things at the cottage, it would be a full house, and thankfully, nothing had happened to upset their careful arrangements.

With Liam and Jason at Westerleigh for the night, Ellie set off for Harbourwatch with a positive stride, Nicki and an excited Anna by her side.

'How's Oliver feeling about being in charge tonight?' Ellie asked as they approached The Lugger, whose lights shone like a beacon in the gathering darkness.

'He's an old hand at putting the twins to bed. It's just I so rarely have a night out without him.' Anna sent Ellie an impish look as they crossed the bridge, their shadows long in the lamplight. 'To be honest, I think Oliver's not sure whether he should worry more about how to keep Nicki's boys happy when he hasn't a clue about gaming, or about my finding my way home afterwards.'

Ellie laughed, knowing full well Anna was hardly the misbehaving type. She was the glue that held them all together.

'Oh, did you hear what happened with Mrs L?' Anna added.

'No! Please tell me she didn't have an accident on that scooter!'

Anna grinned as they walked along the front. 'According to Gemma, Matt had worked out there was a journo in the cove, posing as a dog walker, easing the locals into cosy natter but actually trying to tease out information on Will and his whereabouts.'

Skin prickling, Ellie shot Anna a wary look. Would Will blame her for this as well?

'So what happened?' Nicki asked as they came to a halt outside the Spar.

'He sent Mrs L in her direction.'

Appalled, Ellie stared at Anna. 'Oh no! Not one of Polkerran Point's greatest gossips.'

'You forget,' Nicki cautioned as they entered the shop. 'The cove has more than protective rocks. Mrs L is part of our hidden harbour patrol! I defy anyone not in the know to get any sense out of that woman when she's on duty!'

Only half-reassured this wouldn't become another issue for Will, Ellie tried to forget it as they stopped to collect Bella before resuming their walk along the lane towards Harbourwatch.

'It's a shame Gemma's away,' Nicki mused. 'Oh, how's the trip going?'

'They're loving it.' Anna's tone was subdued, and the others exchanged a puzzled look. 'I'm just worried… Oh, take no notice of me.' She shook her head, but as she turned to move on, Bella grabbed her arm.

'Hey, don't leave us hanging! Don't tell me they're having problems? They always seem so happy.'

'Oh, no! No, it's not that.' Anna's hazel eyes shone as they approached the tall, wrought-iron gates of Harbourwatch. 'I'm being silly. And a bit selfish.' She lowered her voice. 'Matty's going to propose when they get to Milan. It's where Gemma had been heading when her travels came to an abrupt end last year, and she was forced to come home. Without that, she'd never have met him. He felt it would be a nicer memory for her.'

'That's wonderful!' Ellie exclaimed. 'Why does that make you sad or selfish?'

'Matty gets restless. I think it stems from all those years of touring with the band when he was younger. I worry they'll find the perfect place on one of these trips and decide to stay there.'

'Nonsense,' Nicki declared. 'They've found their haven; it's a secluded creek on a tidal inlet.'

'And each other,' Ellie added. 'Besides, didn't Gemma say when they were leaving that she already couldn't wait to come home?'

Anna summoned a watery smile, and Nicki clapped her hands.

'Good. Now, let's get inside and open this wine.'

Ellie made to follow them, then became aware of someone walking up the lane from the tidal beach. In the gloom, it was hard to see who it was at first, but as the glow from a nearby lamppost touched the leather cap, her heart began racing, and she made to hurry after the girls.

What was Will doing, lurking by the beach in the dark? Not having seen him since their row over the photos, Ellie had no desire for a repeat match, or a harsh stare from him as he passed by.

'Ellie, wait.'

Will's voice was low, vibrant with emotion. Was he still angry?

Chapter Twenty-Eight

"Sweet Little Lies"

Conscious the others were approaching the steps to the front door, Ellie hesitated by the open gates.

'What?'

Will removed the hat, turning his head aside and running a hand round the back of his neck. Then he huffed out a breath, meeting her eyes with his own. 'I'm sorry about... the last time we met. I wasn't expecting to see the photos, but you're right. You gain nothing by doing it. Someone did, though, and I've been hiding out since. A couple of the fan groups are rumoured to be scouting around, and I'd prefer it if they never found me.'

Ellie frowned. 'How did you know I'd be here? Now?'

'Oliver. I phoned him earlier about something, and he mentioned you were all coming over to Kate's. I wasn't sure you'd take a call, so...' He raised a hand, then it fell to his side.

Was he sorry about what he'd said, though?

Ellie remained silent, uncertain how to play this. Should she just say, 'okay, thanks'? Should she say sorry too – but for what?

'Look, I'm—'

'Ellie! Come on!' Nicki's voice clattered into the moment.

'I er… I have to go.'

Ellie turned away, but her reluctance must have been obvious because Nicki suddenly appeared at her side, tucking an arm through her cousin's and all but dragging her to join the others, then tugging on the old-fashioned bell pull.

'He doesn't deserve your time or attention, love,' Nicki muttered, then assumed a smile as the door swung open to reveal a beaming Kate.

'Come on in. The place is ours for the night!'

Ellie's simmering excitement wasn't for Kate's declaration as they followed her down the hallway. Will was hard to interpret these days, a conflicting mixture of sincerity vying with his blatant lingering resentment, but there had been something about the intensity of those few moments outside. The fact he'd come all this way to try and catch her, that he'd used the word 'sorry', that he believed her – over the photos, at least – wrapped Ellie in a cocoon of contentment. It might not last, but for now, she'd take it.

'Come on, slow coach,' Kate called, and Ellie smiled and sped up to join the others.

They started with cocktails in the lovely central room with the glass ceiling. Dusk had completed casting its mantle, and candles burned in wall sconces and on the mantelpiece, below which a warm glow emanated from the hearth.

'This is such a gorgeous room,' Ellie murmured, smiling her thanks as Kate handed over a Cosmo. Boy, did she need this! Her heart was still playing ping pong with her ribcage.

'Wait until you see the drawing room.' Nicki grinned before taking a sip of her cocktail. 'Yummy. Thanks, Kate.'

'What drew Dev off to London at such short notice?' Anna took a seat at the large dining table as everyone settled around her.

'Dev wanted to go with Grandy for his next check-up, to get a handle on things.' Kate's features filled with sadness. 'We know he's not going to get better, but he's so much more… at ease since he came back here.'

They solemnly raised their glasses to the elderly gentleman, and the conversation moved naturally on to Hamish and his recovery, and then on to the children, after which Kate led them into the warm and inviting kitchen.

'We could have eaten at the big table in there.' She gestured back along the hallway. 'But this felt better.'

'It's perfect.' Anna hugged Kate, then hurried over to peer into the pots on the stove. 'This is much more informal.'

They dined, amidst much laughter, on grilled chicken with a Greek salad and garlic roasted potatoes, followed by a sumptuous pavlova.

'Wow. That's another one gone.' Kate tossed a second bottle of wine into the recycling with a laugh. 'I fear for my head in the morning!'

'We've only had half a bottle each,' Nicki protested, opening another. 'And we all know the way back home.'

Ellie had relaxed after her first drink. Anna and Kate were such fun and lovely company, Bella was a scream, the food had been yummy, and Nicki had always been able to make her laugh at herself while still letting her know she understood.

Inexplicably, Will flashed into her mind, and Ellie drew in a sharp breath, placing her glass on the table. It was a memory of seeing him the first time when she finally managed to extricate him from that ridiculous outfit; of his youthful good looks, the flash of his smile, those dark eyes boring into hers…

That was unexpected, she mused.

As was the direction of the conversation once they retired to the drawing room.

'Oh my God, this is a dream,' Ellie exclaimed as they entered the square room with its pairs of narrow arched windows facing outwards on three sides, each affording a different view of either the harbour, the bay or the open sea.

Another grand hearth blazed with a warming fire, a glittering chandelier hung from the centre of a beautiful central rose and wall lamps glowed. There was an abundance of elegant furniture interspersed with comfier sofas and side tables, and soon they were settled on two of these on either side of the fireplace, each clasping another glass of wine.

'So,' Bella addressed Ellie. 'What was up with Will earlier?'

Ellie leaned forward to place her glass on a coaster with an unsteady hand.

'Don't you get on?' Kate laughed. 'Dev and I didn't exactly hit it off the first few times we met.'

Unsure what to say, Ellie's gaze darted around, landing on her cousin by her side.

'They have history,' Nicki said, placing a comforting hand on Ellie's arm. 'But it's ancient, not modern.'

'The tensions look quite current.' Kate put a hand to her mouth, her expression mortified as she saw the emotion flooding Ellie's features. 'I'm so sorry! I've touched a nerve, haven't I? I didn't mean to.'

Conscious of Anna's compassionate expression, Bella's encouraging smile, Nicki's comforting hand and Kate's genuine concern — oh, and the wine — Ellie did later concede the wine *may* have been a factor — she decided to open up.

'Please don't worry,' she reassured Kate. 'It's hardly public knowledge. Even Nicki doesn't know the whole story.'

Nicki pretended to bristle, then reached over to hug Ellie. 'You don't need to tell us anything.'

Anna nodded. 'Yes, let's change the subject.'

Ellie, however, shook her head. 'No.' She spoke clearly, firmly. 'It *is* old history, and I'm letting it get to me. I buried it deep, but seeing Will again has brought the memories flooding back. The good and the bad.' She drew in a short breath. 'So here goes.'

Awash with a myriad of sensations as the memories flooded in, Ellie recounted the essence of how she and Will met and fell in love.

'We became inseparable for the rest of the summer.' Ellie sent her cousin a small smile. 'And I wasn't the only one who caught the love bug.'

'Don't look at me,' Nicki trilled, sipping her wine. 'Bella was as bad once she'd seen Alex.'

Bella merely rolled her eyes but Nicki's look was sheepish. 'I really fancied Alex when I first met him. Mind you, he turned out to be a tool. Still is. Sorry Bella.'

Bella gave a throaty giggle. 'Don't mind me.'

Ellie's brow furrowed. 'I thought I remembered you being with him at that party at the manor.'

Nicki laughed, but it sounded hollow. 'We were. Until Bella walked in. It was like one of those cartoons, where the character's jaw hits the floor and the eyes pop out.

Not that I cared.' Her expression became dreamy. 'I left the party to meet Hamish, and since we got together, I've never looked back. What can I say. Posh college boy or hunky fisherman? No contest for me.' Then, she sobered. 'It's probably why I wasn't paying much attention to what was going on around me. I mean, I knew you and Alex were pretty much joined at the hip that summer, Bella. And Ellie being with Will, but none of you were around much once paired up.'

'We walked. For miles.' Ellie's expression became wistful too. 'Along the coast path, discovering a secluded beach. And…' she hesitated, then added, 'on my twenty-first – it was about a week before we had to leave Cornwall behind – he proposed.'

'What?' Nicki sat up so fast, she almost spilled her wine. 'You never told me *that*!'

Nicki exchanged a stunned look with Bella, who had gone strangely pale. 'I thought you were just… having some summer fun, you know, like we all were. Dating but with no great intentions.'

'You were so busy battling with your parents over refusing to return home, determined to stay with Hamish, you were pretty oblivious to anything else.'

'So what went wrong?' Anna asked quietly, her expression pensive.

Ellie sighed. 'We kept it to ourselves. No one but Will and I were to know until we'd told our parents.' She clasped her hands. 'Mum and Dad did everything to persuade me away from the commitment. I was too young, still in education. I said I'd postpone the masters, but the guilt was awful. They'd scrimped and saved to put me through uni. They were worried. Acting was an unstable career. Will had pretty much no income. We barely knew each other. What was two months? And so it went on.'

There was silence as four pairs of eyes stared at Ellie with varying degrees of empathy.

'What happened?' Anna's voice was a mere whisper.

Ellie swallowed hard on the lump forming in her throat. 'I had no doubts about my love for Will. But I'd be a fool if I couldn't see some sense in their advice.'

'You ended it!' Kate exclaimed. 'Oh no!'

Ellie lowered her head, staring at her clasped hands. Then she lifted her chin. 'There's more. His agent had secured him an amazing role in a film in Australia – Will was excited at first.'

Ellie turned despairing eyes on the others as the gut-wrenching pain returned as though it was yesterday. 'He declared we could make it work; he'd turn the role down and keep looking. It was madness. The type of job every actor dreams of and—' She stopped, trying to swallow again, and Bella leaned over to top up her glass.

'I realised the best thing I could do for Will was to let him go – for his sake, not mine. I dreaded he might one day come to resent me.' She lowered her head, awash with the tendrils of grief reaching out to draw her back in time. 'I cited the family opposition, said I had to do what was right by my parents. We had to end the engagement. The masters had to come first. When he realised I was adamant, he was livid. So angry, and he just stormed off.'

The pain was agonisingly fresh as Nicki hugged Ellie again.

'And was that it?' Kate looked appalled. 'I'm so insens-itive, Ellie. Please forgive me.'

'There's no need,' Ellie reassured her. 'You didn't know any of this.'

'You are the least insensitive person I know,' Anna added, taking Kate's hand and squeezing it.

'But *was* that it?' Nicki persisted.

'No. I couldn't bear the torment of seeing Will so hurt. I understood my parents' reasoning, but I was young and so much in love. Why couldn't we do both, Will take the role and me defer the masters? I could follow him once I'd got a visa.'

Ellie quickly related how she'd come to this conclusion during a sleepless night, tried to contact Will but hit a block every time, until she recalled the email address.

There was a collective holding of breath. Ellie's gaze moved from her cousin to Bella, whose expression was unreadable, then on to a sympathetic Kate and Anna.

She stumbled on a weak laugh. 'Lordy, it was an outpouring! I told him everything, how I'd been stupid, that I loved him more than anything. I'd go with him, anywhere in the world, if only he'd give me another chance.'

'Oh my God,' Anna whispered, a hand to her throat and tears shining on her lashes. 'It's a bit like *Persuasion*.'

'If only.' Ellie felt broken all over again. 'There's no happy ending here.'

'What did he say in response?'

'Nothing. I never got a reply to the email.'

'Maybe he didn't receive it,' Bella offered, but even she sounded disbelieving.

'I had a read receipt.'

'Then he can't have loved you enough,' Kate declared.

'Agreed,' Nicki added, draining her glass. 'I told you he didn't deserve you.'

'There's more.' Ellie confessed. 'I went up to London to try to see him. It must have been late October.' Dark memories were crowding in on her, and she drew in a short breath. 'I was told Will had already gone to Australia, flown the day before. What was more, Will had moved on emotionally too, was seeing someone else, one of the production assistants on the film. She'd been on the same flight with him. The message couldn't have been clearer. Still—' Ellie summoned a smile as she looked around at the supportive faces. 'It was the closure I thought I needed. I tried to move on, but no one was ever enough. I haven't found love since. Not as I'd known it.'

There was an awed silence. Anna dabbed at her eyes, and Kate sniffed as she reached under the table to produce a box of tissues.

'Who was it?' Bella's voice was harsh as she moved to the edge of her seat, staring across the low table at Ellie. 'Who told you Will had moved on?'

Ellie bit her lip, but Bella's razor-sharp eyes held Ellie's with fierce determination.

'Alex Tremayne.'

But it wasn't his fault was it, Ellie mused to herself as the drinks were topped up and the conversation moved to other things. Alex was just the messenger, and just because Ellie didn't like what he'd told her, it was hardly his fault.

Chapter Twenty-Nine

"Rain Man"

The weather had turned, with a storm forecast. Dark skies and sudden bursts of wind greeted Ellie as she loaded Fifi, grateful for Mrs Tremayne's agreement to the second mini-session taking place indoors at the manor stables.

Before Ellie went there, however, she parked in town to pick up a sandwich, then spotted some familiar faces gathered in the lane by the former gatehouse – one of the properties now in Oliver's portfolio, along with the adjacent run of almshouses.

Heading over, she waved a greeting. 'Morning.'

'Alright, my lover? 'Tis a proper job they'm about.' Old Patrick gestured at the scaffolding erected around both buildings.

'Master Oliver must have plans,' Mrs Clegg announced from her chair.

'Talking of plans,' Ellie mused, as her eye scanned the bulging bag on the lady's lap and a second in Pat's hand, 'are you off somewhere?'

'Ah.' Ryther – who'd been talking to one of the scaffolders – walked over to join Ellie. 'These reprobates are off to catch the village bus over to Fowey. There's an open call for extras on this production. All ages welcome. Pat.'

He addressed the elderly man, who had begun ushering Mrs Lovelace and Mrs Clegg along the path.

'Wasson?'

'Why the bags?'

Mrs Lovelace stopped beside Ryther. 'They's changes of clothes. Bring some along, the sheet said. Come on, Cleggie. Best get on dreckly or we'm missing that bus.'

Ellie eyed them all with curiosity. 'But why are you wearing those?'

All three had weathered leather camera cases slung around their necks.

Mrs Lovelace tapped her nose. 'Come camera ready, they says.'

'Aye,' Pat grunted as he pushed the wheelchair towards the bus stop. 'Reckons we stand a gurt chance with these bewdies.'

'Oh, but I don't think it means…' Ellie's voice trailed away as it fell on their backs as they moved along the lane, and she exchanged a worried look with an amused Ryther.

'You have to wish the casting director luck,' he mused before following slowly behind the others.

Once up at the manor for the mini-shoot, there were ample features for backdrops, with stone walls, arched windows and wooden trugs of flowers still containing the last rose blooms. All Ellie needed to do was set up her lighting and she was ready to go.

She completed the sessions on a high, despite being exhausted, relieved to finally load her equipment into the car and head back to Westerleigh.

Once she'd completed her routine with the batteries, hard drive and memory cards, Ellie firmly closed the door on the orangery to ensure Heathcliff didn't try to help and headed upstairs for a soak in the beautiful, claw-foot bath in the main bathroom.

Warmed through, Ellie left her hair to dry naturally, donning some soft trousers and a favourite but well-worn T-shirt before being enticed down to the kitchen by the tempting smells drifting up the stairs.

'Dinner will be a few hours yet,' Anna called as Ellie entered the kitchen. 'Fancy a drink to warm you up? I'm just doing a coffee for Oliver.'

'I could do with some water, to be honest.' Ellie added several lumps of ice to the glass, then took a seat at the table, scrolling through her inbox on her phone. 'Where are the babies?'

Anna pointed to the ceiling. 'Wore themselves out at baby and toddler group today, so both decided to have a pre-dinner nap. How was the shoot?'

'Wet, but thankfully, we were inside.'

They both looked over at a firm knock on the boot room door, and as Oliver was passing, he opened it to reveal Will.

Raindrops sparkled on his shoulders and the leather cap, which he removed, brushing a hand through his hair.

'Come on in.' Oliver stepped back.

Her heartbeat picking up a notch, Ellie made to stand, but Anna placed a surprisingly firm hand on her arm.

'It will look like you still care,' she said quietly. 'Act as if it's the most normal thing.'

Anna had a point, so Ellie took a hefty swig of water. The cooling liquid shot down her throat, and she coughed, putting a hand to her mouth as Anna turned a warm smile on the visitor.

'Come and join us, Will. We're just making coffee.'

'I… er…' Will's gaze found Ellie's. 'It's Ellie I came to see. If that's alright?'

'How lovely,' Anna said brightly. 'I'll make you a coffee first, then you can have her all to yourself.'

To Ellie's alarm, Anna headed for the machine, casting Oliver a meaningful look. He narrowed his eyes, looking from Will to Ellie, then back to his wife, who suggested he get the mugs out.

Will took a seat opposite, his attention fixed on the window, down which the rain continued to pour. His fascination with the weather was both a blessing and a curse, as it meant Ellie could admire his profile at leisure, with no fear of being caught out. Today, he wore a linen shirt under a designer zipper, the neckline turned up and caressing his jawline, damp tendrils resting on his collar.

Her heart had begun its habitual silly prance, but before anything could be said, Anna brought Will a steaming mug of coffee and a plate of home-made shortbread.

'Ellie says she got some great photos on the walk to Polridmouth. I wish I could've come with you. It's one of my favourite places in Cornwall.'

Oliver eyed Anna with affection. 'Everywhere is your favourite place in Cornwall.'

His wife merely smiled, taking his hand. 'Excuse us. Oliver needs to get back to work and I'd best go up and check on the twins.'

Left alone, the silence between them swelled, but as Will had said he'd wanted to see her, Ellie decided to wait, reaching for her glass, unprepared for him turning suddenly in his seat.

Rocked by the tortured expression which flashed across his features, she sank back into her chair, the glass of water all but forgotten.

He cleared his throat, and the despair in his dark eyes faded as swiftly as it had come.

'I... er, when will you have some of the photos for me? I'm working on my pieces to camera, so could do with a feel for the best spots. I'd heard you might be leaving soon.'

'Oh.' Not sure who'd shared that little gem, Ellie drew in a shallow breath. 'They're done. I wasn't sure...'

After our last conversation about photos, I didn't feel like rushing into another one...

If Will's unsettled air was anything to go by, he was thinking the same thing.

'Well, I won't go until I've completed the job,' she continued. 'I mean, jobs. I have to edit today's shoot, and I'm finishing up the photography for Tremayne Manor. Umm—' Ellie felt awkward, keen to end the moment. 'Hold on.' She pushed her chair back and shot into the orangery to check the download, relieved to see it was complete. 'Okay.' She popped her head back around the door. 'Do you have time to do it now? You might want to bring a chair,' Ellie suggested, heading back to her own and selecting the necessary folder.

Placing a chair next to hers, Ellie caught her breath as Will's arm connected with hers.

Grabbing the mouse, she opened the folder.

'So—' Why did her voice sound so high? 'Which would you like to see first?' She indicated the labels on each icon.

'Scenery, please.'

Ellie clamped her knees together, wary her leg might accidentally brush against Will's, he was seated so close to her.

The images loaded, and she moved the keyboard and mouse across. 'Just tap on the arrows there to go forward and back. See what you think.'

Silence fell as Will did as instructed, and Ellie's gaze sank to her lap where her hands appeared to be twisting her poor old T-shirt into a ball.

Setting it free, she put her right hand on the table, but instantly became aware of Will's left – still bearing the remnants of a summer tan – resting beside it.

He had long fingers – a sign of creativity, she'd always teased him. Those hands had lovingly held hers as they'd walked the cliff path, lain on the secluded beach or strolled to the pub at the end of a beautiful day on that long-lost summer. Will's hands had pressed her close as he'd kissed her the first time, stroked her skin as he'd made love to her, touched her in a way she'd never forgotten.

Heat spread throughout Ellie's body, and she swallowed hard, finding it impossible to stop staring at Will's hands as he closed the folder and opened the one saved as 'Possible PtoC'.

'I'm sorry.'

Ellie's startled eyes flew to meet Will's as he shot her a quick glance before resuming his study of the screen. 'I meant what I said outside Harbourwatch. I shouldn't have said what I did about those photos. I do believe you, Ellie, even though we can't explain it. Seems to be a theme with us.' He huffed slightly on a laugh. 'I'm as in the dark as you about why anyone would either wish to damage your work or steal from you, but we're far more likely to create a full picture with two heads, not one. Just tell me what you need.'

Focusing on regaining a regular breathing pattern, Ellie took in Will's words, expressed with genuine warmth, and she could have wept at how much she wished she could turn her head into his chest, have his arms come around her, comfort her properly. But this lifeline would have to suffice, and she'd gladly take hold of it.

'I want a friend,' she whispered, her breath then catching in her throat as Will's head turned towards her again.

Ellie summoned a wobbly smile. 'I just need a friend to help me sort this out.'

Will held her tremulous gaze for a moment, then he nodded.

'Deal.'

He reached out his hand. Ellie stalled, then tentatively offered her own, and he clasped it firmly. Heat shot through her body, and she tried to will away the colour she knew would follow. Will said nothing, but nor did he release Ellie's hand.

Was he drawing her closer? No, he couldn't be... *could* he?

A sudden sound caused them both to start as Anna opened the door to the orangery.

'Sorry to disturb. Ellie, Marcus is here.'

Chapter Thirty

"You've Got Mail"

Ellie all but rolled her eyes. What was it today with men not using their phones? Then a thought struck her, and she tugged it out of her pocket.

'Damn it,' she muttered.

'Dead again?' Anna asked as Ellie followed her into the sitting room, conscious as she left of Will's stillness.

'Hey, Ellie.' Marcus beamed at her from by the island. 'Sorry, couldn't get through on the phone, so thought I'd stop by on my way to Looe.'

A wail came from the baby monitor.

'That sounds like Bertie.' Anna excused herself, disappearing into the hall.

'My battery died. Is something wrong?'

'No. It's the opposite. Phyllida... she... I... we're a couple! I wanted you to be the first to know.'

Ellie threw her arms around him. 'I'm so happy, Marcus. The best possible news.'

'It's all thanks to you.' Marcus hugged her back. 'Look, I'd best go. Don't want to be late for the girls.'

They headed for the door into the hall, but Marcus stopped and turned to face Ellie, his face serious, then took her hands in his.

'I want you to know,' he said quietly, 'that although we've only been friends for a few months, you've given me the impetus to change my life, and I'll be forever grateful.'

He pressed a firm kiss on Ellie's cheek, and impulsively, she did the same to him.

'I'm so happy,' she exclaimed, emotion welling behind her eyes.

Returning to the kitchen after waving Marcus off in his car – Anna following, with Bertie in her arms – Ellie was surprised to see Will picking up his cap from the chair in the sitting room.

'Oh. Did you see all you wanted to?'

He said nothing for a moment, and Ellie's brow furrowed. Was he displeased with her work?

'Yes. I think I've seen enough.'

He opened the boot room door, called his thanks to Anna for the coffee and – fixing his hat into place – reached for his coat.

'But—' Ellie hesitated. 'What do you want me to do with them? I can file share the folders or send you specific images.'

She was speaking to the air as the outer door shut on Will's back, and she walked slowly back into the kitchen, closing the door in confusion.

Anna came to stand beside Ellie, Bertie on her hip. 'Jane Austen once wrote that friendship is the finest balm for the pangs of disappointed love.' Ellie drew in a short breath as Anna added, 'Unless it's misinterpreted. That's my addition, by the way.'

With that, she turned away, and Ellie walked as though in a trance back to the orangery, sinking into Will's vacated chair and staring at the screen of folders.

What now?

The following morning, Ellie was on tenterhooks, wondering if Will might get in touch, and when a notification pinged, hope sprang to life, only to sink back into place as she realised it was from the newspaper.

They were returning the two photos they'd been sent. They were unable to divulge the email address that had been used because of data protection, and with the dead ends over the anonymous posts on socials, she wasn't sure teaming up with Will would achieve anything.

But it helps. Like Anna said, it's a balm.

Opening the returned images, Ellie put them side by side.

The one of Will was possibly her favourite of all the ones she'd taken, the other photo being a portrait image of him by the cottage at Polridmouth Bay. The walk seemed an age ago now. She peered a little closer, rubbing at what looked like a mark on the screen, then rummaged around on the table, in the drawers below the small bookcase and in her bag.

Where was her screen cleaner? She opened her camera bag, then let out an exclamation.

'I'd forgotten about you.' Ellie picked up the spare memory card tucked into a side pocket, setting up the hard drive and leaving it to download. She'd clean her screen later.

Leaving it to do its thing, she made a cup of tea, settling at the island with her iPad. The house was quiet while Anna was out with the twins and Oliver was up in his den, and with time to kill, and Will firmly in the forefront of her mind after their tentative rapprochement, she began scrolling back through her sent items again.

Ellie eventually reached the year in question and, tummy clenched in anticipation, she slowed her scrolling. Not recalling the email address was a hindrance, but she'd never forget the date they'd split up. The email had been sent the next day.

Her heart dipped and rose in swift succession when she found it. She wasn't going mad, and she hadn't dreamt it. Here was the proof, in black and white... but Will was adamant he hadn't received it back then, and he'd checked recently too. If he wasn't lying, what on earth had happened?

'Right.' Ellie hit 'Print', then shot into the orangery, staring in fixed fascination as not one, not two but three pages slowly emerged. She'd not been wrong about the length!

Skimming through it as she returned to the island, a sense of dread and discomfort swelled within Ellie. The reminder of how she'd felt as she frantically typed those words and sent them off in the hope it would help Will understand – forgive her – brought feelings of regret and distress, and she carefully folded the pages, tucking them into her bag, feeling slightly nauseous.

What was the point? Another week and she'd be free to leave. Any remaining editing could be done from Oxford, and her time in Polkerran Point would be ended. Finished. Over...

'Thank goodness you're here!'

Ellie started as Anna burst into the kitchen.

'Oh my God! What's wrong? Is it the twins? Where are they?'

'Asleep in the buggy outside, although how they stayed that way with the speed I just ran up the lane with them... Look, it's Will.'

A hand shot to Ellie's throat, her skin tingling in dread. 'What's happened to him?'

'Nothing,' Anna said breathily, leaning on the island. 'Nor is it likely to, the way you two are carrying on.'

'I don't understand...'

'I saw Kate in town. She's been trying to call you but it's going straight to voicemail.'

'My phone's on charge.'

'Please go and check it. Now.'

Puzzled, Ellie opened the door to the orangery, heading over to the charging station and picking up her phone. Three missed calls and two WhatsApp messages...

Wandering back into the sitting room, she could see the missed calls were from Kate – as was one of the messages. The other was from Will.

Heart thudding loudly, Ellie's head shot up to meet Anna's steady look.

'Listen to your messages. Hopefully it's not too late.'

'For what?'

'To catch Will before he leaves.'

'Where's he going? He never said anything yester—'

'Back to London. He'd been round to let Dev know the cottage would be empty for a while. Kate saw him as he was leaving, on his way to load the car up. She got the impression he's going away until you've returned home.'

Ouch!

Ellie's legs weren't prepared to support her, and she collapsed onto the nearest chair.

'But... but we...' She raised tortured eyes to Anna. 'We'd become friends. I thought. He said we—'

'Ellie, love.' Anna took the adjacent chair. 'I suspect Will believes you and Marcus are an item. Kate said she didn't think his parting comment was meant to be heard,

275

but she's absolutely certain he said, "there's nothing here for me now".'

Coldness pervaded Ellie's skin as her head dropped into her hands. 'No, no, no! I'm not... Marcus and I are *friends*. That's all it is.'

Hadn't she told Will that? Maybe not...

Anna's lips twitched. 'I'm not sure that's what Will thinks. Now check your messages. This is the twenty-first century, not a time when things can't easily be resolved.'

The small flicker of hope that had glimmered at times, flaring with expectation at others, stirred within Ellie, and she gave Anna a fierce hug before heading up the stairs with her phone.

Will's message was a voice note, beginning with him clearing his throat in that way he had.

Ellie almost couldn't breathe.

> *Hi. I wanted to say goodbye. Something's come up.*
> *So... I mean, yeah. File drop those folders. You'll*
> *be gone when I come back. Just wanted to say...*

There was another pause and... was that a muttered expletive?

> *I wish you all the best. I mean it. For the future.*
> *For your life. And...*

A slow, heavy sigh.

> *Be happy, Ells. Bye.*

The message ended, and Ellie's head spun with a heady mixture of confusion and hope. What on earth was this about? So what if Will thought she was with Marcus? Why would that bother him? Unless…

Desperate now to catch Will before he left, Ellie whizzed him a message – 'wait for me' – grabbed her bag and keys, called goodbye to Anna, and shot Fifi down the lane so fast she startled a couple of gulls sitting on the wall, and they rose noisily into the air. She drove more slowly up the track towards Peaches, as it had limited passing places, heart thumping in anticipation of coming nose to nose with Will's car as he made to leave.

'Please don't have gone yet,' she begged under her breath, and the sheer relief of seeing the car still in the driveway almost stole it away. Ellie brought Fifi neatly to a halt, effectively blocking him in.

It was a beautiful day for November, the sea the blue of a warm summer's day, with woolly clouds scattered over the vast blueness of the sky like sheep in the fields at the top of the cove. Ellie eyed the leather bag and coats in the back of the car with sadness, then approached the house, conscious of the lack of smoke from the chimney.

Barely had Ellie stepped over the threshold into the porch when Will came thundering down the stairs, only to grind to a halt as he saw her.

Calm down, she cautioned herself. *Friends, Will had said. Not 'throw yourself at me the next time we meet'.*

'What are you doing here?'

'Did you get my message? I got yours.'

Awkwardness filled his features. 'No. I— er… You'd best come in.'

He gestured to the sitting room, but Ellie ignored Will's invitation to take a seat, especially when he ran a hand round the back of his neck and paced across the room before turning around and repeating the action.

She studied him in confusion for a moment, then walked over and stepped in his path, effectively halting it.

'Will, what did your voice note mean?'

For what felt like an eternity, his rich, expressive eyes held her own. 'I think it was pretty obvious.'

Men!

Come on, girl. It's time to be brave.

'Is this about my friend, Marcus?'

The discomfort filling Will's features was all the answer she needed and, courage rising, she took a step towards him.

'We're not an item, Will.'

'But I've seen you with him so many times, you always look so happy.' He scanned her face, with tortured eyes. 'Are you—' Will swallowed visibly. 'I thought you'd fallen in love with him.'

Ellie began to shake her head. 'No. I mean, yes. I do love him, but purely as a friend. That's it. Friends, Will. He's delighted to be dating someone he's liked for a very long time. That's what he came to tell me yesterday.'

Will's eyes closed as he released a long breath. Then, he swung around and walked over to the window, staring out.

'I've been a damned fool.'

Hope filtering through the confusion, Ellie recalled her earlier discovery and dug around in her bag.

'I found it. The email I sent you.'

Will's body stilled as she pulled it from the bag. Then, he turned slowly to face her, his gaze dropping to the pages she held out, then back to her face.

Walking over, Will took the pages from her. Then, without even glancing at them, he started to tear the paper into shreds.

Chapter Thirty-One

"Ever After"

'What are you doing? It's proof! It tells you everything about why I broke my own heart to do what I thought was right! How I realised my mistake within hours of you leaving, begged you to forgive me, to get in touch.'

'If the fire was lit, I'd burn it,' Will bit out, tossing the pieces of paper onto the sofa.

Ellie's mind was in turmoil, her heart quivering.

'Why?'

Will hadn't taken his eyes off her, and Ellie tried to modify her breathing, but it was as though someone had reduced the oxygen in the air around them.

'Because I've realised arguing about an email sent twelve years ago is futile.' He stalled, drew in a short breath, and she could see the pain of the past deep in his eyes. 'I tried to forget you, to move on, but something always held me back. I can't stop thinking about you, or what we had.'

Will's gaze burned into Ellie's, his face fully expressive of his turmoil. 'I'm in pieces, torn between hope and agony... but I'm scared to ask—'

'Ask me anything,' Ellie interrupted, her heart off on one of its capers again.

Only hurry up, or I'm just going to go for it.

'Your love…' He swallowed visibly. 'How you felt. Has it… have those precious feelings gone forever?'

Ellie took a step forward. 'I've borne them here,' she pressed a hand against her breastbone, 'for all this time. The love may have slumbered, but it never died.'

'Nor did mine for you.'

'You… you still love me? You…' She shook her head, disbelieving. 'You should have stuck with acting, Will. I'd never have known.'

Will started to laugh, but then he sobered, reaching out to capture both her hands in his. 'It was my own pig-headedness. If I'd only listened to you, trusted in you…'

Freeing a hand, Ellie placed a finger against his lips. 'Don't. If an ancient email doesn't matter, nor does anything else before this moment. Right here. Now.'

'If I hadn't blocked you— I'm an imbecile.'

Tendrils of delight began to circle around Ellie, wrapping her heart in a gentle, encouraging embrace. Her throat was tight, her eyes wide as she fought back tears.

'It's fine, Will,' she all but croaked. 'I don't blame you for being so angry you didn't want to hear from me.'

Will shook his head vehemently. 'You don't understand. My temper soon abated; my true emotion was gut-wrenching despair. Grief. I blocked you out of self-preservation.'

Ellie stared at him, confused. 'But—'

Taking her hands in his again, Will stepped nearer, holding her gaze intently. 'I couldn't bear the pain of knowing you'd never tried to contact me, of checking and checking and there being nothing. At the time, it made sense – it was an act of survival.'

'Oh,' Ellie managed to whisper as the enormity of the distress he'd endured hit home. 'I'm so sorry.'

The dark eyes holding Ellie's were the ones she remembered – warm and full of fire.

'It's done. In the past,' Will said softly, shuffling closer. 'But somehow, there are pleasanter things on my mind just now.'

He pulled Ellie into his arms, his mouth descending on hers, tentatively at first, as though he couldn't quite believe it, but then with increased urgency. Dormant sensations stirred within Ellie as her hands travelled to Will's shoulders, returning his kisses with equal fervour. *This* her body remembered.

Drawing the kiss to a close, Will dropped a trail of them across Ellie's cheek, then whispered in her ear, 'I feel like crying. I can't believe you still love me.'

His voice broke on the word 'love', and Ellie leaned back in his arms.

'Try.' Her lips curved upwards as his gaze met hers.

'After all this time… and the way I reacted to you.'

'Yes.' Ellie gave a rueful smile. 'Constancy appears to be my middle name.'

Will made a small sound. 'Idiocy seems to be mine.' She laughed shakily, but he shook his head. 'I have loved none but you, Ellie.'

Will silenced her with another kiss, but she couldn't help amusement rising in the midst of her delight, and he pulled back to look at her.

'What?'

'It tickles. You didn't have a beard when we were last kissing.'

'Nor did you,' he retorted as Ellie's amusement increased. 'I never forgot you. I meant to, but you had burrowed deep into my heart, and it wasn't prepared to let you go. Nor should *I* have been.' He rested the back of his hand against Ellie's soft cheek.

'Will? You there? We need to talk.'

They broke apart, staring at each other as Alex's voice permeated the air between them. A momentary fear gripped Ellie. Could history be about to repeat itself?

'I'll go,' Ellie reassured Will, even as he began to shake his head, but Alex had opened the door and stood on the threshold.

'Call me,' she whispered, kissing his cheek before stepping past Alex without looking at him.

'Put your damn phone on charge,' Will called, but then Alex closed the door, and Ellie shot outside, trying to comprehend everything that had happened in the last half-hour.

Alex's flashy sports car had pulled up behind Ellie's, thankfully leaving her enough room to extract Fifi, but as she opened the door, Bella emerged from Alex's car.

'Thank God you're here!' she exclaimed, throwing her arms around Ellie, who hugged her back in astonishment.

'But I thought you weren't coming back until next week? You were so vague the other day, and I—'

Bella put a finger to her lips, casting a swift glance towards the cottage.

'I told him to get in there.' She jabbed a finger towards Peaches. 'He's got some explaining to do, but I think it best he talk to Will on his own. He wanted me to go in with him, but I told him no way. Look.' Bella fixed Ellie with her keen amber eyes. 'Can I come and see you in a bit? There's something I need to say as well.'

Hoping Will would be calling later, Ellie bit her lip, then nodded. Bella seemed both earnest and, worryingly, anxious – a characteristic she rarely displayed.

'I'll be at Westerleigh for the rest of the day.'

She did, after all, have some daydreaming to do.

–

'You're back!' Anna greeted Ellie with enthusiasm as she entered the kitchen. 'And?'

Ellie dropped her bag on the island, walking over to watch Anna as she resumed mincing some vegetables. How could such mundane things be happening when she'd just been in Will's arms again, heard him say he still loved her?

Anna nudged her. 'You've gone pink.'

Smiling faintly, Ellie slid onto a stool. 'I keep trying to be cautious, in case things aren't what they seem, but there's definitely progress.'

Removing the lid, Anna stirred the mushy mixture, then looked up. 'What's holding you back?'

'Nothing on my side, but we were interrupted.'

'Oh no!' Anna exclaimed. 'Talk about bad timing!'

'It was Alex.'

Anna almost dropped her spatula. 'What's that man up to? Oliver took a call from him earlier, but he hasn't emerged from his den since. Oh.'

The door opened and Oliver came in.

'Our presence has been requested at some sort of summit. In our own home, no less.' His tone was dry, but Ellie suspected he wasn't much amused.

'Do you need me to go out? I could do with stretching my legs and I'll take—'

Oliver shook his head. 'No. I'm afraid you've been asked to be there too. Three thirty. Is that okay?'

Ellie exchanged a puzzled look with Anna, but Oliver's face remained impassive. Was that it?

284

'What's it about, Oliver?'

He shrugged at his wife. 'No idea. Tremayne requested it. Said he had things he wished to talk about.'

Anna looked thoughtful. 'Maybe he's got hidden depths.'

Oliver rolled his eyes, walking off to scoop Bertie into his arms as he tried to pull himself up on the sofa arm. 'We might need to call in Douggie's dredger to find them.'

Anna turned to Ellie. 'Has Will mentioned this?'

'No, but he's—' Ellie glanced at her phone as it pinged. 'Oh, hold on. This is him.'

Can you call me? It's urgent xx

Ellie hurried back into the orangery and closed the door as the call connected. Her heart had begun to pound, but not in a good way.

'Will? What's happened?'

'Alex.' His tone hardened. 'I could kill him!' Ellie blinked, but Will released a heavy sigh. 'Not really, but I'm sure you understand the sentiment. Look, he's just confessed to having done something which explains a lot. Twelve years, dammit! I loved you so much, Ells. Splitting up broke me in two.'

'What's Alex done?' Ellie's own voice sounded distant, as though it belonged to someone else, her mind flying towards the last time she'd seen Alex Tremayne back then. He may have been the one to tell her Will had already left, moved on, but he was trying to let her down gently…

A huff of breath. 'Can I come over? Alex said something as he left, about being at Westerleigh later, but I don't want you having to see him without me.'

'He's been in touch with Oliver. We're summoned to some sort of gathering here at half three. What's he done, Will? It's not to do with Bella, is it?'

A disgruntled sound came from Will. 'Not directly. Look, I'll fill you in when I see you. I've no idea what the idiot is up to now.'

'Well, there's safety in numbers.' Relief made Ellie's voice wobble.

'Hey.' Will's evident concern was almost too much after all this time. 'Ells, don't let this get to you. I'll come over a bit earlier, if Anna and Oliver don't mind.'

'They won't.' Ellie sniffed, then gave a watery laugh. 'They are the loveliest people.'

Three thirty couldn't come soon enough, whatever Alex Tremayne's purpose.

—

Ellie killed the time before Will arrived, trying not to overthink things and deciding to keep busy having another go at tidying up her workspace.

It was only when she discovered the missing pack of screen wipes tucked under the edge of the sofa that she recalled what she'd been doing earlier that morning, and tugging one out, she opened up her laptop, giving the screen a quick clean, then tilted it to see if the fingerprint smudge had gone.

She couldn't see it now, so she settled back at the table and logged in, the images from the newspaper still on the screen. Ellie's eyes narrowed as she tilted the screen.

The mark was back and— wait! It was in exactly the same place on *both* photos!

Ellie flopped back in her chair, staring at the images. Then she picked up the laptop and headed for the hall closet, closing the door. In totally blackness, the screen stood out starkly, and so did something else.

With a jolt of shock, she closed the laptop with a snap and groped for the door. 'These aren't my photos,' she muttered as she emerged into the hall again. 'At least, they *are*, but these are photos *of* the photos.'

Unable to get her head around what might have happened, it took all Ellie's willpower, when Will walked through the door at three o'clock, to not throw herself at him. Were they truly close to untangling the mistakes of the past, to finding a new future?

They escaped up to Ellie's attic room, but as she closed the door and leaned against it, Will swung around to face her, his face tortured.

Then, without warning, he swept her into his arms.

'I'm sorry,' he whispered, his chin resting on her head, holding Ellie close to his body as she tried to catch her breath, corral her capering mind. 'My God, Ells, I'm so *so* sorry.'

Brow furrowed, Ellie forced herself upright, leaning back in his arms to scan his contrite features.

'For what?'

Will didn't answer, steering her over to the bed and pulling Ellie down beside him. Her heart beating a hopeful tattoo, she watched as he entwined his fingers with hers, awash with memories of the past and the immediacy of this precious, present moment.

'Can you ever forgive me? For not hearing you out, back then or now? Damn it.' Will ran his free hand through his hair, leaving it in charming, tousled disarray.

Emboldened, despite her confusion, Ellie did what she'd longed to do, brushing his hair back into place with her hand, only for Will to capture it in his and bury his mouth in her palm.

'I thought we'd agreed to forget the past,' said Ellie. 'The missing email. All of it.'

'I've just heard the truth of it. From Alex.' He almost spat the name. 'We were both right. You sent an email, and I never saw it. Because *he* did. That's why you got a read receipt.'

Chapter Thirty-Two

"Tales of the Unexpected"

As the mundanity of the truth hit Ellie, she paled. 'How...' She swallowed hard. 'How did he get into your emails?'

'Exactly what I asked. Alex said he'd gone into my room at the house one morning to rant on about something, a few weeks after we'd left Cornwall behind. I hadn't told him we'd split up, it was too raw, having happened the day before, but he'd been in a right stew for days because Bella had dumped him. Foul mood, lashing out at everyone, drinking too much.'

Will put an arm around Ellie, and she rested her head on his shoulder, trying to take it in.

'I'd not slept, hadn't even wanted to get out of bed, so I'd only just gone for a shower, but my laptop was open on the desk. He saw a notification. An email from you. Just arrived. He says he skim-read it, got the gist – saw the read receipt flash up – then deleted them both.'

Ellie's heart shot upwards and so did her head, as she turned frantic eyes to meet Will's saddened features.

'If you hadn't left the room...'

He leaned forward, pressing a firm kiss against her quivering mouth.

'Don't, Ells.' He brushed away a shimmering tear, then drew her head back onto his shoulder.

'Would you have… read it?' she croaked out, closing her eyes in case the answer was unbearable.

'Without question.' Will's voice trembled. 'My anger had soon dissolved, swept away by such despair and longing. If I'd heard from you at any time in those endless weeks before I went away – if you'd found a way around my stupid idea to block you to tell me you'd changed your mind, that there was a chance…' He drew in a shaking breath. 'I just never dreamt it might happen. Damn, I was such an idiot, if only…'

His voice seemed to fail him, and sitting up, Ellie took Will's face in both her hands. She could barely speak herself, lashes wet with unshed tears. 'I love you so much. Please don't *ever* let me go again.'

Will lowered his mouth to Ellie's, kissing her gently at first, his hands moving to her waist, under her shirt and onto her back, pressing her close.

Ellie's kisses became feverish in return, the pent-up emotion of so many years, the missed opportunities, the hand fate had dealt them, pouring in, wave after wave.

As they drew apart, Ellie's cheeks damp from her tears, Will raised a hand to tuck a strand of hair behind her ear.

'There's something else.'

'I don't think I can take any more,' Ellie whispered.

'You said you came to London, but I'd gone abroad.'

'I did. Besides, Alex…' Ellie almost choked on the name as the enormity of lost time struck her. 'He told me you'd taken someone with you.'

Will's face was sufficient for the truth to be clear. 'Damn him. It's not true. I went alone.'

Confusion deepening, Ellie spoke hesitantly. 'But why… I mean, he was so nice to me. He could see how upset I was. He was on his way out, walked me to the end of the road, watched me catch the bus.'

Expression darkening, Will pursed his lips. Then his gaze narrowed. 'When was this, exactly? Do you remember?'

Ellie tried to think. 'End of October? Yes, I remember all the Hallowe'en decorations in the windows on your street. It was about a month after I sent the email. I longed to come earlier but I'd just started my master's and couldn't get away. I wish it had been sooner; I might have caught you before you left.'

'I didn't go to Australia until late November. The visa didn't come through before then.'

As the reality struck Ellie, her face crumpled, and unable to prevent the tears, Will wrapped her in his arms until the emotion was spent.

'All these years,' she quaked through shallow breaths. 'If I'd known you were still in London, I'd have waited. Stayed, until you heard me out.'

'And I'd have listened.'

The sound of the doorbell floating up the stairs caused them both to check the time.

Ellie drew in a short breath. 'It must be him.'

'Come on. Let's get this over with. Then we can start the rest of our lives.'

Ellie quickly repaired her face, and Will didn't release her hand as they fetched up by the kitchen door, but then he turned her to face him.

'I've still been a classic fool.' He pulled Ellie back into his arms, and she went willingly, resting her head against his chest as he stroked her hair. 'Fate threw you in my way, after all these years. What did I do? Act like a prize ass and not grasp the opportunity with grateful hands.'

Moved deeply by the emotion throbbing in Will's voice, Ellie lifted her head to look up at him, then raised her hand to caress the side of his face. 'But we both blamed the other, and with good reason. You weren't to know the truth, nor was I.'

He sighed, placing a hand over her own, and her skin tingled in anticipation at his touch. 'But your anger had dissipated. Despite what you believed, you never acted like a sulky little brat.'

A small sound escaped Ellie, and Will's lips twitched. 'I might have. Just not in front of you.'

–

The man who walked into Westerleigh Cottage that afternoon, Bella on his heels, was definitely Alex Tremayne, but it wasn't any version Ellie had yet seen, and judging by the confused expressions of those around her, they hadn't either.

Alex's golden tan had assumed a grey tinge, and while his arresting good looks were all present, his cocky, assured strut had dimmed.

Oliver took charge, taking Alex to his den while Anna did as she always did, setting out an array of home-made fare as the others busied themselves making pots of tea and coffee. Nicki – delighted to have a few days off to help get ready for the move to the other cottage – had taken the twins out in the double buggy to fetch the boys from school, so it was an adults-only assembly.

Bella wouldn't be drawn on anything when Ellie pressed her, merely asking that she wait to hear Alex out first.

It wasn't long before Oliver and Alex came back. Some of the latter's confidence seemed to have returned, although he still wouldn't meet Ellie's gaze, and she exchanged a look with Will, relieved to see he was struggling to hide a smile as he pulled out a chair for her.

A sudden growl came from the hearth, and Anna hurried over to stroke Dougal, who'd barred his teeth at the new arrival. Heathcliff wasn't in any mood to be consoled, however, scooting over to the cat flap into the boot room, hissing at Alex as she went.

'Alex and I have just had an interesting conversation,' Oliver began as everyone settled around the table. 'Which will remain between us, but let's just say, hostilities between Tremayne Estates and the Seymour Trust are on hold.'

'Permanently?' Anna essayed, her expression quizzical.

'We can hope,' Oliver concluded. 'Alex, you said you had a few other things to say?'

Alex got to his feet, looking around the table, but a pointed stare from Bella had him hastily reclaiming his seat.

'Yes. Of course. Sorry.' His look wasn't so much contrite as more humble than usual, and Ellie glanced at Will to find his gaze fixed intently on his old friend.

'This is long overdue,' Alex began, pausing to run a finger between his shirt collar and his neck. He cleared his throat, casting a fleeting look at Bella beside him, before his eyes roamed around the rapt faces staring back at him. 'I've an apology— ow!' He bent to rub at his ankle. 'Sorry. Apologies. Several of them. To make. For various…' he cast around for a word, and Bella did a good impression of a gangster, muttering 'transgressions' out of the side of her mouth.

Ellie's head dipped as she strove to conceal her amusement, only to see Will's hand reaching for hers. As his fingers encircled her own, her heart swelled, and she struggled to listen to Alex, thinking only of being alone with Will again once this show was over.

'I— er, I've spoken to Kate and Dev about last year. And Matt,' he added, addressing Anna, before turning to Will. 'I threw my toys out of the pram over a deal Matt secured for Oliver and took it out on the others by putting the village fayre at risk. It's all connected to a bit of a…' He huffed on a breath. 'Vendetta – is probably the best word – I waged with Oliver over the selling and purchasing of estate properties.'

Will's brow furrowed. 'Why, Alex? What's been driving it?'

Alex slumped back in his seat, then looked to Anna and Oliver. 'This is your home, and you've kindly allowed me in to try and sort things out, but I'd really like to talk to Will… and Ellie.' He threw a quick, culpable look towards her. 'In private.'

'Seems fair enough.' Oliver stood, Anna at his side. 'We'll talk more in a few days, Alex.'

'Yes, that would be great.' Alex sent Oliver a grateful smile.

'We'll go for a walk,' Anna said, tucking her arm into her husband's. 'See if we can find Nicki and the twins.'

A profound silence fell as the boot room door closed behind them, Dougal trotting at their heels. Then, Alex turned to Will as Ellie grasped his hand more tightly.

'You asked why. Stupidly, two things, but they're connected. I've always been a player. You know that, Will, from years ago. Not just at work, standing on anyone I could to get to the top, but in relationships as well. Too much attention from the fairer sex. Vanity working on a weak head produces every sort of mischief.' He stopped, drew in a short breath. 'Well, about six years ago, I brought my jaded temperament here, to the cove. A place I hated for everything it stood for, except there was a property.' He scanned the beautiful room. 'This one.'

He outlined how he'd been after securing it from the then owner, Meg, for a rich client desperate to own it, but she'd refused outright to sell. Frustrated by both the failure to earn a substantial commission and to force an elderly lady to do his bidding, he'd set out to gain it by other means – namely romancing the person who inherited it from Meg when she passed away: Anna.

'You're joking,' Will exclaimed. 'Please tell me you're making this up.'

'He's not,' Bella interjected. 'He told me all of this earlier. Oliver confirmed it to me.'

Struggling to take it in after everything she'd learned about Alex recently, Ellie busied herself pouring teas and coffees as Alex continued to outline how he'd started to feud with Oliver, who had around that time commenced his philanthropic property venture.

When Oliver and Anna had got together, and he'd moved into the house that had lost Alex so much – not just in terms of financial gain but in reputation and kudos at work – his resolve only hardened. Never would a Tremayne asset – several of which he'd sold off over subsequent years – benefit the community by becoming part of Oliver's property portfolio.

This had led to last year's spat with Matt, and by default, Dev and Kate.

Ellie's stunned gaze met Bella's resigned one, and the latter shook her head.

'I had no idea any of this had happened, Ellie. Like you, I vowed never to come back here after Alex and I split. Then, when Matt reached out a couple of years ago to help Oliver with his research, I decided to risk it. It had all been so long ago, and it seemed general knowledge that Alex still had an aversion to the cove.'

'What she didn't realise was that my father decided to retire last year,' Alex continued. 'Hand the estate over to me. I ended up coming back more than usual, and that's when I saw Bella again. The first time since that summer all those years ago.'

The look he sent Bella gave Ellie pause as her sympathies were unexpectedly roused. Whoever he was, whatever he'd done, one thing was clear: Alex Tremayne was deeply in love with her friend.

'And so, we come to the second reason I've behaved as I have lately.' Alex drew in a long breath, and Ellie's brow creased as she noticed his hands shaking before he clasped them together on the table.

'It's taken me a long time to work out why, aside from being who I was at work, I also became the boyfriend from hell. And I take full responsibility for it. I did something I hadn't believed possible: I fell in love. A long time ago.' He flicked an imploring glance at Bella, but her attention remained with Ellie. 'I didn't realise at the time. It was an amazing few months, but it wasn't until we went back to our own lives, mine in London and Bella heading off on her teacher training, that I realised how much I wanted to be with her.'

'So what happened?' Will looked from Alex to Bella and back. 'What split you up?'

Chapter Thirty-Three

"The Traitors"

'You've never talked about this, Bella,' Ellie added, confused by the uncharacteristic trepidation on her friend's features.

'Some things get buried deep.'

As Ellie knew all too well.

'When Bella dumped me many years ago, neither of us appreciated the impact it would have on my idiotic, immature character, but sadly, it resulted in me making sure no one around me was happy either, hence my interference in Will's relationship with Ellie.'

Bella winced. 'I had no idea you'd been a victim of his backlash at the time, Ells.'

'So why did you end things with Alex back then?'

A dull red colour infused Alex's cheeks, but he nodded at Bella, and she held Ellie's gaze steadily.

'City Alex was a complete contrast to the one I'd seen that summer. I went up to London for a couple of weekends, in between starting my studies. I'd really liked him, become a bit smitten even, and I thought it might be worth pursuing. But…' She hesitated, and Alex stirred in his seat.

'She had the good sense to find the showy, braggy and shallow version of me wasn't quite to her taste.'

'I had a fascination, almost admiration, for him at first, but then I started to see through him Alex constantly tries to outdo people, even his so-called friends. Impressing others was more important to him than anything. I couldn't find any kindness, compassion or desire to help others.'

Alex sank back in his seat, eyes cast down. 'And Bella was the opposite. She was genuinely caring, believed in volunteering, did unpaid hours for Citizens' Advice. And I laughed in her face when she told me, saying it was pointless.'

'And I knew instantly he wasn't the man for me; wasn't the fun and funny person I'd had a blast with, been drawn to, in Polkerran. He'd disintegrated into ashes. I became ashamed. Of myself, for being so taken in by such shallowness.' Bella sighed, casting Ellie an apologetic glance. 'It's why I've never spoken of it.'

'Damned idiot that I was, I lashed out at those around me, set about driving apart anyone around me who was happy. I can't change the past.' Alex looked from Will to Ellie. 'All I can do is try to do better in future and not repeat those errors of judgement. I'm no angel, and I doubt I ever will be, but I am determined to make changes where I can, and I look forward to working with Oliver instead of against him.' He smiled faintly. 'I'm still interested in making money, but I'll try to make more balanced decisions when it comes to estate disposals.'

He drew in an audible breath as his attention fixed on Ellie.

'I did you probably one of the worst disservices, Ellie, preventing you from reconciling with Will all those years ago, and when I realised who you were — back here in the cove at the same time as us — I initially feared the truth coming out. I was desperate to repair things with Bella. If she'd found out how I split you and Will up… it had to remain in the past.'

Astounded, Ellie threw Will a shocked look, then addressed Alex. 'Were you trying to ruin my businesses? Slagging off my photography and posting horrid reviews on my artwork so I had to go home?'

Will's grip on Ellie's hand tightened.

'No!' Alex's response was vehement, his expression confounded. 'I swear. I had no idea that was happening. I've got my faults, but I wouldn't… I actually admire you, Ellie. I know how tough business is. My intention at first had been to try and keep Will away from being in your company, but that concern faded once I'd seen the two of you together. There was enough animosity there to power a speedboat and effectively keep you apart.'

Strangely, Ellie believed him. It meant her suspicions on the culprit were probably right, though she still couldn't understand their motive…

'I need some air,' Bella interjected. 'Come on, you.'

She opened the door to the boot room, and Heathcliff stalked past, tail erect and nose in the air as she passed Alex.

'There, kitty. Nice kitty,' Alex essayed, warily extending a hand to stroke the cat's back.

Heathcliff eyed him balefully but didn't hiss. Bella urged Alex out the door as Will's phone rang, and he walked into the sitting area to take the call.

Ellie could see Bella talking to Alex out on the terrace. Arms wrapped around her body, mentally pushing aside the two of them and their recent admissions, Ellie headed into the orangery, then recalled what she'd been doing earlier.

Someone had taken photos on their phone of each of Ellie's images displayed on that screen – the reflection and the smudge proved it – and it was time to find out why.

'This is going to sound a bit mad, but I need to talk to Chloe.'

Will looked at Ellie uncertainly as he put his phone aside.

'Why?'

'It's tricky. I need to ask her about those photos in the newspaper.'

Will put a hand under Ellie's elbow and steered her back into the orangery, his eyes flashing when he caught sight of Alex outside. Bella had her arm around him now, and Ellie shook her head in disbelief.

'Ells?'

'Sorry.' Ellie tried to cast her mind back. 'I was editing the walk photos, and she called in to collect a book. It took me a few minutes to find it, and then she left. My laptop was open on the island, and I'm sure there were images of you on the screen. Look.'

Ellie pulled up the photos the paper had returned to her, then opened the originals.

'See this.' She pointed to the mark. 'This was a finger-print smudge on my screen, and it's just about visible on these photos, but not on mine. If you look closely, here, there's also a slight reflection of someone, see?'

'I can, but I don't get it.' Will turned her to face him, his hands resting on her arms, and Ellie's heartbeat quickened at his expression. 'I've no idea where this is going, but I wish it was all over and we could be alone again.'

Ellie wrapped her arms around him, resting her head against his chest as he held her close, relishing the sound of his heart beating steadily beside her ear.

'I could stay here forever,' she murmured. 'But—'

'You need to know. *We* need to know.' Will released her with a sigh. 'I'll contact Chloe, see if she's free to pop round. You don't think Anna will mind?'

'I'll message her, but I'm sure she'll be fine about it.'

Anna was quick to respond, saying it was okay, but they'd be back in about ten minutes. Ellie watched Will step into the living room, tapping into his phone, then started as the door to the terrace opened and Bella entered the orangery.

'Ellie, we need to talk.'

'About what?'

She followed Bella into the kitchen, and Will gave a thumbs-up from where he stood by the window.

'What's up?'

Bella huffed a breath, folding her arms as she leaned against the island. 'I'm sorry, okay? I didn't know half of this crap until recently. But I feel partly to blame for what happened to you and Will.'

Ellie was taken aback. 'I can't imagine for a minute you need to, but I'm listening.'

'Don't mind me,' Will called, heading for the boot room.

'When we split, Alex said I'd be sorry. I thought it was an idle threat. I mean, what could he possibly do? I had no idea you – and Will – were part of the collateral damage. I didn't know you'd got engaged or that you were facing parental opposition. None of it.' Bella's troubled features became even more solemn. 'I honestly thought the summer romance had ended, as they usually do. Like

301

mine had. Until you opened up to us the other day, said you'd been engaged and admitted the break-up was behind you dropping out of your MA.'

Bella's luminous eyes were wide, her smile tremulous now. 'I couldn't work out why Alex was so wary of you when he realised who you were, but when you spoke out about the past… at Harbourwatch that night a horrible suspicion took hold. I'd spent all these years walking in the opposite direction to Alex whenever I came across him; this time I finally faced him head-on.'

Ellie laid a gentle hand on Bella's arm. 'You still feel something, though, don't you?'

Bella sighed. 'I'm not sure. I mean, it really was just a holiday fling, and once I'd seen him in his natural environment, I couldn't run away fast enough. He had absolutely no regard for anyone but himself, or for the aftermath of anything he did. Did you know I caught him with someone? His defence was that I was always studying, so he got bored. When I finally saw him again, here in the village last summer, the distrust and dislike came flooding back. He tried to lay on the charm, but it left me cold. I shoved him – quite literally.' A small smirk appeared. 'Away.'

Ellie grinned. 'I did hear about his dip in the harbour.' Then, she sobered. 'But now… you seem… a bit more supportive?'

Letting out a huff of breath, Bella shoved her hands in her pockets, still leaning against the counter. 'Leopards don't change their spots, and we all know you should never think you're going to be able to do it, but…'

Feeling for her old friend, Ellie gently squeezed her arm. 'You always did like a lost cause.'

Despite herself, Bella laughed. 'True, but for whatever reason, Alex is genuinely trying to improve.'

'For you.'

'So he says. And I feel as though I'd like to hang around to help, if I can.'

'Well, he's made quite the start, ceasing hostilities with Oliver, apologising. Even Heathcliff looked as though she might come round.'

A smile softened Bella's firm mouth. 'There's something here.' She pressed a hand to her chest. 'An inner desire for him to become the person he aspires to be. It won't be an easy road, and I suspect there'll be a few potholes to come...' Her gaze drifted towards the window, where Alex could be seen still leaning on the wall, staring out to sea.

'But you want to hang around to see if they can be filled?'

Their eyes met, and the corners of Bella's crinkled as her normal smile returned. 'I'm up for the adventure, I think.'

Before anything else could be said, a commotion arose as the door to the boot room opened to reveal the return of Anna, Oliver, Dougal and the buggy, just as the front doorbell rang.

'That must be Chloe.'

Ellie was about to head for the hall, but Will overtook her. 'I'll do it.'

'They're fast asleep,' Anna whispered as Ellie joined her. 'I'm just going to wheel them into the snug.'

'I'm so sorry for the disturbance.' Ellie felt awful as she unfastened Dougal's lead, giving his ears a thorough rub. This was *their* home, after all.

Anna shook her head. 'Not at all.'

Just then, the door to the hall swung aside as Will ushered Chloe in. Oliver's eyes narrowed, steely blue as they swept over the new arrival, who'd frozen just inside the room, colour flooding her cheeks.

'Oh no,' she squeaked.

'What's *she* doing here?' Oliver growled, turning to Will.

'Shhh,' Anna whispered. 'You'll disturb Bertie and Emma.'

'Sorry.' Oliver gestured to the others to move out of the way so Anna could wheel the buggy into the hall, closed the door and swung round to face the others. 'What's going on, Will?'

'It's a bit complicated.'

'What is?' Chloe all but croaked. 'I thought this was about another guided walk, or something.'

A sound near the boot room door drew Ellie's attention. Bella, who'd been out to retrieve Alex, stalled with him on the threshold.

It was impossible to miss the momentary alarm in Alex's eyes as he spotted Chloe, his gaze then flying to the others. 'Shall we go?'

'*We?*' Chloe exclaimed, suddenly coming to life, brushing past Oliver. 'Is she… *Alex?*'

'No!' He responded firmly. 'We're not a "we" in that sense. Sadly.'

Chloe paled, halting in her progress across the room.

'I'd appreciate an explanation.' From Oliver's tone, it wasn't an invitation, more an order.

'It's my fault,' Ellie admitted. 'Will did check with Anna about asking Chloe here. I'm sorry if it's caused a problem. We just wanted to talk to her about something.'

Will reached for Ellie's hand and squeezed it. 'We'll take this somewhere else.'

The door opened and Anna returned.

'Still asleep, bless them.' She looked from her husband to Chloe, frozen part way across the room.

'Shall I put the kettle on?' Anna was already moving towards the kitchen, pausing by Chloe. 'Hello. You must be the Chloe that Ellie mentioned in her message. I'm Anna.' Then, she faltered. 'Have we met before?'

'She worked for me before you did,' Oliver informed his wife.

Ellie and Will exchanged a confused look. This wasn't going entirely as they'd anticipated.

'Oh gosh! I remember now.' Anna's face pinkened as she shot a look over at Alex.

Chloe bowed her head. 'Yes, Oliver fired me.'

Anna's eyes widened. 'I remember now. For snooping through his papers. We later found out it was to get information for Alex. For the estate, when Oliver started his philanthropical venture.'

'I'm so sorry,' Chloe raised a mortified face to them.

Anna, in the meantime, turned her attention to Alex. 'The two of you had a fling, didn't you, when you were dating me?'

'I… er…' Alex puffed out a breath. 'Yes.'

'A fling!' Chloe choked out. 'You said I was your *girlfriend*. We dated whenever you were in the cove. I was working at the council then, and you asked me to help stall the paperwork for Anna's B&B.'

'I'll own up to that one,' Alex said, sending Anna an apologetic look.

'Look, I really think we should go,' Bella insisted, grabbing hold of Alex's arm.

'No, wait.' Oliver turned to Will and Ellie. 'There's obviously something you wanted to talk to Chloe about. Why not go into the orangery? We'll make some coffees for when you're done. Strong ones.'

Bella ushered Alex back towards the boot room door as Anna and Oliver began preparing drinks.

'I'm scared,' Chloe said as Ellie invited her to go with them. 'Can't you give me a clue about this?'

'It's just a few questions about some photos.'

'Oh my God!' Chloe's hand shot to her throat, and she threw Alex an agonised look across the room. 'Don't go, Alex.'

Brow furrowed, he and Bella exchanged a puzzled look. 'Why?'

'I did it all for you. For *us*.'

Chapter Thirty-Four

"The Good, the Bad and the Ugly"

Chloe's words fell into a profound silence. Then, Will took charge.

'Into the orangery. You too, Alex.'

He led the way, Bella and Alex sinking onto the small sofa as Ellie encouraged Chloe to take a seat by the table containing her laptop and a scattered array of papers, notebooks, memory cards and charging leads.

Will brought in two chairs from the dining table, then closed the door to the main house.

'Over to you, Ellie,' he suggested, taking the seat beside her.

It didn't take long to explain how she knew who had taken the photos, and Chloe made no effort to deny it.

Ellie, however, wanted to find out more, and with a little prodding, Chloe also confessed to all the other things she'd tried to chisel away at Ellie's businesses, from the initial attempts of calling the shops to remove the cards, then leaving the anonymous negative comments and reviews and onwards to flooding socials claiming Ellie used AI rather than her own talent to create her images.

An awkward silence hung heavy in the air, mixed with a heady dose of puzzlement. Bella was the first to voice everyone's immediate thought.

'But why? What has Ellie ever done to you, that you wanted to harm her in this way?'

Chloe twisted in her chair to stare at Bella. 'I told you, I did it for Alex.' She sounded surprised anyone could think otherwise, but Alex's flabbergasted countenance told another story.

'What the hell are you talking about?' he exploded, shooting out of his seat beside Bella. 'I'd never do that.' He paused. 'Well, maybe years ago, but not *now*!'

'But you *did* tell me, remember? When we bumped into each other last month? You bought me a drink.'

'Alex is always buying drinks for people. It's his way of breathing,' Will chipped in.

'We talked about nothing. I don't remember anything. And I sure as *hell* didn't ask you to do any harm to Ellie's businesses.'

Alex looked around helplessly, but Chloe sent him a pleading look, and Ellie bit her lip. Was she yet another conquest Alex barely noticed?

'You were feeling low,' Chloe persisted. 'There was something you'd done in the past, and you dreaded Will, or someone called Ellie finding out now their paths had re-crossed. You wished something would happen to drive her out of the cove, sooner rather than later.'

Alex slumped back into the sofa.

'I had a good old moan. But I *never* asked her to do anything.' His repentant gaze fastened on Ellie. 'I promise.'

'Did he, Chloe?'

She flicked a glance at Will, then reluctantly shook her head before turning pleading eyes on Alex. 'You were used to me helping you. I thought we'd be together again, but we won't, will we? Because of her.'

Chloe pointed a shaking finger at Bella.

'Alex?' Will spoke firmly. 'Anything to add?'

Alex seemed flabbergasted, eyes flitting from Ellie to Will. 'It's true. I did say I was in fear of you both somehow finding out I'd done something. But I did *not* ask Chloe – or anyone else – to intervene.'

Chloe sniffed, raising her chin and glaring at Alex now before turning her attention to Ellie.

'I'm sorry. I thought if your efforts to earn money here failed, you'd have to return more quickly to your old life, and Alex's secret – whatever it was – would remain hidden.' Chloe dabbed at her eyes. 'The photo thing wasn't planned, but everything I'd done so far to hamper you hadn't worked, and I'd seen you at the walk. Both times you and Will talked, the chemistry was obvious. I grabbed the chance. Took those snaps of a few images to send to the paper. You had no clue.'

'This is what happens when you toy with people's feelings, Alex.' Bella spoke with sadness as she looked at him, slumped by her side.

'I didn't know,' he repeated, his skin ashen now, hands shaking. 'I promise. I didn't know.'

'He didn't,' Chloe interjected. 'I've been stupid. I thought he loved me once, that if I did this, he'd renew his interest in me. I love him.' Her voice became a wail as she buried her face in her hands.

'Shouldn't we report this? It's malicious, if nothing else.' Will looked to Ellie, and she hesitated, then shook her head. Chloe's behaviour had been questionable at least, not just towards Ellie, but also Anna in the past, but her punishment – the irrefutable truth about her chances with Alex – would hopefully teach her a lesson.

'I think this is something you need to discuss between you,' Ellie said, getting to her feet. She looked over at

Chloe. 'I wish you hadn't done it, and I can't say I'm feeling particularly sympathetic after what you tried to do to my businesses, but that's your problem, not mine.'

Bella nodded. 'Come on, Alex. Let's talk this out. Then you're free to go.'

Alex shot her a startled look. 'Not without you!'

'That depends,' she retorted. 'On what you now say and do.'

-

The following morning, Ellie woke slowly, her eyelids opening and closing as she savoured the wisps of the most enchanting dream. Wrapped in a comfortable cocoon of bedding, she stretched her legs, eyes flicking wide open as her feet encountered firm, warm flesh.

'Morning.'

Rolling over, her entangled legs dragging the sheets with her so that Will was barely covered at all, her heart swelled with sheer happiness.

Will's head remained on his pillow, his gorgeous dark eyes smouldering as their gaze held.

'Hey, stranger.' Ellie's mouth curved. 'It's a while since I've woken to your handsome face.'

'I bet you say that to all the boys. Before you steal their bedding.' He tugged at the duvet, which had become scrambled by the sheets, effectively pulling Ellie towards him. 'I think you need to apologise.'

Ellie hefted the covers over his all but naked body, then closed the final gap to snuggle next to him, resting her head on his chest.

'I'm sorry, I don't think I heard you.' Will's words reverberated through Ellie's cheek, and she smiled, keeping her eyes closed. That way, she could almost see again the most precious moments from the previous night.

'There's this loud thumping in my ear. It's affecting my hearing.'

A rumble in Will's chest indicated his amusement, but then—

'Aargh,' Ellie squeaked, as he flipped her onto her back, burying his face in her neck, then began showering kisses along her throat until he reached her chin, but as he raised his head to claim her mouth, she ducked under his arm and rolled off the bed.

Laughing, Will flopped back onto his pillow, but as she became aware of his gaze travelling the length of her exposed body, she snatched up his shirt from the floor and headed for the bathroom.

Staring at her reflection, Ellie rubbed at a smudge under her eye, then ran her hands through her mussed-up hair, adjusting Will's white shirt. She had an inner glow, as though someone had lit something within her.

After hastily brushing her teeth, she peered round the bathroom door, then frowned. Will was no longer in the bed.

'Will?' She stepped out, shrieking when he scooped her up in his arms.

'Every day should start with some timely ablutions, but I fear it's a little chilly for a dip in the sea.'

Reaching up, Ellie clasped her hands around his neck as he carried her back into the bathroom, kicking the door shut with his foot, and as his mouth claimed hers, she slid to the ground and began unbuttoning the shirt.

After all, Will was right. One should start the day with a shower, and this one looked like it had plenty of room for two.

Will cobbled together a breakfast of toast and orange juice and, afterwards, they took their mugs of coffee out onto the small terrace facing the sea.

Sinking onto the bench beside each other, they stared out over the azure water. It was a sheltered spot, and despite the weakness of the early winter sun, Ellie could feel its touch through the thick throw Will had placed around her shoulders.

A fishing boat could be seen in the distance, cresting the undulating water as gulls wheeled and cawed overhead, the smell of woodsmoke from the newly lit log burner drifting up into the sky, and Ellie sighed with contentment.

'I wish I could live here. In the cove, I mean.'

Will leaned forward, elbows on his knees as he cradled his mug. 'It's inspiring, isn't it?' Ellie rested her hand on Will's leg, and he sat back, placing his own hand on top. 'So, why can't you?'

Ellie peered up into Will's face. 'Here? With you?'

Putting his mug aside, Will shifted in his seat. 'You did say your email promised you'd follow me anywhere.'

Ellie rolled her eyes, laughing. 'Don't tell me you're going to quote an email you never read.'

'Probably. For the rest of our lives.' He combed his fingers through Ellie's hair, then held her chin. 'I don't intend to let you go a second time.' He kissed her thoroughly, then turned back to look at the view.

Her heart almost too full to bear, Ellie couldn't stop smiling. She slipped her hand into Will's and he squeezed it.

'I'd love to live here, at Peaches, but...'

'Your life is in Oxford.'

'Well, yes. And no. Will—' Ellie tugged on his hand, and he turned fully to face her. 'It's a place, that's all. I ended up there by default, not design. I've worked hard to build up my business, but I can do it again.' Ideas were coursing through Ellie's mind, followed by the buzz of anticipation, opportunity. 'I mean, I've already made a start. And it's not so far away that I can't still do the odd job for existing clients, is it? Besides, Cornwall's a smallish county. I can work farther afield than just the cove and this could still be home. But what about you, *your* work?'

She held Will's intense gaze as he studied her thoughtfully. Then the edges of his mouth began to curve upwards.

'I'm lucky I can pick and choose, and if I don't mess up in my first foray into producing, there's always the chance of a follow-up, focusing on *Jamaica Inn* and Bodmin Moor.' He grinned at Ellie. 'Anna says Matt has quite taken to life down here. He's about as publicity averse as I am. He's got his hidden creek, we've got our hilltop idyll.'

It was true. Gemma had told Ellie how Matt loved the way the locals just accepted him as Anna's brother and left him in peace.

If that was what Will wanted, then they were in accord.

'Then I'll start making plans as soon as I go back.'

Will kissed her swiftly. 'Which is when?'

'I've got a week until I have to be there, but I can come down as often as work permits.'

'Perfect.'

They had seven wonderful days ahead of just Ellie and Will…

Resting back against the bench, the hazy sun's rays caressing her face and Will's hand firmly holding hers, his thumb stroking her palm, Ellie willed away the sudden pressure behind her eyes.

This was no time for tears, happy or otherwise. This was *their* time. Hers and Will's. And nothing would persuade her otherwise.

Epilogue

"Love, Actually"

Six Months Later

The Fiat struggled up the hills as the A30 wound its way through Devon and into Cornwall.

'I'm sorry.' Ellie broke off from singing along to her playlist to pat the dashboard. 'Not far now, Fifi darling.'

Instinctively, she glanced in the rear-view mirror, then shook her head. She could barely see a thing back there, so laden was the little car with her entire portable life from Oxford.

Heart pattering almost in time to the music, Ellie turned off the trunk road. 'Thirty minutes to go,' she mused.

One long half-hour until she'd be back in Will's arms again after almost a month apart.

With the filming wrapped on his docu-drama, he'd been buried in post-production in the studio in London, and Ellie had been swamped by cutting ties with her flat, life and work in Oxford – culminating that morning with a long-ago booked photoshoot – and networking madly to establish a footing in the South-West.

Delight over the change in her circumstances pulsed through Ellie's veins as she took the turning for Polkerran

Point and approached the winding descent, skimming past the cemetery near the top of the hill and almost holding her breath as Fifi finally rounded the corner which would afford a vista of the cove's protective arms of land reaching out into the sea.

It was a stunning Saturday in mid-May, with a cloud-free, linen-blue sky, and Ellie lowered her window as she reached the harbourfront, a soft breeze stroking her bare arms as she followed the lane parallel with the water to take the track up to Peaches Cottage.

Hedgerows bursting with tiny white hawthorn flowers heralded the upcoming wedding, long grasses waving as she passed by until she slowed Fifi and pulled into the gravel driveway beside Will's car.

He came out of the stable door to the cottage as she turned off the ignition, then grinned as she flung the door wide and tried to get out without unfastening her seatbelt.

'Aha!' he exclaimed, bending down as though to lean in and help her. 'You're my prisoner.'

Will captured Ellie's willing mouth in an intense kiss and she wrapped her arms around his neck, the belt straining as she leaned into him.

'Come on, let's get you out of there.'

He led the way into the cottage, then took her in his arms, and conversation pretty much fell by the wayside for a while.

'I feel properly welcomed home,' Ellie sighed when he finally released her, leaning her head against his chest. Was it possible to burst from happiness? Probably a bit messy, even by Ellie's standards.

Sensing her amusement, Will set her back, his dark eyes finding hers.

'And that's funny why?'

'Nothing.' She reached up and pressed a firm kiss to his mouth. 'Poor Fifi is stuffed to the gunnels. I've no idea where we'll put everything.'

Will steered her out to the charming terrace facing the sea. 'It doesn't take much to fill Fifi. Besides, there's always that small bedroom. They used to call them box rooms, so it seems a fitting place.'

'I've missed this,' Ellie sighed, taking in the expanse of ocean, deep blue and scattered with sunlight-kissed diamonds, dotted here and there with the white mast of a yacht.

Wrapping his arms around her, Will rested his chin on top of her head, then brushed her hair aside to place a firm kiss on her neck. Ellie shivered, leaning against him as the trail moved round, Will turning her in his embrace until he had reached the base of her neck.

'Stop,' she gasped out reluctantly as shivers surged through her body.

'Spoilsport,' he whispered against her mouth, savouring a long kiss before letting her go.

'I hate to be a bore, but we're short of time, and I need to get my dress out. It'll be like a rag if I don't hang it up soon.'

Will sighed resignedly as he followed her back into the cottage. 'Well, we can't have that, can we. No one wants to go to a wedding dressed in a rag.'

–

'What do you think? I found it on Vinted.'

Ellie held out her arms as Will made a good show of examining her outfit, hand to his chin as he walked around her.

'Will?'

He'd stopped out of sight.

'Shh. I'm just working out how to get you out of it later. Those fastenings look complicated.'

A pulse thrummed in Ellie's neck in anticipation, although she swung around and tried to swat him, but he was too quick for her.

'You're in luck. They're fake. The tiny buttons conceal a zip.'

Will, she had to admit, looked gorgeous in an open-necked black shirt and trousers teamed with a linen jacket.

'Seriously, though. Do you like it? I picked the colour because it went so well with my ring.'

Ellie held up her hand, still delighting in the weight of the large, square-cut emerald flanked by two tear-drop diamonds, which had replaced the plastic ring at Christmas. She turned back to the mirror, turning to and fro to inspect the effect of the floaty, layered fabric as it swirled around her bare legs, brushing her ankles above her favourite strappy heels.

Will's hands snaked around her middle as he pressed a kiss to her cheek.

'You look far too enticing. It's a beautiful dress, made more so because you're wearing it. Do we really have to go to this thing?'

'Yes, I promised.' She sent him a contrite look. 'It's just a shame it fell on this date.'

The depth of passion in his dark eyes was almost enough for Ellie to say, 'ah sod it. We won't be missed,' but he dropped a final kiss on the tip of her nose.

'There's no way I'm letting you out there looking like that on your own. I'm coming as your bodyguard.'

Laughing, Ellie followed Will out to the car. 'I hardly think Old Patrick's a threat these days.'

'Ha!' Will held open the door for her, scooping up the ends of her dress to ensure it didn't get caught as he closed the door. 'He's not the only single man left in the cove, you know.' Will fastened his own seatbelt, then reached out to squeeze Ellie's hand. 'Matt's got some of his old band mates staying. They're playing a set at the after-party. All Gemma's persuasion, I'm told.'

'Oh, that should be fun. I used to have a massive crush on the drummer.'

Will shook his head resignedly as he reversed the car out of the driveway and swung it around to head down the lane. 'So Nicki and Bella told me. He's the one who's newly available.'

–

'Everywhere looks *so* beautiful, Kate.' Ellie hugged her friend as she welcomed them inside the tastefully converted property in the grounds of Tremayne Manor.

Thick wooden struts supported the arched roof, and white lights, soft pink roses and greenery adorned the beams and tables. Candles flickered in large glass urns on the circular tables set around the outside of the space, while uniformed staff cleared the debris from the celebratory dinner.

There must have been a hundred people there. She returned an enthusiastic wave from Phoenix, chatting to a man Ellie didn't recognise.

'That's the new teacher. Started after Easter. Phee brought him along as her plus one. The venue's becoming so popular,' Kate enthused. 'And due in no small part to your stunning photography. By the way, did you see what's on the walls?'

Ellie turned around. 'Oh!' A hand went to her throat. 'I had no idea!'

'Mrs Tremayne wanted it to be a surprise. She loved the black-and-white images you took of Polkerran and its community, including the manor, so had them enlarged onto these canvasses and the downlights installed to spotlight them.'

Slowly, Ellie viewed the entire room where her photos hung on the whitewashed stone walls, each with a small plaque crediting her.

'Come on, you need a drink,' Will urged, smiling at Kate as she greeted more guests arriving for the evening party.

Once equipped with an obligatory glass of fizz, Ellie scanned the sea of faces.

'There are so many people here. I'm so happy for them. Let's go and say hi.'

Will followed Ellie across the room to where the happy couple held court.

'You made it!' Jean swept Ellie into a warm embrace, then turned to her companion. 'Good to see you again, Will.'

Will leaned forward to kiss Jean's cheek. 'Happy wedding day.'

'You look gorgeous, Jean.' Ellie admired the ankle-length fitted ivory dress. 'As does all of this.' She waved a hand at the splendour of the room.

Jean cast a quick look over her shoulder. 'Greg paid for almost everything, but don't tell Mum. Bless her, she gave me an account book – years old – that she and Dad set up when I was a teen, saving for a wedding that never happened. She stopped paying into it, of course, but the fund sat there all this time. I think she thought it would cover the whole thing, but…'

She pulled an awkward face, and Ellie sent her a sympathetic look. 'It only bought the cake?'

'Thanks to Anna, that was covered, and you did an amazing job on the invites, but at least it paid for the champagne.' She turned back to Will. 'How's the post-production going?'

'A lot more smoothly than filming whenever your mum and her cronies were on set. I'm not sure the sound man will ever recover from Mrs L telling him she wasn't having any man called Mike coming near her cleavage.'

'I did warn you they would be the most challenging extras you were ever likely to meet.'

Laughing, Ellie shook her head. 'I still can't believe they gave her a few lines.'

'It was that interview with the journalist poking around. Went down a storm on the socials, with everyone claiming Mum should go into politics, evading every question and coming out with some classics. Someone's even set up an Instagram account in her name: @MrsMalaplops.'

Jean plucked at the sleeve of the man talking to a couple near their table, and having shared their congratulations with Greg, he expressed his excitement about their new future together up in Newcastle.

'Oliver is an angel with his property schemes,' Greg added, placing an arm over Jean's shoulders and dropping a kiss on her cheek.

Ellie's heart felt as though it was smiling. 'It's set you free, Jean.'

'I know. I'm so lucky.' Jean's voice wobbled as her eyes misted over. 'With Mum, Cleggie and Old Patrick in an almshouse each, and this qualified warden moving into the gatehouse, they'll be better looked after than with me up at Potter's Meadow.'

More arrivals came to express their good wishes and, excusing themselves, Ellie spotted Anna and Oliver at a table with Matt and Gemma, so she and Will headed over.

'Come sit by me,' Anna urged her. 'Lauren and Daniel have gone off to mingle. Love your dress! The fastenings down the back are so cute.'

Warmth filled Ellie's cheeks when she saw Will's mouth twitch as he turned to speak to Matt. She knew exactly what he was thinking!

Catching up with everyone after having been away for a month, Ellie sipped her champagne, her gaze constantly drifting towards Will. He and Matt had fallen into a swift friendship based on mutual respect and a shared desire to keep their once-public lives as private as they could. The cove appeared to be the haven they both sought, and Ellie – catching Gemma's amused eyes on her – raised her glass in salute.

Anna dragged Oliver over to talk to the locals who usually frequented their kitchen table, and Ellie moved round to sit by Gemma.

'So how's the planning going?' she asked.

Gemma pursed her lips, then grinned. 'Let's say it's ebbing and flowing like the tide just now.'

'Oh, why's that?'

'This.' Gemma waved a hand round at the happy faces, the contented murmur of conversation punctuated by laughter and the clink of glasses as greetings and congrat-ulations were shared.

'I thought you were going to disappear somewhere secluded?'

'Oh, we are.' Gemma turned sparkling green eyes on Ellie. She had the most splendid auburn curls, which were caught up in pearly combs either side of her face and cascaded down her back. 'We've found the perfect place – a tucked-away villa on Lake Como.'

'Nice.' Ellie smiled and lightly touched her glass to Gemma's. 'Here's to weddings away from the crowd.'

'Italy was a must, after Matt proposed there. It's going to be a small event – about thirty people – at Villa Balbi-anello in this tiny cove called Lenno.' Gemma grinned. 'It was the cove that sold it to me. But Auntie Dee isn't really up to the journey, so we've decided to do something like this when we get back. Not so big, of course.'

There was a disturbance then, as someone Ellie vaguely recognised arrived to claim Gemma's hand for a dance.

'This is Roddy. He's an old bandmate of Matt's,' Gemma explained before allowing him to bear her off to the dance floor. Ellie's astonished gaze followed them.

'Am I in danger?' Will said softly in her ear as he took Gemma's seat.

'Definitely not. It was a teenage crush. I'm far too mature for such silliness these days.' She raised her chin, sending him a sideways look, trying not to smile, and Will leaned down and kissed her swiftly.

'Good.'

'Nice to see you two lovebirds back in the cove.'

Will shook Hamish's hand as Nicki sat down.

'You look well,' Ellie exclaimed, giving Hamish a hug.

'Been out on the boat a few times. Not solo, mind. But it's a start.'

Leaving the men to talk, Nicki turned to her cousin.

'It's a shame you missed the service. Not a dry eye in the house, mostly from laughter.'

Ellie laughed. 'Don't tell me. Mrs L up to her tricks?'

'The whole lot of them. You know they've all moved into the renovated almshouses?'

They chatted about village news for a while, including the latest on Jean's ice cream shop, which Phoenix was taking over. Then, Nicki sent Ellie a keen look.

'Have you spoken with Bella lately? I haven't heard a squeak.'

'She called me last week. She'd been in London, so we met there for lunch. She's still somewhere between friendship and a relationship with Alex, did you know?'

'There are rumours.' Nicki winked as she drained her flute. 'You know the cove.'

'Apparently, she's roped him in to volunteering at the nearest pet rescue centre, which seems a bit unfair to the animals. Do you think it has legs, Alex and Bells?'

'Hmm,' Nicki mused. 'Let's just say they might need to borrow Cleggie's mobility scooter now and again. Time will tell. I suspect all this philanthropy conceals a hidden desire to make Bella's point. At least Alex is being true to his word here. Anna says the truce with Oliver is holding, and he's getting actively involved in the community. He's the driving force behind the changes the estate's making.'

'Did you hear he's offered me a retainer? I'm going to be resident photographer for events here at the manor.'

Nicki grinned. 'That's great! He's also appointed Lauren as the part-time estate manager, so he can stay in London more. Did you know Daniel is his cousin? That way, he feels he's keeping it in the family.'

They excitedly discussed how much fun it would be to live so close, then Nicki clutched her midriff. 'Come on, something's telling me we need to find the buffet.'

They'd almost reached the long table displaying a tempting array of nibbles and light bites when Ellie's eye was caught by someone waving. She sent Nicki ahead, telling her not to hoover everything up, and walked over to the nearest table.

'Alright, my lovely?' Mrs Clegg reached for Ellie's hand and dropped a kiss on it.

'Hello everyone,' Ellie greeted them, smiling round at Old Patrick, looking rather dapper in a tweed blazer that was surely too warm for the day, Mrs Lovelace, sporting a jaunty-looking fascinator in her silver-grey curls, and Ryther, pale but smiling.

' 'Tis good to see you back in the cove, young'un,' Patrick said, raising his glass of beer in Ellie's direction.

She mouthed 'thank you', then took the vacant seat beside Mrs Lovelace.

'And how are you? Nicki says you've all moved into the almshouses now.'

'Aye, young Ellie, and she's not wrong. A bit of an upheaval, but we'm right proper sorted. Not often at our time of life we get a fresh start like this. All mod cons and the like, and no stairs. And Ryther, there,' she nodded across the table, the fascinator wobbling precariously, 'gave us all enemas, he did. One of they Japanese types.'

Ellie's startled gaze flew to the man in question, who seemed oblivious.

'Anemones, you silly mare,' Patrick chuntered, turning to Ellie. 'For the communal garden.'

'Master Oliver has seen us to rights,' Mrs Clegg added, reaching for a piece of wedding cake. 'We all have one of those pull things in case we need anythin' day or night. There's this lovely warden lady moving into the gatehouse next week.'

'It's not for *anything*,' Patrick scoffed, taking a slurp of beer. ' 'Tis for emergencies only. The maid'll be useful, mind.'

Mrs Clegg smiled at Ellie. 'When's your big day, then? It's all about weddings lately, with Jean and then Gemma next.'

'We're still talking about it,' Ellie said gently, turning to Mrs Lovelace, whose beady eyes were transfixed on her daughter, now taking to the dance floor in the arms of her new husband. 'You'll miss her.'

'More than I would ever let her know, young'un. But bless my Jeannie. It's her time now, and I've got Gemma not too far away. And Cleggie and Pat – they'm family, as like as not. Jeannie will visit, mind. The cove gets under your skin, becomes part of you. She'll not stay away too long at a time.'

Will remained deep in conversation with Matt, so Ellie excused herself to join Kate and Dev, who had come to sit beside Ryther.

'Kate's fretting. Mollie has her first beau,' Ryther said, eyes sparkling in a tired face.

'I'm fine,' Kate said firmly. 'It's just she's starting her GCSEs, and I don't want her distracted.'

Dev merely shook his head as he met Ellie's amused look. 'She could do worse, Kate. The young lad happened to mention he'd visited Hever Castle, and Mollie was immediately smitten.'

They chatted about Dev's son, Theo, for a bit, then Ellie turned her attention to Ryther, who was watching the dance floor.

'What's that?' She indicated a small, copper-coloured object he held in his fingers.

Laying it on his palm, Ryther revealed a pretty shell. 'It's a flat periwinkle, quite common in Cornish rock pools.'

At Ryther's invitation, Ellie examined the polished shell, admiring its rich colour and the distinctive pattern on its surface as best she could in the ever-changing light inside the barn.

'It was Meg—' Ryther stopped. 'You know of the lady who lived in Westerleigh and her connection to Anna?'

'Yes. At least, a bit.'

A wistful expression settled on the elderly gentleman's features. 'This was her favourite type of shell. It looks like a miniature garden snail, see?' He took it from Ellie and held it up to catch the lamplight. 'But this, like Meg, is – despite its delicate appearance – tougher and brighter. There are so many shades and variations, but she only ever found two of this particular hue, and I discovered not so long ago that she gave this one to Anna, who kept it in the bowl in the hallway.'

'It means a lot to you. Like Meg did.'

'Indeed.' A soft, nostalgic smile touched his lips. 'She gave the other one to me, though I'm not sure she knew it, when she was in the hospice. Her mind had all but gone, but it was as though she suddenly knew me. She told me to follow the shells. It was a message I didn't understand at the time.'

'And do you still have it?'

'No. I gave it back to her. After she passed away.' Ryther tucked the shell into his waistcoat pocket, raised Ellie's hand to press a kiss on it, and she leaned over to return the gesture on his cheek.

'You had a chance to change the story, Ellie, my dear.' He inclined his head towards where Will stood in conversation. 'I can't tell you what peace it brings me to know that the cove has healed the both of you in a way it never could me and Meg.'

Tears pricking the back of her eyes, Ellie stood, then leaned down to hug him. 'I'm so sorry.'

'Don't be, my dear. We will soon be together again. Now,' he cleared his throat, his keen eyes brimming with emotion, 'be off with you. And be happy, Ellie.'

With a final squeeze of his hand, Ellie released Ryther and looked around for Will. He and Matt had moved over to the entrance, where she could see them talking to Daniel – the husband of Anna's best mate, Lauren, who sat beside Anna now, a hand resting on her bump, tapping it in time to the music.

Ellie made her way over, Will reaching out to take her hand, drawing her to his side.

'We're hatching a scheme.' He nodded towards Matt and Daniel, who'd headed off towards the bar. 'I'll tell you about it later—' He broke off. 'Hey, are you okay? You look upset.'

'I'm fine. Can we get some air?'

'Gladly.'

Will led Ellie across the manicured lawns, then up some ancient stone steps.

'I used to come up here when I wanted to get away from the multitudes in the house.'

Dusk had come sweeping in across the sea, draping a silken mantle over the cove, its gentle touch caressing their skin as they reached a stone platform, which in turn led onto the castellated rooftop.

Ellie raised her face to the soft breeze, relishing in the now-familiar salty air and the faint chug of a boat heading out to the nighttime fishing grounds.

Lights flickered across the far side of the cove, and faint music could be heard emanating from The Lugger. Owls hooted hauntingly in the tall trees above Tremayne Manor, and sail lines rattled against masts in the harbour below. Draping an arm across her shoulders, Will held Ellie close, then pointed across the water.

'See that, up there?'

Ellie followed Will's hand, pointing to a large, stone building still visible in the fading light, lit up by the lamp-posts along the lane below.

'What is it?'

'It's one of the estate properties Alex wants to offload. Used to be a grain store for the farms up on the hilltop. It's got planning permission for a stunning barn conversion. It's too large a project for Oliver's community scheme.'

'I bet it will be gorgeous when it's done.'

Will turned Ellie to face him, his dark eyes probing hers in the dim light. 'That might depend on you.'

Her brow furrowed. 'How come?'

'We did say Peaches, much as we love it, isn't practical size-wise. Dev still doesn't have any local takers for it, and if he does, we'll give it up, but I thought we could keep it as a bolthole for now and live there while the renovations on the grain store take place. Daniel's keen to be involved; he loves a bit of DIY.'

Ellie's eyes widened as her heart skipped in delight. 'For us? We could live there?'

'Only if you want to.'

She silenced him with a kiss, which became prolonged, arms wrapped around each other as they sealed the pact.

'You could have a whole room to yourself to mess up.'

Laughing, Ellie allowed Will to drag her over to a low stone wall against the cliff behind the manor house, and she settled beside him, hands clasped, her eyes fixed on the barn. Their future home. Here. In the cove.

'Matt gets it.' Will spoke softly. 'He says Polkerran Point has become the home he'd always longed for. The locals just accept him, leave him in peace. Here, he's just Matt, Anna's brother. Well, unless you're Mrs L, to whom he's just Matt, the "magician".' Will grinned. 'He says he's tried to convince her his wizardry is on the guitar not with a wand, but she's not having it.'

Ellie drew in a contented breath. She loved the cove with all her heart, the perfect blend of scenery and silliness. Thank heavens she'd had to return.

Her smile was tremulous as she turned to face Will, more content than she could ever imagine herself being. 'I lost my heart here. To you. I didn't understand, all those years ago, that I needed to return to find it again.'

Will placed a palm against her cheek, those rich, dark eyes fastened on Ellie's.

'Nor did I. But Anna says this place has a way of encircling your heart, cocooning you in its warm embrace so that you never want to let go. Of it, or the way it makes you feel.'

'She may well be right,' Ellie breathed, her gaze dropping to Will's firm mouth as it edged closer. 'I've totally fallen for Polkerran Point, and without it, we'd never have met.'

'Or been reconciled,' he whispered, lips almost upon hers. 'It's fate. The cove offered us a second chance at first love. We were always meant to be.'

And Will sealed the declaration with a kiss.

Acknowledgements

And that's a wrap!

It's been a whirlwind few years, hanging out with the locals in Polkerran Point, and I'm going to miss them very much. It is, however, time to say goodbye for now, and as always, I have a long list of people to thank for their help during the writing of this last instalment in the series.

I'll start as I always do, with Emily Bedford, my fabulous editor at Canelo, without whom this series may never have seen the light of day. I've never met anyone so kind, upbeat and positive, even when delivering the difficult news of what needs to hit the cutting room floor! Emily, thank you doesn't seem enough to express how grateful I am to you for your patience, support and encouragement over these last few years, especially for your confidence in this last book.

I feel obliged to mention my four-legged demanding assistants, Tig and Tag. Despite your best endeavours, I finished writing the book. I forgive you.

Onto the research. I'm not a TV producer, have no talent for artwork, zero medical knowledge and take all my photos on an iPhone, so it will be no surprise to hear I had to call in a few favours on this one.

Firstly, I'd like to thank my lovely friend, Jeannie Peters, for the advice on back injuries, the associated treatment and possible side effects. You helped me find a credible way to keep Ellie in Polkerran Point beyond her intended stay.

In the same vein, thank you to all the lovely authors who responded to my cry for help in the Savvy Writers' Snug on Facebook about the role of a TV producer. Claire Seeber, Melissa Oliver, Alison Stockman and Jennifer Page, you are all stars in my eyes!

Susi Mount, of Coppertop Cards, I can't thank you enough for the lovely video chat to talk through how you make your gorgeous cards and all the background info, from the source materials to sales outlets. Although a smaller part of Ellie's work, I hope I've done you proud.

Lastly on the matter of research, but by no means least, I must thank my very dear friend, Adrea. Many of you will know her as Ada Bright, my co-writing partner on our time-travel adventure series featuring Jane Austen, but Adrea is also an incredibly gifted photographer, taking the most stunning images, both of people and landscapes.

She responded to my cry for help in typical Ada-style, inundating my WhatsApp feed with short videos, not only talking me through every aspect, from actual camera and lens types, charging stations, memory cards, shoots and the challenges but also demonstrating how to hold the camera, change the lens etc. She talked me through downloads, editing, mini-sessions and much, much more.

Emily's very lucky she didn't receive my idiot's guide to photography instead of a cosy Cornish romance!

I'm grateful to everyone mentioned above and, as is always the case, any mistakes in interpreting the help you gave me are my own!

My penultimate thanks go to all the readers and reviewers who've joined me on this journey to Cornwall. I can't tell you how much it means when you share your thoughts, badger me for more background on characters, try to guess whose story will be next or simply get in touch to say you enjoyed the read. Without you, there would be no point in telling these stories. To me, you are the best.

And finally, I'd like to thank my husband, Julian. I've probably said all I could possibly say in previous acknowledgements, but for me, it bears a repeat. Julian, you do make everything possible. Your love, support, encouragement and sense of humour are invaluable. I couldn't have written this series without you, so I – and the entire community of Polkerran Point – send you our love and thanks for making dreams come true.